Other work by the author:

Novels:
Jesusville
Catholic Boys

Story Collection:
A History of Things Lost or Broken

Screenplays:
Love in the Age of Dion

DARK ROAD, DEAD END

PHILIP CIOFFARI

LIVINGSTON PRESS
THE UNIVERSITY OF WEST ALABAMA
LIVINGSTON, AL

*The author wishes to thank Joe Taylor, the staff at
Livingston Press, and Jaden Terrell for their help in preparing
this manuscript for publication.*

DARK ROAD, DEAD END

PART ONE: THURSDAY

----*ONE*----

MORRISON STOOD ON THE PORCH of the River Hotel finishing his third whiskey of the evening, wondering how they would kill him. It would be an accident, of course. That was the way with agents who fell out of favor. *An unfortunate tragedy of circumstance, a situation that was unanticipated.* That would be the wording in the letter to the aunt he hadn't seen in years. *With our deepest regrets. . . .*

The whiskey had gone sour on his tongue. Death had never been so real to him. Over the years he had, of course, attended his share of funerals. But his own death had remained a nebulous thing, remote at best, undefined.

Until now.

The realization that it was imminent astonished him, as if he'd lived his entire life without regard for its terms and conditions, its limited warranty. As if he'd failed to read the small print of the contract.

Farther down the porch, hotel guests gathered around a piano bar, the maudlin tinkling music and their chatter of no interest to him now. In this heat even the smallest gesture was an effort, but he waved his glass at the waitress coming toward him, the young perky one—LeeLee or DeeDee—who always offered him a smile.

"Eve-nin', Mr. M."

Under the yellow porch lights, his face with its watchful eyes and strong chin seemed on the verge of discovery. His eyes flicked toward her and he smiled briefly before looking away. Pretty women always made him feel he should apologize. For what, he wasn't sure.

She took his glass and moved toward the door without

breaking stride.

He turned now to the river and the gold disc of the sun suspended above an horizon of slash pine and palm. Usually he didn't have his fourth whiskey until the sun had set and the sky had turned an iridescent silver. But tonight he didn't have to wait for the colors of dusk to unnerve him.

When the girl brought his whiskey he moved to the end of the porch with its view of grey bungalows and beyond that, beyond the row of trees with their brush-like blossoms of pink and white, the ball fields of the high school where a handful of Guatemalan boys played soccer. Tonight Emilio was not among them, and he felt as if something necessary had been ripped from him. The sons of fishermen and migrant workers on temporary visas, the boys came from the trailer park up river. Watching them at play had been the solace of his evenings.

On the field, the ball arced high, the boys' cries rising in the darkening air. He took satisfaction in the youthful motion of their bodies, arms swinging freely, brown legs flashing as they followed the ball this way and that across the field. At 51 he could still remember what it was like to be young and he looked back to that time with regret. He wished he could have been carefree and joyous like these boys.

Across the river the swamp grew darker, a chaos of shadow and night sounds. In a matter of hours he would be out there, on patrol again, his nightly ritual. Except that tonight there was a special shipment coming in. Emilio had alerted him to that. The anticipation added to his anxiety, sharpened his fear.

But first he had to meet with Caruso. He drained the whiskey and turned back one last time to watch the boys, ignoring the romantic notes of the piano and the laughter that drifted dismally in the air around him.

IN his government-issued grey sedan, he drove through town, the streets unlit, the main business district—hardware store, luncheonette, post office, and grocery market—shut down for the night. It made him feel lonelier than he was, *especially* at night, this outpost in the bottomlands, this mile stretch of dirt and coral wedged between two branches of the St. Thomas River. The dark streets lay prostrate beneath a black sky, and all of it—sky, river, buildings, trees—held hostage by the endless miles of swamp.

2

South of town, scrub pine grew in dense stands against the marsh. The whiskey had heightened his senses, and night's voices rose around him like a threat.

The turnoff, though he had been here before, came upon him unexpectedly. He checked the rear view before cutting his lights and swinging the car onto the dirt. The heavy Ford rocked in the tire ruts; hard-packed sand hissed against the hubcaps. He drove slowly, the sandy surface pale against the tangled darkness of the trees.

There was a break in the foliage where Caruso's car was parked, nosed into tall grass at the water's edge. Morrison killed the lights and watched the surface of the bay materialize from the blackness.

A shadow detached itself from a tree. Caruso stood at the edge of the road, snuffing out a cigarette with his foot. He came alongside the car and smiled, his handsome and younger face playfully mocking as always.

"We have to stop meeting like this, *Walty*," Caruso said.

Two nights ago Morrison had made the mistake of confiding a childhood secret: what they had called him in the housing project in St. Louis where he'd grown up. Not Walter or Walt. *Walty,* said then, as now, in derision. "Serves me right, I guess, for telling you."

Caruso laughed. "Hey, that was our moment. Self-revelation, human contact. Not just two anonymous, soul-less grunts trading agency secrets in the dark."

Anonymity protects us, Morrison was thinking. It was one of the rules he'd lived by. But maybe he'd only been fooling himself. Maybe that too, like a long and productive life, was simply another illusion.

He looked toward the bay where a crescent moon had risen above the water, sharp and thin as a chalk mark. "This operation I've been watching at the Blue Lagoon—"

"Forget about it." Caruso swatted a mosquito on his hand. "They're loving me tonight. It's a damn orgy out here." He came around to the passenger side and slid in.

Morrison raised the window and turned on the engine so that cool air blew from the vents. Caruso leaned back in the seat and sighed. He was a big man, broad face and shoulders, a body that was no stranger to the weight room.

"What do you mean, forget about it?"

"Pendleton's got all he needs from the reports you and the kid filed. He wants to terminate the investigation."

Morrison swiveled in his seat to face him head on. "But that's absurd. There's more here. I want to go after the big guys."

"Pendleton's not interested."

"How could he not be interested?"

"He wants to move on the fishery. *Now*." The shadows blacked out his eyes, hardened the edges of his face. He sat there impenetrable as the darkness of the marsh.

"*I'm* supposed to decide when."

Caruso raised his hand to stifle a yawn. "That's been changed."

"Why wasn't I informed?"

"You *are* being informed." Caruso gave him a lazy smile, his eyes glinting in the sliver moon's light. He stretched his arm along the door frame, his fingers—thick and capable of inflicting great pain, Morrison thought—tapped the vinyl: a slow, thumping rhythm marking time.

Morrison searched the man's face to see what he wasn't telling him. "When?"

"Sunday night."

"*This* Sunday?"

"That's right. The night of the next big shipment. Perfect timing."

"But—"

"*You're* going to take us in."

The words came at Morrison like a fist.

Caruso yawned again and this time made no effort to cover it. He smelled of an aftershave Morrison found cloying. He shifted in his seat to distance himself from the man, the relentless beating of his fingers.

The car seemed more like a coffin now than an object capable of motion, a final resting place where he was doomed to hear forever the hissing wind of air conditioner vents and the distant throbbing of a motor going nowhere.

His eyes raked the face of the man on the seat beside him. How much did he know? What was he *not* saying? But the face that looked back at him was broad and empty in the faint light of the moon. Morrison saw no trace of the mockery he usually found there or the promise of terrible cruelty yet to be delivered.

"We never cut off an investigation this early. We're still in the initial stage," he said. He'd been watching the Blue Lagoon fishery less than a month. All they had so far was the boy's, Emilio's, reports from inside the warehouse—conversations overheard, names and places dropped—as well as what both he and the boy had observed: fishing boats arriving at the fishery all hours of the night, their "unofficial" cargo transferred to smaller skiffs that traveled upriver and vanished somewhere in the vast spider web of tributaries and channels that criss-crossed the swamp. All of this, Morrison knew, amounted to nothing that would go beyond implicating the fishery's staff.

"There's so much we don't know. Where the wildlife is coming from. Who else is involved. Where the main distribution point is. What, if anything, this guy Alexander Crimmins has to do with it—"

There was no point in going on. The Division knew this as well as he did. Caruso knew it, too. It was the oldest strategy in the apprehension of smugglers: *controlled delivery.* Anytime you caught a mule in transit, you let him pass. Follow him and he'd lead you eventually to the king snake.

Caruso leaned toward the window, his smile growing wider. "I worry about you sometimes, Walty." He straightened up and stared with heavy eyes at the darkness outside, as if he might really be concerned. A mosquito hummed inside the car. He swiped the air, a gesture that quieted the hum only a moment. "You don't understand the nature of the game. You're still thinking somebody's gonna win and somebody's gonna lose."

"This might be the biggest operation we've—"

Caruso looked at him without expression. "Pendleton's not interested in your suppositions."

"Tell him—"

"Sure, whatever," Caruso said. And for the first time something crept into his eyes that Morrison thought might be pity or disdain, or both. He had tried to like the man; he really had. But beneath his surface arrogance, his cock-of-the-walk attitude, Morrison sensed something even more disturbing: a burnt-out corner of the man's psyche devoid of compassion for *any*thing, human or animal. And that was the hardest thing for him to accept about Caruso: that he had no concern for the wildlife the Division had been created to protect.

Morrison looked away at the maze of leaf and branch beyond the windshield. Beside him, the man sighed wearily.

"I'm beat," Caruso said. "Gonna get me a woman *and* some

shut-eye. I'd advise you to do the same. Take it easy these last few days before the hit. Life, as they say, is short." He swung his large frame to the side and pushed at the door. "Enjoy," he said with a light-hearted laugh.

Morrison watched him, death's slick messenger, move among the shadows toward his car. He had known they were going to kill him. He just hadn't thought it would be this soon.

HE stayed that way, arms resting across the steering wheel, eyes fixed on the dark maze of the forest as if it were a veil he might penetrate. What he had now, in place of a future, was a wall.

What was it Caruso had said? That he didn't understand the nature of the game?

He wondered if that were so.

But work, *his* work, he understood. It had been his guiding principle. He had believed in it the way others believed in God. He liked the order it bestowed upon his life. He liked the simplicity of goals to be accomplished, ends to be met.

Even now he could remember the hopeful excitement he felt when—fresh out of grad school, starry-eyed with good intentions— he'd joined the Fish and Wildlife Service, or the "effen W" as the local hunters and fishermen preferred to call it. For fifteen years he'd gotten out of bed before dawn, slogging through wetlands to apprehend duck hunters who'd exceeded the limit, or tramping through woodlands in the dead of night in pursuit of poachers.

Nor did he lose that enthusiasm later with the Customs Service where he worked out of the port of Miami as an inspector before signing on with this Special Operations Division, an elite enterprise designed to take on the most serious violations of customs law, to take more risks, to work under deep cover, not stepping outside the law per se, but if necessary skirting its edges. *If necessary.*

And there were times when it certainly had been necessary, when the dangers he'd faced would have toppled a weaker man. It was his belief in the cause—preserving the world's vulnerable and endangered species, protecting those living creatures who could not protect themselves—that had kept him steady.

But what should he believe now?

Over the years he'd had a grim running joke with Krebs, his only real friend at headquarters. *Remember Ed Callahan.* Krebs had teased him with that whenever he thought Morrison was getting too comfortable in his job. *Remember Ed Callahan*—one of the Division's top agents killed under mysterious circumstances in Arizona. He'd been sent out there to monitor a drug smuggling operation. Morrison was brought in a week before the bust, at which point he found Callahan in a highly agitated state. Over a bottle of Sour Mash they consumed one night, he'd confided to Morrison his suspicions that top levels of the Mexican government might be involved in the smuggling, exactly how he wasn't sure, but he'd seen enough evidence to point in that direction. But headquarters, he said, had turned a deaf ear to his reports; they were blind eye-ing him to his face. Twenty-two agents from the D.E.A. and Customs took part in the bust. Callahan, who was chosen to lead the raid, was the only one who didn't make it out alive.

The rumors, never verified, that circulated at HQ were that he'd become a serious embarrassment, his "accidental" death—he was shot from behind on the road to Nogales—someone's way of eliminating the problem.

Now, Morrison thought, it's my turn.

You're going to take us in, Caruso had said.

The order still rang in his ears.

The car before him, nearly identical to his own, roared into life, slipped backward from the shadows, turning to reveal Caruso's face framed in the window. In the dashboard light his lips twisted into a cruel, mocking grin—or did Morrison interpret the grin that way because of the man's gesture? Before the car lurched onto the road Caruso raised his hand, shaped like a gun, and held Morrison in his sights. Then the man and the gun were gone. The car jounced in the ruts and then the car itself was gone, swallowed by the dark canopy of trees, the rumble of its engine already lost in the ratcheting sound of insects.

----*TWO*----

THE VOICE INSIDE HIS HEAD said, *run!* It was a voice from childhood, from the time street gangs would corner him, beat him in the alleys. *Run! Run! Keep running till your feet are bloody stumps, till there's no breath left in you!*

But he hadn't run. He'd stood his ground, taken the beatings, until the gangs tired of him, turned their attention to the weaker, less durable boys in the neighborhood. Nor would he run now. There was not only his own life to think about. There was the boy, Emilio, who had laid his life on the line by going undercover. No way was Morrison going to abandon him.

At Souvenir City, north of town on the state highway, he pulled into a dark lot—one of the places in this section of south Florida where there was an outdoor pay phone. Cell service was erratic here, at best.

Waiting for the Admiral to pick up, he stared ahead at the cluster of thatched-roof chickee huts made to resemble an Indian village. By day, during tourist season, the place was jammed with sight-seers, their mini-vans and over-sized SUVs crowding every corner of the lot—more traffic here than at the authentic Seminole villages farther down the highway. It was one of the ironies of American life that always amused him: our preference for imitations in lieu of the real thing.

"Yes, sir, I'm confirming for tonight as scheduled," he said when the retired Coast Guard admiral picked up.

A GRAVEL road ran alongside the canal and Morrison followed it a half-mile in from the highway until he reached a break in the wall where a small sandy beach doubled as a boat landing. Twenty minutes passed before he heard the boat, the slow *putt-putt* of the engine in the canal waters, an occasional skip in the rhythm like a missed heartbeat; then he could see it, riding the shadow of the canal wall, coming from the direction of the Coast Guard marina.

It was at Morrison's insistence that they met here. He didn't want to be seen coming or going on his nocturnal patrols. To the people of Mangrove Bay, he was down here selling Bibles. Only the Admiral, who now edged the skiff close enough for Morrison to board, knew the truth—or some of it, at least.

Before he'd left the hotel, Morrison had traded his suit for a lightweight vinyl windbreaker and a peaked cap, the kind favored by the locals. To the casual observer they were two more anglers plying the night waters of the bay.

The Admiral eased the boat back into the dark canal where bulrushes towered above the sea wall. The engine puttered quietly through the no wake zone. "You got me good tonight, Walter," he said from the stern.

Morrison glanced behind him where the man sat with his shoulders hunched, a grin on his fleshy, full-bearded face. He had a wide open, almost shocked look in his eyes from staring too long at reflected light. "How's that?"

"Me and the mizzus, we was, you know, just getting happy when you called. Happens sometimes, once in a blue moon. Old farts like us. May not get another go at it for months. You know how it is."

But Morrison had never gotten that far in his marriage. Too short-lived, and now too far in the past for him to calculate the shelf-life of love's intimacies. He'd always thought he'd be given a second chance, get things right the next time around, have the wife and children he secretly longed for.

The sharp ache of remorse left him feeling more uneasy than he already was. So he turned his thoughts to the present moment, the information Emilio had given him about the shipment coming in. "Something's going down tonight," he said to the Admiral.

"Fact or hunch?"

"Fact."

"That's good." The Admiral chuckled. He enjoyed baiting this man he worked for. "Because you've got more *hunches*, more *instincts*, than any man I know."

"Sometimes they're even right," Morrison said with a self-mocking grin.

It was cooler on the water, something bitter-sweet in the air from the vegetation nearby, and when they reached the end of the canal, the Admiral opened the throttle, the skiff veering toward an archipelago of dark shapes. As they wove between the islands, the pressure inside Morrison's head eased for the moment and he was lulled by the engine's drone and the steady rush of water against the prow. These islands were small, unnamed and uninhabited, anchored to the sea by nothing more than the arching roots of mangroves. Alongside one of them, the Admiral cut the engine. The mosquitoes would spare them if they kept a distance from the shoreline.

Across the water loomed a larger island, Hells Island, its shoreline thickly treed. A *real* island, the Admiral liked to call it, not one of your flimsy mangrove types good for nothing. There was a dock with a blue light, and a path that ran up from the dock. On a small rise above the tree-line a house was visible, a low-slung building with siding of weathered wood.

Morrison trained his night-vision glasses on the house where, in one of the rooms, a single light burned.

The Admiral yawned and said, "You find out anything more about that fellah from Texas who owns it? That Crimmins fellah."

That was as much as the locals knew. The island was owned by *some fellah from Texas*. He was rich; he was powerful. Some kind of big-game hunter. Those were his categories. And they knew a little of the island's history. Its previous owner was Richard Hells, U.S. Ambassador to Nicaragua or Peru, one of them South American places, they weren't sure which. They knew he'd sold it a couple of months back to *that fellah from Texas*.

Morrison kept the glasses trained on the house. "Wish I could tell you."

The Admiral had never quite accepted his role as uninformed ferryman but he kept his complaints to a minimum. "Not like I'm gonna run off and tell the whole town," he griped good-naturedly, more to get Morrison's goat than anything else.

Morrison moved the glasses slowly across the small island. It wasn't that he didn't trust his boat captain. The old man was a decent fellow, with a long history of government service, and he had been unswervingly faithful in his duties as boat man. But in undercover operations the unnecessary circulation of information always proved to be dangerous—in the long, if not the short, term—and Morrison wanted to protect them both.

Nor had Morrison offered much information about the Division or the danger he was in. How his suspicions had been growing from as far back as early spring when Pendleton had stopped inviting him to meetings of the Special Ops Committee. No more trips to the Southern District's HQ in Atlanta. Not even to the local meetings when Pendleton came into the field. And then they'd stopped sending him new recruits to train, stopped asking for his opinion on sensitive issues. And now, in the three-plus weeks he'd been here in Mangrove Bay, they'd been over-ruling him regularly, tonight the prime example: within six months they'd gone from seeking his input, from *following his lead*, to outright rejecting his concerns—*blind eye-ing* him to his face, as Callahan would have phrased it.

Now he scanned the grassy field around the house then back to the house itself with its long porch, and a terrace off to one side. Shadows flickered at the far end of the porch, or so he thought; but when he steadied the glasses no human form materialized. Only once, several nights ago, had he seen someone unmistakably. On the porch, at the edges of the window light. What he thought was a support post. Until it moved, a twitch, a shudder, sliding beyond the edge of light.

That had been the only sign the island was being used. No choppers had descended upon or taken off from the helicopter pad adjacent to the house. According to Krebs, though, headquarters in D.C. had been aware of Crimmins' dabbling in the wildlife trade for almost a year now.

When Morrison asked why the man wasn't under investigation, Krebs had shrugged it off. "The usual reasons, Walt, you know. The guy's big enough and clever enough to hide his direct involvement. To say nothing of the fact that probably some of what he's importing is legal. Most likely not all of it's black market. And since no one knows the full scope of his operation, it's pointless to nail him on one or two shipments. The way the laws are set up, it's just not worth the department's time and effort."

And that's where things stood at the moment: stalemate. If Crimmins *was* using the place to monitor his smuggling operation, Morrison had no evidence thus far to support it. Was it, as the Admiral might have said, *just another hunch?*

He held the glasses as steady as the lapping tide would allow. The boat's motion and the eerie-green magnification of the lens made him dizzy. He lowered the glasses and held them between his knees, blinking to clear his vision. The lemon peel of a moon had risen higher in the sky, dripping a narrow trail of light across the bay. He tried to find comfort in the easy, lapping sounds of the water and the warm salty air, but the vastness of the dark horizon overwhelmed him. Against the panorama of the southern night, he felt shrunken and ineffectual.

Caruso would have laughed at that. It's the nature of the game, he would have said. The mere fact that man is such a tiny speck in the infinity of the cosmos tells you all you need to know about whoever or whatever designed the ground rules. We're pathetic, let's face it. Talk about being over-matched, under-equipped, and constitutionally ill-prepared. You create a creature with needs—aching, relentless needs—then give him half what it takes to fulfill those needs. I mean, come on, the sheer perversity of it, the audacity of it all. And it was because of that—the perversity of it, the audacity of it—that made Caruso howl with delight, made him want to raise his fists and clobber his way to extinction.

The breeze off the water, despite the warm night, made Morrison shiver. He turned in his seat and caught his ferryman in a yawn.

"Thinking of the missus," the old man said with a lazy smile.

MORRISON leaned into the wind as the skiff made its way back through the maze of islands. At the mouth of the river, the Mangrove Bay airport's blue runway lights were visible beyond a fringe of palm and cypress. Soon they passed the River Hotel with its gabled roof and its long porch edged with tiny yellow lights. Piano notes drifted across the water. Laughter and chatter accompanied the sound, more raucous than earlier.

How foolish man's efforts to entertain himself seemed to him now that he was under sentence of death. Or maybe, he considered, *he* was the foolish one for not having taken more pleasure from his life when he'd had the opportunity.

I would live differently, he vowed to himself, *if given another chance.*

He turned his attention to the Blue Lagoon fishery and packing house coming up now on the skiff's right side: a long narrow building of corrugated steel with its series of cranes and winches set up along the sea wall for unloading the fishing boats that arrived with cargoes of crab, redfish, mullet, pompano, and grouper.

A half-dozen men were unloading a company trawler—white with blue trim and the logo *Blue Lagoon* written in curlicued script across the stern. One of them leaned defiantly against a mooring post to light a cigarette, blowing smoke in their direction.

A short distance upriver they passed the trailer park where Emilio lived. His eyes scanned the huddled cluster of dwellings, half-expecting to see Emilio moving on the silent streets, though he knew of course this time of night the boy was working at the fishery. In a matter of weeks, the boy had become like a son to him. So effortlessly, so unexpectedly, it had taken Morrison off-guard. He smiled now at the wonder of it. Maybe the boy *was* his second chance, the family—or at least part of it—that he longed for.

From that point on, the black trees made the river seem smaller and darker. He instructed the Admiral to back the skiff into a tiny inlet enmeshed with mangrove. From there, with the help of night goggles, they had a prime view of whatever traffic the river might bear.

What kind of exotic wildlife and how much of it was being shipped this night, Emilio hadn't been able to determine. He had overheard only that a shipment was arriving.

Sometime after midnight.

Via Gun Rock Bay.

The air forced itself like a clammy hand against Morrison's skin. It was difficult to breathe in such close quarters. Hunched forward because of the low-hanging limbs, he heard a hiss and the air filled with the acrid odor of repellent. The Admiral tapped his shoulder and held out the spray can but Morrison waved it away. In addition to wearing insect-repellent patches and specially treated clothing, he'd taken the time to give himself an extra-dosing of Deet before he left the hotel. His concern that the smell of drifting spray out here might give them away was short-lived. The marsh gas took care of that. In no time at all, the sulfurous odor of methane rising from the black peat around them seemed to erase all traces of the bug spray.

A few feet upstream, a gator slid from the bank, parting the water with a soft, swishing sound.

Morrison checked his watch.

Twenty-two minutes till the witching hour.

----*THREE*----

AN HOUR PASSED BEFORE THEY heard the low throb of an outboard. The sound grew louder and expanded: several outboards echoing in the hollow spaces of the mangrove forest. Morrison caught a flicker of movement, something grey and fleeting between the trees, and the first of the boats passed by. It was a skiff not unlike the Admiral's, with one man aboard. The cargo it carried had been draped with a canvas tarp. Behind it came three other identical boats, each with its lone occupant and its draped cargo: a ghostly parade in silhouette, slowly vanishing upstream.

When the sound of the engines was some distance ahead, they pulled at stumps and roots for leverage, freeing the skiff from the inlet. The engine kicked on and they followed the louder sound deeper into the swamp.

In the prow of the boat Morrison leaned forward, arms wrapped close to his body as if hugging himself. Moments like this he liked to reassure himself with the feel of his 9 mm tucked beneath his jacket. It wasn't uncommon for a game warden, or even an enterprising local sheriff, to blunder his way into oblivion in this part of the world.

He turned to look at the Admiral, the only back-up he had, whose steadfast gaze was on the darkness ahead. Beneath the blanket at his feet, the old man kept a 30.06 hunting rifle on these nightly sojourns. Once, because Morrison liked to know what was moral ground zero for the men he worked with, he had asked him why he bothered with this kind of duty, this part-time employment with the Division. Surely not only for the money, given the pension he drew from his years in the Guard and the money he'd made as a tour boat captain during his retirement. Surely not, the old guy had replied, surely not. As he was thinking it over, coming up with the words to explain himself, the light buried deep in his eyes had grown brighter and an amused grin played on his lips. It's like this, he said. You know the way your heart beats when you're falling in love, that wild beating that makes you feel it's going to break right through your chest? Maybe you feel it once or twice in your life, *if* you're lucky. Then you spend the rest of your days hoping you'll feel it again. Closest I ever come to that nowadays is times, moments really, when life's on the line, when the hair on the back of your head stands up and your heart beats so hard from whatever danger's out there you want to cry out because you feel so damned alive.

Looking at the old man now, his shoulders taut with a military authority, his eyes straining for clarity in the darkness as he guided the skiff upstream, Morrison saw that he had found one of those moments again.

SOME, the Admiral among them, might have argued that the landscape they traveled through possessed an eerie beauty, the twisted limbs of the mangrove the fibers of a web that held together this earthly universe of darkness with its finger-like streams and waterways. Morrison, under other circumstances, would have agreed. Tonight, though, notions of beauty were an indulgence he couldn't afford. Tonight his mind moved in the most direct and linear way: there was an objective and there were steps he would follow to meet that objective. First *this*, then *that*. The boundaries were logic and common sense. You kept between the lines, you followed the light, such as it was, at the end of the tunnel. Tonight he viewed the wilderness around him simply as one more labyrinth to be negotiated, one more maze of secrets to be isolated and unraveled.

For days he had pored over maps of the region, noting—in some cases committing to memory—the paved and unpaved roads, the tributaries and lakes, the designated canoe and hiking trails, the campsites and campgrounds, the pinelands and hammocks and strands, the sloughs and marl prairies. North of here, Highway 41 crossed the wilderness, connecting the state's east and west coasts, and it was in that direction they were now heading.

After several minutes the darkness upstream turned milky, then Morrison saw the thin slant of moonlight on water and the creek opened into the wide pond called Gun Rock Bay. When he had first come across that name, while studying the maps, he asked the Admiral about it. "Oh yeah," the old man had said. "The place has quite a history. Outlaws, shootouts, you name it. In the old days there were stills along here that ran whiskey up to Miami, till the Feds came down and busted them up. Later, in the 70s and 80s, the cartels used these same routes to smuggle dope in from the Gulf."

From the shadow of the trees, they scanned the shoreline for movement. Halfway Creek ran off to the left and wove its way to the highway. The old man tipped his head toward that side of the pond. "There's a foot path that parallels the creek."

Keeping close to the shore they paddled quietly, gator eyes like sullen coals aglow on the pond's dark surface, until they reached the far side and pulled the skiff onto dry land near the large rock that gave the place its name.

"Stay with the boat," Morrison said.

"Not on your life." A fiery light burned in the old man's eyes. He unwrapped his rifle from the blanket and stood looking ahead at the path.

Morrison's first thought was for the old man's safety.

"Didn't get this far in life being a pussy," the Admiral said. "Can take care of myself."

And because Morrison believed that was true, he gave in. "All right, then. But stay behind me. In case they get trigger-happy out there."

The ground was solid here, the trees no longer mangrove but a mix of pine and holly and water oaks. The path wound northwestward away from the pond and within several minutes they heard the wind-like sound of traffic on Highway 41. As the road noise grew louder, isolated male voices rose intermittently from the trees ahead.

They heard the creek before they saw it, a low gurgling sound to the left, then they were alongside it—the black water darker than the surrounding forest, its smell a mix of dampness and rotting ferns—and they walked until the voices sounded dangerously close. The boats were suddenly visible, four of them in a row, beached nose-first on a sloping muddy bank that rose to a clearing where two white panel trucks were parked.

The men had formed an assembly line of sorts, lifting wooden crates and metal cages from the boats, and passing them along to two black men who loaded them into the trucks. The light came from a pair of six-volt flashlights resting in the dirt midway up the bank. The beams illuminated the hulls and, from time to time, the men drifting in shadow around them.

By this point in the night's activities, Morrison's shirt hung like a wet towel on his frame. He crouched on the path and motioned for the old man to get down as well. Not a hundred feet away the men labored in silence, except for the exhortations to hurry coming from the black men. Their words leapt into the dark above the highway noise and the constant hum of mosquitoes.

For a few minutes, Morrison watched in silence, the moisture in the air so thick it fell like mist upon him. An occasional mewling or chuffing sound emanated from the crates, or the strident voice of a parrot—once the tarp had been removed—repeating the men's muffled curses. In the metal cages, he glimpsed several varieties of parrots. And Macaws, too, red, blue, yellow and green ones, and the highly prized hyacinth macaws which would command a price of up to $20,000 on the black market.

There were rare varieties of monkeys as well, crowded into small compartments, frantically chattering and squealing as the men flung the cages up the line as if they were bags of rice. As many times over the years as he'd witnessed this kind of scene, he never failed to be sickened, *physically* sickened, at the sight. Dryness in his throat, sweat on his palms, an ugly feeling in the pit of his stomach. This was the job he'd signed on for: to protect these creatures, to prevent this kind of exploitation.

But the ever more disheartening fact, he knew too well, was that what he was witnessing represented not the worst phase of the process. Many smuggled animals never got even this far. The boats that transported them from their point of origin often threw them overboard, to avoid detection by the Coast Guard. Recently fishermen in the Caribbean had hauled in more than two hundred and fifty drowned animals—birds, monkeys, porcupines, ocelots—in their nets, the fifth such time that had happened in as many months.

If the animals weren't cast off into the sea, they often suffered other equally cruel fates: being crowded into such tight containers, for instance, that they would kill and eat each other.

So these were the lucky ones.

To ease the ache in his knees, Morrison shifted position then abandoned the crouch altogether because he hurt too much. He waved his hand around his face. The mosquitoes were vicious here, relentless. Through the trees he watched the men begin to unload the last of the boats.

Abruptly they stopped working and the assembly line broke apart when the man pulling the cages from the boat stepped back on the bank, cursing and bending over slowly with his hand pressed to his spine. Morrison was able to identify him now: Bobbie Dawson, the Blue Lagoon's night shift foreman. Flat top haircut, broad face. Squared shoulders and a squared trunk of a body to match.

One of the black men, the heavier of the two, shouted from the top of the slope, "Ain't no time for a break."

Dawson ignored him and walked in a slow circle, stretching his arms and tilting his shoulders one way and then the other. The two black men grumbled to each other in low voices.

Morrison studied the faces of the other boatmen, two of whom he recognized as Dawson's co-workers at the Blue Lagoon. When he stepped across the path for a better view, a twig snapped under foot. He froze.

Dawson stopped stretching and turned to stare in his direction. He had moved in such a way that the light cast a dim glow on the lower portion of his face and as he continued to stare idly at the darkness, a half-smile oozed across his lips.

It was that slow smile Morrison kept seeing on the trip back through the mangrove. The man's face—staring into the trees and smiling as if he'd reached a decision—became Caruso's face, the knowing smile an alternate form of the hand raised in the shape of a gun, both gestures reminding him his days were numbered.

It wasn't simply the fear of losing his life that concerned him, but the worry of leaving behind unfinished business. Though not a man who'd spent a lot of time pondering the hereafter, he felt sure of this one thing: if there *was* any kind of after-life, among the most restless and troubled souls would be those who crossed over *before* fulfilling their purpose.

So it was that every flutter of a bird's wing, every rustle of leaves in the wind consumed him as he sat hunched forward in the prow, gun drawn, senses at high alert.

"Easy," the Admiral said behind him, "let's go nice and easy."

The smugglers' boats were somewhere ahead of them. The Admiral had waited until they were well out of earshot then gave them an additional ten minutes head start. We should be fine, he'd assured Morrison. Those boys sure as hell aren't going to dawdle out here. They're going to keep right on moving.

But the silence tormented Morrison, raised one of two possibilities: either the boats were safely at a distance, as the old man maintained; or one or more of them had stopped, were waiting in ambush around some turn of the creek. He stared beyond the inert, indifferent hulks of gators half-sunken into the muddy banks and tried to penetrate the maze of vine and branch. And then he did see something, no mirage this time, the pale dull glint of a man's face in the dense fabric of mangrove and the barrel of a shotgun raised against that face.

Morrison fired. The face and shotgun disappeared. A cry of pain rang through the hollow spaces of the mangrove and Morrison was thrust backward violently, thrown from his seat as the Admiral gunned the skiff into the black watery tunnel between the trees.

----*FOUR*----

REGINA HAD BEEN OUT OF his life nearly five years. What Rowan had of her now, compliments of her sister Beth, was an address in the Bronx and a few unsavory tidbits of bio: she was living with a Puerto Rican guy named Willie who bred dogs, a rare variety of the Pomeranian Spitz, and who treated the dogs a hundred times better than he treated her. Over the years the news of Regina that had trickled his way, always via Beth, had been consistently disappointing. A series of problems: men, jobs, life in general. "You know Reggie," Beth once remarked, "ever since you guys split she's been hell-bent on—on what?—I don't even know anymore." Beth stopped short of blaming him, but he finished the job on his own.

And here he was, on a Thursday in October, showing up at her door unannounced, asking for help—after the way he'd treated her. Pathetic. But he needed money, fast, and there was nowhere else safe to turn. He stepped from his aging Caddy and crossed the street to a grey brick building, 1375 Zerega, the entrance buried in an interior courtyard, sun-deprived and gloomy.

His body tensed against the onslaught of unwelcome memories. He had grown up near here, they both had; in fact, they had lived on this same street, several blocks down, for the not quite four-year stint of their marriage. Treeless, all concrete and brick, this end of the street had never been inviting and time had shown its buildings no mercy. The brick had darkened, grown more melancholic; graffiti curled along the walls like ivy. In the lobby most of the name tags were missing from the directory.

Out back he found the Super kneeling on the pavement painting a child's dresser white. Rowan launched into a description of Regina as if she'd been frozen in time: long brown hair, a thin dancer's body, pretty face, real pretty. . . . He stopped. The Super's small brown face focused on the dresser; he was daubing paint around the drawer handles and seemed not to be listening. "She might look older now, of course," Rowan explained. "She's living with a guy raises dogs."

"*Them*." The super stopped in the middle of a brush stroke. Something flamed in his eyes and he spit onto the pavement. "They stink the place up. I call the cops. This ain't no zoo. I make them get out."

"Where'd they go?"

"Not far, I think. I see her sometimes. On the Avenue." He pointed with his brush at an upstairs window. "That place there, 2C, I paint it three times, I scrub, I wax the floor. It still smells bad."

ON the Avenue he peered through store-front windows darkened by the EL's shadow. Back when, Regina had expensive tastes, far above these cheap dress shops and bargain basement clearance centers. From the beginning they had talked about getting out—Westchester, Connecticut, *some*where—it was only a matter of time and money. Who would have guessed she'd still be here? At least he could say he'd escaped. For a while, at least, he'd lived in Manhattan.

Following the EL he walked a few blocks toward Westchester Square, past bodegas and bars and a super market, before turning back. He hadn't passed anyone who even remotely resembled her.

He was running out of time.

In the car he cruised the entire length of Zerega, beginning at the western end, the house where Regina grew up, a flat-roofed brick two-family that her grandfather had built when he came from Naples. She and Rowan had lived in the basement apartment. Metal grates masked the windows now and the yard's lone tree, bearing magnolias each spring, had been cut down. He drove past without a second look, the sick feeling in his gut a reminder of hopes betrayed.

When he passed beneath the EL the street turned industrial: warehouses with loading docks and asphalt yards cordoned off with chain-link fences. The area seemed disturbingly lifeless, the buildings silent and in varying degrees of decay. A half-mile of this before the street dead-ended at a muddy field, a poor excuse for a waterside park. He stopped the car and stared at it. After yesterday's fiasco, a consequence of his bad judgment and his usual dose of misfortune—he'd failed to arrange the fix and important people had lost money, *serious* money—he figured this was how he'd end up: his body dumped at the end of some forlorn street.

The full weight of his hopelessness fell upon him; for a moment he couldn't think or breathe.

Around the field's edge a bike and jogging path threaded through a fringe of trees. Good place for someone with dogs, though there was no one in sight at the moment, and he didn't have time to wait. He drove back slowly, watching for her on the way.

For once, luck was on his side. A flurry of movement in one of the asphalt lots caught his attention. A dog, no two, small and white and yapping non-stop, chased each other inside the fence. Across the yard a woman stood on the steps of a trailer set against the windowless wall of a warehouse. She leaned against the railing and smoked, looking into the yard's open space.

He stood outside the fence, his fingers curled around the chain-links. It took several moments for her to notice, to realize there was something distinctively familiar about him, and once she did she flicked away the cigarette and stared. He walked along the fence until he reached a gate and pushed his way through. The dogs came running to him, yapping at his feet, but he kept his eyes on the woman.

"Hello, Reggie," he said when he drew near the trailer.

"Jesus!"

"Not quite." Something eased inside him and he smiled for the first time in days.

"How'd you find me?"

He nodded in the direction of the dogs who were barking through the back fence into a yard of shuttered storage units.

"Traitors." She raised a hand to shade her eyes as she studied the strain in his face, the raincoat thrown hastily over a wrinkled dress shirt and pants, the scuffed shoes. His face flushed. He thought it must be obvious he'd been on the run all night, afraid to go home even for a shower and shave.

"You've been to hell and back," she said.

"You, too." Her face looked as though it had been sandblasted with misery. Her eyes, once her dominant feature, seemed on the run in the deep hollows of her sockets but she had a compact body that still took control of a pair of jeans. "You'll always be a knockout, though."

"What do you need, Nicky?"

"Who says I do?"

"You're here, aren't you?"

He felt his face flush again. "Missed you."

"Missed you at times, too. How does that change things?"

"Thought you should know, that's all."

"Yeah, well, thanks for coming all this way after all this time to tell me." She stood with her hands stuffed into her back pockets, her chest straining against the gray fabric of her T-shirt, as she watched him with a cool, even stare.

He offered a weak smile and ran his hand through his head of thick, black hair. "Thought we might talk."

"O God, Nicky. Five years and now you want to talk?" She shifted her weight on the steps, shifting her gaze too across the rough surface of the pavement, mica chips glinting in the morning sun. The dogs had settled down, napping in the thin shade of the fence. "So talk," she said.

But he couldn't. Not out there in that barren yard with its bland horizon of metal fences and warehouse walls, not with the sun beating down so pitilessly. He felt ripped open, exposed; shame ate away at his nerves. He didn't want her to see how fragile he was, so he asked if they couldn't go inside. There would be shadows, a cool darkness where he could hide. Just for a minute. She said neither yes nor no, watching him as if she were estimating something.

THE trailer smelled of dog. It was narrow, cramped, hot. She opened one of the bedroom doors to show him: the mother spread out on the floor, six pups curled against her in a mass of white fur. "My babies."

Behind them, against the far wall, three cages sat side by side on a table. The dim light made it difficult to identify the cages' occupants but he thought at least one of them held a snake. She had always been an animal lover. When they lived together she kept asking if she could get a pet. Anything, she didn't care. She couldn't pass a pet store without staring through the window, falling in love with whatever was on view. *Some day*, was his stock response. He had no room in his life, then or now, for animals.

The stench was overpowering. Newspapers, urine and feces-stained, served as carpeting in the otherwise bare room. "I change the paper three times a day," she said in defense of her housekeeping skills.

The mother raised her head to look at them in the doorway. Rowan saw the look in her eyes as a plea. "Oh, she's a beggar, all right," Regina agreed. "Aren't we all."

He asked what was in the cages. "My menagerie," she said. "They wouldn't interest you."

She closed the door and led him into the dining area. Originally the trailer had been used as the foreman's office for the warehouse next door, she told him. When the company went bust and the warehouse closed, the landlord figured he'd make a few bucks renting the space out until a new tenant came in. She glanced at the shabby room and shrugged. Good for the dogs, she said, the yard and all.

"The dogs, sure." He looked around in disappointment. There were leftovers from their married days: a coffee mug with blue tropical birds; familiar dishware in the sink; and the Formica dinette set he stood next to, the color of curdled cream.

"You've got no right, Nicky—"

"I didn't say anything."

"You're thinking it."

"What am I thinking?"

She flopped onto the worn love-seat and lit a cigarette, blowing smoke straight ahead at the wall. "I did what I did."

Me too, he thought. I did what I did, and here I am: broke and out of luck. He lowered himself into a chair and ran his hand over the table's chrome rim. He'd never liked this table. Too plain, too ordinary. He didn't want his life to be ordinary. It was the one thing he'd been sure of back then. He'd fallen in love and he thought that would make a difference. But finally he'd had to choose: an ordinary life and Regina's love, or something more dangerous, more unpredictable. "This guy Willie, he's—?"

"At work."

"Not you, though."

She smiled, no warmth in it. "Not today. I'm taking care of the dogs." She saw he was waiting for more, and added: "Willie's the jealous type. Only lets me work part-time."

"That's all right with you?"

"Why wouldn't it be?" She drew hard on the cigarette, mouth pinched, eyes narrowed. "Just want something steady," she said so softly he had to lean forward to hear her. "After what I've been through."

"You mean, what *I* put you through."

"You weren't the only one."

He squirmed in his seat and looked around for something to distract him, but the yellow walls blocked his escape. That, and the overbearing stench of dog which seemed to mock him, seemed to say: this is your cage, too.

"Willie comes home every night. I can count on that. And between his job, my part-time stuff at the pet shop and the dogs we breed we get by. Almost."

"You used to want more than that."

"Would have settled for love." She smiled weakly. "Still would. But facts are facts."

"Facts can change."

"Mr. Hopeful."

He laughed at that.

She stood, moving to the open doorway, staring toward the street. "Still driving Caddies, I see."

"Old one."

"Hope you've got better friends these days."

No friends, he wanted to say, least none that wouldn't rat me out in a situation like this, that's why I'm here. But he kept his mouth shut. No sob stories. No sniveling. He'd promised himself that. He'd had a woman, *this* woman, who loved him; he'd had a life full of promise. That wasn't enough. Now he had an escape route instead of a future.

She watched him from the doorway. "How much money you need?"

"Who says I do?"

"The look in your eyes."

"I'm fine." When they split up, he'd let her keep their bank account: fifteen, sixteen thou. For the trouble he'd brought her, for capsizing their dreams. He'd come here with the thought— what did they call it when they were kids, *Indian-giver*?—he'd come here thinking, if she hadn't spent it all, maybe he could borrow some, enough to go south, a few thou maybe, to tide him over. "I'm good. Just wanted to see you, you know, for old times' sake."

SHE flicked her cigarette into the yard, watched it fold into a curled wisp of spent ash. Behind her, he sat hunched against the dinette. She heard him say, "What?" and she turned back to him, said she didn't say anything. He looked small, shriveled-up. Not like the tall, handsome lover she first knew: the buttoned-down, know-it-all college boy who, for reasons she never understood, fell in with low-lifes. *Why?* she had asked more than once back then, you've been to school, you should want more. He would shake the question off, an annoyance not worth his time. College had been something he'd tried on like a cap in bad weather, easily removable. It was street-life that beat in his veins.

Under other circumstances he might have passed for a rumpled actor, down and out on his luck; but here, in the shabby domain of the trailer and with his hang-dog expression, he looked simply like a guy who'd fled somewhere fast. She wouldn't allow herself to pity him. "Look at you."

He had his hands in his pockets and he opened the raincoat as if to say *yeah, look at me.*

There was a humility about him that was new to her. She sighed, stared back into the yard, checking on the dogs roaming along the storage yard fence. He was like the dogs, she thought. He needed to be penned-up to keep him out of trouble. Back then it had been stolen car parts, head lamps and air bags. After that he started running with an older crowd. God knew what they were into—the ponies, she thought. By then she had already decided to leave him and she didn't care anymore what he did with his nights. "How bad is it?"

"Not bad."

"You used to put greater effort into your lies."

"I'll spare you the details."

"How broke?"

"Flat." He'd never kept more than a few hundred dollars in the bank. There was always a horse who couldn't lose, a bet he had to make.

"You leaving town?"

"Not only town."

"Oh, Nicky," she said, understanding. In her voice, he thought he heard her tone from the old days. A mix of sorrow, regret, pity.

She moved past him down the hall and came back with a mewling and wriggling pup in each hand. In the cramped space around the dinette she held them out to him. "Best Pets on Fordham Road—where I work sometimes. Ask for Ricardo. He'll take care of you, no questions." She cuddled and kissed each of the dogs—he saw the tenderness in her eyes, sadness too—then she pushed them toward him and he opened his hands. They made high, whimpering sounds, almost a squeal, as they greedily licked the salt from his fingers. They seemed happy. They seemed, he thought, like they'd found a home.

"I've got the papers." Regina reached for a metal box on the table. She handed him the AKC forms. He had to set one of the dogs down to tuck the papers into his pocket. The abandoned pup trembled at the table edge, whining until Rowan picked it up again. "Don't take less than 1600. Apiece."

"What about Willie?"

"I'll tell him they slipped through a hole in the fence."

"He'll believe you?"

"Gonna make me suffer either way."

"Hit you?"

She laughed. "No touch, no talk. Like I don't exist. That's the kind of guy I hook up with these days. No more hitters."

"Only that once."

"Once was enough." She held his eyes without yielding.

"I'm sorry, Reg—"

"I know, I know, you were under a lot of pressure. You already told me that."

"No excuses," he said. "I quit them."

Something flashed in her eyes—amusement? mockery?—he wasn't sure. "Well then, I guess you're right. Facts *can* change." She went back down the hall and returned with a cage. Inside was a white snake with yellow markings. He recoiled when she set it down on the table.

"What's that for?"

"You need to leave the country, right? There's a guy in Florida Ricardo deals with sometimes. A private distributor. Bobbie Dawson. This," she said, touching the cage, "is an albino ball python. Extremely rare. " The snake—about the size of a baseball bat, he figured—had curled itself into a tight circle. "They do that when they're frightened," she said. "Their version of the fetal position."

He had been standing a good step back, eying the reptile warily. "Poisonous?"

"Not this one." She placed her hand near the wire and, slowly, the snake came out of its curl and flicked its tongue at her fingers. "His name's Freddy. He's worth thirty retail. Dawson might give you fifteen."

"Hundred?"

"Thousand."

"Where'd you get it?" was all he could think to say.

"Gift from Ricardo. He thinks I bring him luck. Business has been good since I started working there."

He stood there staring at the dangerous-looking creature with the eerie, iridescent-yellow markings. "I hate snakes."

"They're really quite beautiful, if you look at them closely." She allowed the snake a few more flicks against her finger. "Bye, Freddie."

She went outside to stand on the steps, resting her hands on the rail.

Gripping the pups, he hiked his shoulders wearily and stood in the doorway. "I owe you."

"No, you don't."

"How you figure that?"

"That fifteen thousand you left me. My—severance pay. We're even now."

She hadn't bothered to turn to face him, nor did she watch as he descended the steps. He carried the pups to the car, then came back for the cage. She handed him a second, smaller cage with three white mice. "Dinner. One every other day."

He grimaced at the thought. But one of the truths from his playground days came back to haunt him, the humbling taunt he and his buddies used to toss at one another whenever the occasion warranted it: *beggars can't be choosers.*

She gave him instructions on how to care for the snake, and the dogs too, for the short time they would be in his possession.

"Thanks," he said. She turned away again, resting her hands on the rail, watching the dogs play along the fence.

Crossing the yard, a cage in each hand, he had to laugh at the weird turn his life had taken. Here he was, the man who never had any use for animals, suddenly turned zookeeper. Strangely enough—despite the bitter facts of his life—he felt a spring in his step, the stirrings of hope. At the gate he looked back to see Regina who stood in the same position, leaning forward, hands on the rail, the vacant yard between them like five wasted years.

----FIVE----

THAT EMILIO'S INFORMATION HAD PROVED correct was the only consolation Morrison could take from the night's activities. With only three days left until Sunday, time had become his most unforgiving adversary. And now the added complication of having been seen in the swamp. Had he killed the man? If not, had he been recognized?

What he knew so far of the operation, or what he could at least presume based on his experience and what Emilio had overheard, was this: the animals were poached, most likely in this case, in the wilderness areas of Central and South America, then transported in crates or cages to a central distribution point before being shipped, along with legitimate goods, in the holds of large cargo ships bound for ports along the Gulf where they were met by the Blue Lagoon trawlers.

The cages would be off-loaded at the Blue Lagoon and transferred to the smaller, unmarked skiffs that Morrison and the Admiral had seen first-hand. From the highway the white vans would carry the live cargo—those at least that had survived the grueling trip—to various destinations across the country.

And here, Morrison could only speculate. Roadside zoos? Wildlife Safari parks? Hunt clubs and private game reserves? Exotic pet lovers? Non-traditional healers who wanted not the live animal but one or more of its body parts, ground or powdered, for medicinal purposes?

Any or all of the above.

In the crates tonight, in addition to what he'd been able to identify, there might have been: toucans or other exotic birds worth anywhere from a 1000 dollars to as much as 90,000 dollars apiece; a variety of monkeys with a market value of 15-30,000 dollars apiece; and snakes. Pythons most likely, which were worth a minimum of 2000 dollars apiece on the black market but as much as 20-30,000 for the rarer varieties.

Whatever else had been in those cages could be drawn from a long list of possibilities: sea turtle eggs, or sometimes the sea turtles themselves; chameleon lizards; hummingbirds; birds of paradise; butterflies; gorillas; panthers. The list went on and on. Anything a smuggler could turn around for a profit.

The sad fact, of course, was that the rarer, most exotic, most endangered species brought the highest prices. As one of his fellow agents in Customs once remarked, "Pound for pound, there's more profit for smugglers in exotic animals than there is in cocaine."

"So why," Emilio had asked in his endearingly passionate way soon after they met, "are there not stricter laws, stiffer penalties? Why do we allow bad men so easily to rape the forests and prairies of our world?"

All Morrison could provide by way of explanation was the obvious, practical reason: that though there was an international convention, to which a hundred and seventy-five nations belonged, that regulated the trade and movement of endangered animal and plant species, it had no law enforcement capabilities. Seizures, fines and imprisonment for offenders were left to individual nations. In most countries, punishment consisted of paying a small fine or, at worst, serving a short jail term.

Under U.S. law, the Lacey Act made it a federal crime to import or export wildlife in violation of any state, federal, Indian, or foreign law. There were loopholes to the law, however, and over the years Morrison had lost many a case because of those loopholes, or because the prosecutors in the U.S. Attorney's Office in Miami were simply too overwhelmed with high profile narcotics cases to bother with wildlife smuggling.

Morrison could not answer the larger question, however: why we placed such a small value on protecting our fellow inhabitants of this earth. He had simply stared into the boy's dark, beseeching eyes and offered an apologetic shrug.

What he *did* know from experience was that to be successful in the war against smuggling, you had to break the larger network. Why Pendleton would sacrifice the greater goal for hauling in a few redneck grunts in the Everglades he couldn't explain, except to believe that there was someone or something the Division was trying to protect. And that he, in his investigation, was getting too close. Which, of course, would explain why they were terminating said investigation, and why they had to eliminate him.

THE mobile home park, four or five rows wide, stretched along the river, separated from it by a thin band of trees. At its edge a man was cursing and beating a dog with a stick. The small brown and white mongrel cowered beneath the blows, yelping sharply each time the man made contact.

Morrison, on his way to meet Emilio, told him to stop.

The man, unkempt dirty-blonde hair curling from beneath his cap, stopped long enough to glare at him and spit in the dirt. "You gonna do somethin' about it?"

Morrison came toward him. "If I have to."

Something in Morrison's eyes scared the man enough to drop the stick. He glared a moment more then opened the door to his trailer, muttering "Ain't none of yer damned business," before disappearing inside. The dog, whimpering, settled in the dirt along the trailer wall and rested its head on its paws.

Morrison had never been able to endure the sound of an animal's pain. He knelt beside it and stroked its head until the whimpering stopped. Then, sad-eyed and straining on its leash, the dog watched from the trailer's shadow as Morrison moved slowly away.

This was such a tight-knit community—Crackers at one end, Guatemalans on the other, virtually all making their meager living off the river—that he felt like an intruder. Yet once inside the local watering hole—a wood-shingled box of a building known only as "the Shack"—there was an atmosphere of welcome, the good will of the down-trodden and dispossessed.

At long plank tables Florida natives and Guatemalans sat side by side, the heated and beer-fueled conversations a mix of Spanish and swamp English. The jukebox offered both Latin American ballads and plaintive Country love songs—one song more overwrought with sentiment than the next. Through the smoky haze he spotted Emilio who came here each night after his shift. He sat with two dark-skinned men against the back wall.

Morrison sipped his beer and rested his weight against the dark, scarred rim of the bar. Beside him two fishermen he'd met here before were deep in conversation. "One thing I would never do, one sure thing," the one next to him was saying. Red-faced, grey-bearded, he leaned heavily toward his bar-mate. "I don't bait hooks for no Yankee fishermen."

"Right on," his companion said.

"Swear to heaven, them Yankees wanna be led around like babies. Find the bloody fish for them, bait their hooks, clean the bloody fish so their hands don't get smelly." He lifted his mug but stopped short of drinking. "Been humiliated too much already in this life. Ain't baitin' no Yankee's hook. Swear on my mother's grave, I ain't."

"Me, neither." The two men clinked mugs and drank deeply, slapping the mugs down hard on the bar.

The talkative one looked around, noticed Morrison and broke into a grin. "How's the Bible business, man?"

"Fair to middling."

"Fair to middling—I like that. Kinda sums up my life." He turned to his companion.

"Whaddya say, Ed? Pretty much sums up the whole mess, don't cha think?"

"Pretty much," Ed said.

The man, still grinning, turned back to Morrison and studied him. "Fair to middling, huh?"

"I'm semi-retired," Morrison said. "I'm not in it full time anymore." He smiled politely then excused himself, saying he had to go to the can.

Edging through the crowd, he braced himself against the assault of sweat and beer and tobacco. He took a seat against the back wall beside Emilio. The young man flashed a wide grin. Morrison's nod was intentionally curt, formal: they were casual acquaintances who happened to be sharing the same bench. But inwardly he was both deeply pleased and relieved to be with the boy.

"These are my countrymen," Emilio said, indicating the men at the adjoining table. "From my town, Santiago Atitlan, the land of towering volcanoes. They have arrived only today. To work in the fields at Homestead."

Morrison shook hands with Rodrigo and Diego who nodded enthusiastically, white teeth lighting up their dark faces. They were younger versions of Emilio, seventeen- or eighteen-year-olds, and they shared with their townsman the same broad forehead and close-cropped hair. Emilio leaned back in the seat beside

Morrison. "It is no problem. They do not understand English." His own English was nearly flawless, if at times overly formal. He hadn't yet been corrupted by American slang.

Morrison's face showed his concern. The noise level this time of night was conveniently loud and the jukebox provided additional cover, but still. . . .

"Trust me," Emilio said. "They know only *hello* and *goodbye*. I will teach them more, in time." He smiled at Morrison's consternation. "Perhaps you would like to join us for our soccer game tomorrow."

"I'd like to. Another time, maybe." Though he wondered when that would be. In some other life, he thought, the way things looked now.

Soon after Morrison had arrived in Mangrove Bay, Emilio offered to teach him the fundamentals of the game. And so he'd made an exception to his usually inflexible rule against fraternizing with his sources. On the high school field, in the company of a half dozen other Guatemalan boys, Emilio had taught him how to manipulate the ball with his foot, how to kick it, receive it, how to move it downfield. Though he was in good shape, Morrison was no athlete. When he kicked the ball, it dribbled weakly off to his left or right. Rarely could he get it in the air for any distance.

But Emilio never gave up on him. Again and again he would demonstrate the proper way to kick, the angle of the foot, the point of contact, the follow-through. He was patient, encouraging, never patronizing or disparaging. In the make-shift games that followed, he played alongside Morrison, exhorting him, shouting instructions, covering when Morrison failed to make a play. When their team won, he threw his arm around Morrison and patted his back, as if he'd been instrumental in securing the victory. For those few moments, despite his inept playing, Morrison experienced the warmth of belonging to something, Emilio and his ragtag group of boys his one and only source of community.

And later, at the Shack, they'd laughed together at some of Morrison's more bumbling plays. "It's not in your blood, the way it is in mine," Emilio would say to make Morrison feel better. "In my country we learn to kick the ball before we learn to walk."

Across the table now, Emilio's two friends had turned away, huddled close, speaking excitedly to each other in Spanish.

As if they knew something.

Morrison dismissed the thought. He had no reason to

distrust them or Emilio. In Miami, during their initial meetings, he'd cross-examined the boy endlessly in an effort to sniff out deceit or treachery of any kind, requiring him to submit finally to a polygraph test. The boy, by nature, was straightforward and honest. One of the many things Morrison loved about him.

It had crossed his mind that, because of the danger he was in, he should work alone from this point on. But the plain and simple fact was he needed this boy. Not only for the information he could provide, but for the comfort too.

"Did you confirm—?"

"Yes." Morrison directed his eyes toward the center of the room, as if talking to himself. "The hand-off was at the highway near Gun Rock Bay, as you said."

"To whom?"

"Two black men. One heavy-set, one thin," Morrison said. "Two white panel trucks. I'm having the plates checked now." He spoke to the smoky haze and the mounted marlins and tarpon above the bar. "I identified three of the four boatmen: Dawson, Connors and Cantrell."

"The fourth, was he tall and thin like a basketball player?"

"Yes."

"Lonnie Wells. Another friend of Dawson's. He, too, works the overnight shift at the fishery."

Morrison nodded. He had assumed as much. "Sunday night," he said and drew in his breath. Until now he would never have violated a Division confidence. *Until now*. But with Emilio he had grown accustomed to letting down his guard. And at this point, confiding in him was a necessity. "The Blue Lagoon will be hit."

"So soon?"

"I've asked for more time. They won't give it."

"The shipment will be large that night."

"That's the reason they gave me. That's why, they say, they want to go in then."

"Such a pity."

"We'll have to move faster. Still nothing on Crimmins?"

"Only what you already know. The Blue Lagoon is owned by one of his subsidiaries."

"I need *some*thing more."

Emilio, grave with concern, nodded in assent. "I will try with all my heart."

The boy's sincerity and apparent guilelessness once again

impressed Morrison. There were times when he had the impulse to throw his arm around him in a comradely way, to laugh with him as if their histories were conjoined, fellow countrymen like Diego and Rodrigo who had been reunited in a new world.

"I will pray for God's assistance."

"I need all the assistance I can get." Morrison said it without levity or humor and then berated himself for sounding so desperate. Was it pride that kept him from revealing his life was on the line? Or fear? Fear of frightening the boy off. Because if they were after Morrison wouldn't they be after his accomplice as well?

Now Emilio's eyes were turned inward, thinking hard or praying, perhaps. The boy had a simple, primitive faith that Morrison found both endearing and incomprehensible. At their first meeting he had told Morrison that the illicit trade in wildlife was proof the devil existed, that he was active in the world today and more powerful than ever, and that he, Emilio, would thank God everyday for this opportunity to battle Satan and his disciples. At the time, Morrison had found that commitment comforting, another reason to believe the boy was an ally he could depend upon.

He asked now, out of concern for the boy's safety as much as his own, "Are you in touch with anyone else in Customs these days?"

Emilio shook his head. "Only you."

Morrison was grateful for that. "There's one other thing. I shot at someone in the mangrove tonight. I may have hit him."

"I will keep my eyes pulled."

"*Peeled.*"

"Yes, I will keep them peeled as well."

Morrison laughed for the first time that day.

BEFORE he left the Shack his mind wandered dream-like, image to image: he saw himself standing on the back deck with Emilio, walking with him in the shadows along the river, talking in low voices at a table in the cramped confines of a trailer: things too dangerous in real life.

There was so much to tell the young man about his life, the time he spent alone, the part that no one knew. And he wanted to hear in depth the story of how a small-town boy from the mountains of Central America came to realize his dream of living in the

United States; because at this point he knew only the few details Emilio had offered when they first met: that while at the university in Guatemala he had gone to the U.S. embassy and offered his services. It was a brash, idealistic and naïve thing to do, Emilio said, but he had seen first-hand the ravages of the animal trade in his own country—not only the plunder of the forests but what it had done to his own sister, an animal rights' activist who had been murdered under mysterious circumstances—and he wanted to help anyway he could. Guatemala was weak; it could not win the war against the smuggling of wildlife. But America was strong. In America, he believed, all things were possible.

The embassy never contacted him so he saved enough money and arranged his own passage here and became part of the Guatemalan community in Mangrove Bay. One day, he told Morrison, I will prove I am worthy to be a citizen of America. And that was yet one more reason, Morrison assumed, why he had put himself in danger as an informant. To prove his worthiness to be called an American.

A love song whined from the jukebox as Morrison considered how much they had in common; because he, too, had never stopped believing in his power to make the world, in some small way, a better place.

Before leaving he stole a last look at the young man beside him—the broad forehead and flattened nose, the dark shining eyes—and pushed himself up reluctantly from the table.

"*Vaya con Dios*," Emilio said behind him.

Yes. *Vaya con Dios*, he muttered to himself, stepping out into the night.

But as he passed through the trailer camp, he didn't feel the presence of God alongside him. If anything, he felt more alone than ever and the feeling chilled him, made him shudder despite his jacket and the warm tropical air.

The brown and white puppy was still chained outside the trailer which was dark and quiet this time of night. At Morrison's approach the dog whined softly. From inside the trailer a voice yelled "Shut the hell up, you damn mutt."

Its tail beat joyously as Morrison freed the pup from its tether. He knew people at the animal shelter in Homestead who would find it a better home.

----*SIX*----

ON THE ROOF OF HIS bungalow that faced the river, a vulture flapped its wings and flew into the night. So far Morrison had been fortunate to have no neighbor next door. But apparently that had changed. A light shone in the room attached to his.

The two units shared a common porch and he stepped onto it gingerly, moving quickly and with a light step to his door. With the room adjacent to his quiet, he hoped he might be able to sleep, but lying in the dark, the dog curled on the floor beside the bed, his mind kicked into high gear, looking for answers to the crisis that had descended upon him, wondering how he might protect the boy.

Then his new neighbors, apparently after a night of drinking, arrived giggling and talking in loud voices, and *shushing* themselves which resulted in louder and more intense giggling. Once inside their room they grew even noisier, banging into things, dropping their shoes heavily onto the floor. Giggling even harder.

He heard water running in the bathroom and more giggling and then the bed creaked noisily. The woman said, "Aw, come on, Johnny, you promised."

A man's groan.

The woman said something he couldn't hear. Then the bed springs creaked more violently than before. The headboard slapped the wall and the woman was laughing. "Thank God," she cried. "Oh, thank God."

The headboard thumped the wall again and again; the woman shrieked in joy—the thumping in perfect time with her cries. A few moments passed before the man said, "Wait, wait, just hold on." His footsteps made a clunking sound as he crossed the room. The A.C. hummed into life and he clunked back across the floor.

Even with the machine running Morrison could hear them, and even after he got up to close the bathroom door. Holding his ears, he sat wearily on the edge of the bed. Finally he pulled on his pants and stepped onto the porch where he thought it might be quieter, but they had left a window open and, if anything, their noises were louder here, remarkably insistent, untiring.

He'd always been a stranger to such desperate passion, determined as he had been to keep his emotions in check. Solitude, his chosen shield.

A shield from what? he asked himself now.

Nothing he conceived by way of explanation seemed adequate. *This* was the consequence: a man alone, at the most critical point in his life, eavesdropping on the intimacy of others.

Hearing them so intimately in the still air he felt indecent, as if he were the one at fault. He walked toward the hotel where a single light shone in the lobby. At the path's end the Tiki Hut sat dark and still, windows boarded for the night. Along the river, pelicans stood guard atop the mooring posts. The light of a fishing boat grew larger as it came off the bay. It passed him slowly, engine throbbing low, heading upriver to the packing house. More contraband? Or was it what it appeared to be, a boat delivering its day's haul of seafood?

When Morrison returned to the bungalow the yellow porch light had been turned on and the man, Johnny, shirtless and holding a glass of whiskey, lounged in the doorway. "Crazy out there, isn't it?" He raised his glass toward the swamp and its noises. "Nature. Always stirring things up. Pushing us to the edge."

"I wouldn't know." Morrison sensed the man was trouble and, crossing the porch, stood at his door, fumbling for the key.

"How's that? That you wouldn't know."

Morrison only half-turned. It seemed indecent to look at him, bare-chested as he was, the door to his room open behind him. "I've never paid much attention to the workings of nature," he lied.

"That a fact?"

The way he said it—aggressively, mockingly—aroused Morrison's curiosity and he stopped searching for his key. "Yes, it is."

The man's smile was friendly, disarming in a boyish way. He

was younger than Morrison had thought. Early to mid-twenties, at most. Well developed chest, his skin smooth and tanned. A kid, really, trying to fake the bearing of someone older. Behind him there was no light in the room, no movement. The girl must be in the bathroom.

"So why's that?" Johnny was saying. His eyes glinted playfully in the dull yellow light. He was still waiting for an answer.

"I can't say. I've never given it much thought."

"More important things to think about, right? Man like you."

"Like anyone, I guess. You get busy." The young man's scrutiny made him uncomfortable but he stayed where he was, staring back at the probing eyes that watched him.

The skin around those eyes had tightened. The voice came at him like a threat. "It's you quiet, unassuming types—"

"I beg your pardon?"

"Don't mind me," Johnny said quickly, flashing a smile. "Just blowing off steam. The heat, you know. Been a long night."

"I think I'll go inside."

He turned toward his door but the kid came forward, grabbed his arm. "No, really, man. I'm sorry, really. Just passing the time." He was all boyish charm again, eyes faintly mischievous. "Name's Johnny-O. That's Johnny hyphen O."

He offered his hand. Morrison took it reluctantly.

"No hard feelings, man." Behind him the bathroom door opened. Light spilled onto the floor and the woman, dressed in a short gauzy robe, stepped into it.

Morrison stared, transfixed, then caught himself and pulled his gaze from her. "Walter," he said to the young man.

"Aggie," Johnny-O said over his shoulder, "Come on out here. Give Walter a better look at that new robe I got you."

She stood in the doorway, hip cocked in a mock pose and smiled at Morrison. The robe, vaguely transparent, fell to mid-thigh, exposing her tanned legs. It was open at the neck and he could see her breasts beneath the gauze. "Feels real good on my skin," she said, then leaned down to kiss Johnny-O. "Thank you, baby. You're so good to me."

"Bring us that bottle. Walter here needs a drink."

"No, I—"

"One drink."

"No, thanks."

"One drink, man, that's all. Neighbor to neighbor. It won't

kill you."

"No use arguing," Aggie said. She was beautiful in a slatternly way. Her dark hair had been blow-dried carefully into waves. Her face, heavily made up, had a fallen angel quality with its wide eyes and perfectly formed nose and mouth. "He won't take no for an answer. We got that in common, don't we Johnny?"

"You got that right."

She came back with a bottle and glass and poured a drink. Johnny-O took the bottle from her, doubled the whiskey in the glass, and handed it to him.

"You two have a nice chat now, you hear. I'm gonna cozy up in bed." She gave Morrison a slow, lazy smile that seemed to linger in the air even after she'd turned away. She closed the door part way, but not enough to prevent him from seeing her—with the help of the bathroom light—as she stretched out on the bed, the robe riding up on her legs, falling open across her chest.

The porch ceiling fan stirred the slow, heavy air. "So," Johnny-O was saying, "what is it you said you do, *Walt*?"

"I didn't say."

"No, you didn't, now did you?"

A smile, slow and laconic, smeared across his lips and Morrison wondered if the two of them worked on their smiles together, standing before a mirror perhaps, seeing whose was slower, lazier.

Johnny-O scratched a bite on his neck from a mosquito that had made it through the porch screen. "It's okay to call you 'Walt,' isn't it? I mean, you don't mind my saying so, Walter's a little lame. But Walt, Walt's got some heft to it. Used to have a gun I called Walt. A Walther .45. Little Walt. 'Cause of its size, you know. Tiny. Fit the palm of my hand." He held out his palm as though he were feeling Little Walt right there in his grip. Then he closed his fingers around it and smacked his lips in a satisfied way. "So you a player or what? You some kind of go-getter?"

"Salesman."

Johnny-O cocked his head and squinted at him with an exaggerated look of suspicion. "You been trying to sell me something here behind my back?"

"Not unless you're in the market for a Bible."

"You're a *Bible* peddler?" Johnny-O threw his head back and laughed. "Real quaint. Real ancient. Us living in modern times and all. Godless world, you know."

"Not down here in Dixie."

Johnny-O sipped his whiskey and regarded him with bemused curiosity. "You a holy man, Walt? That what you are?"

"I just sell the things. I don't read them."

"Hypocrite, huh?"

"Man's got to make a living."

"That he does." He raised his glass to his lips and watched Morrison over the rim.

" 'Course it's still dishonest, isn't it? What kind of country we gonna have if everyone's a fraud in the work they do? What does it say about us? America, I mean."

The punk as moral critic. The absurdity of it amused Morrison. "You're right, of course," he said in a reasonable voice. "We all have a responsibility." He sipped his whiskey, eyes fixed on the man. "What about you? Your line of work."

"This and that." Johnny-O's lips uncoiled in a smile. "Let's just say, I see opportunity where others don't. Right now I'm temporarily unemployed, you might say." He glanced into the room. "Ain't that right, honey bell?"

Aggie lay in bed, head propped with two pillows. Daydream position. One leg was bent at the knee and she wiggled it slowly from side to side. "Everything's temporary with you, Johnny-O."

"Not everything."

Morrison couldn't take his eyes off the slow movement of her leg and Johnny-O, catching him at it, gave him a comradely wink. "Women, they own us, don't they?"

Morrison set down the glass on the railing and said good night.

"Night, neighbor. See you in the morning."

There was a hint of menace in the man's voice which made the "neighbor" reference all the more ironic for Morrison. He'd never had neighbors, only people living next door, as unknown to him as he was to them.

The puppy greeted him at the door, followed him into the bathroom. In the night light's glow he bent over the sink to spray on more repellent. Living here, he'd quickly learned, meant having to protect yourself constantly. If it wasn't the bugs, it was the sun or the snakes or the gators. Or the vultures threatening with their slow-motion circles in an endless sky. You couldn't escape them.

In the mirror his face stared back at him. With his fingertips he smoothed his straight dark hair. Except for his intense eyes and strong chin, it was an unremarkable face, or so he had always believed. A face, despite his years, not yet defined. He covered it now with a towel and patted it dry.

Through the bathroom wall he heard the woman laugh again, so clear and close she might have been standing beside him. Her companion said something muted and indistinct. The woman laughed again in a way that suggested she was taking exception to whatever had been said.

In his underwear he lay on damp sheets, his hand reaching out to scratch the puppy's head.

Through the wall he heard Aggie's voice. "Come on, baby," she cooed, "be sweet to me, okay. Be sweet to your baby."

A combination of loneliness and dread, an unyielding ache, nagged at him. He felt a sudden, child's longing to go home; but there was no place he could truly call home. Certainly not the apartment he kept in Granite City across the river from St. Louis. He had not spent more than three or four weeks there in the years he worked for the Division. And certainly not his aunt's new place in Tampa. Home had long ago ceased being a place for Morrison, had become instead another of the countless things he'd lost in childhood.

If our capacity for love, both the giving and the receiving of it, is conditioned by childhood, by our first experiences with love, as he had once read somewhere, then perhaps that—even more than the nature of his job—helped explain the loneliness he'd lived with, that he felt so acutely now.

Again he reached down to pet the puppy. The dog lay on its side, nestling its head against Morrison's open hand. Tomorrow, before he became more attached to it, he would bring it to the shelter.

He tried to close his ears to mute the jangle of bed springs, the cries of delight that issued from the woman in breathless gasps. He would have laughed again, for the second time that day, had the situation been different: if the clock wasn't ticking on what might be the last seventy-two hours of his life, if he knew what he should do about Emilio.

The question begged for his answer.

How are you going to protect the boy?

----*SEVEN*----

ROWAN, WITH ONE EYE ON the rear view, was heading south on 95. Heavy traffic, as usual. Not much chance to gun the Caddy.

Damned Ricardo.

He had hoped to be down past Philly by now, but the guy had been out of the store when Rowan arrived. The kid cleaning the dog cages wasn't sure when he'd be back. "Nice dogs," the kid had said, extending his hand to touch them. Rowan had yanked them back out of reach.

The kid, whose breath reeked of garlic and tobacco, looked plainly hurt. "Just wanted to pet them."

Rowan mumbled something about how valuable the dogs were and went outside to wait. He tried keeping them on a newspaper spread next to him on the front seat but they kept climbing on him, licking his face. When one of them began scratching at the leather, he scooped them up and prowled Fordham Road in search of a tree with a patch of dirt. He traveled two blocks in each direction. Not a tree in sight.

Afraid they would run off if he let them loose, he bent down to hold them over the curb by the scruff of their necks, urging them to "Pee already, will you!" when they stared up at him with bewildered eyes. Passers-by gave him weird looks. But he continued to shake them over the lip of the curb—hey, it worked for piggy banks, didn't it?

Not a drop.

Finally he straightened up; his back was killing him. On the return to the store, the one cradled in his right arm peed on his raincoat. He could laugh about it now but at the time it wasn't funny and to make things worse Ricardo hadn't shown for another half hour. Regina was right, though. No questions, no hassles. He'd walked away with $3200 in cold cash.

"Find them a good home," he'd said before leaving.

Then he'd returned to his car, casting an apprehensive eye on Freddy in the back seat. The snake paid him no attention, fixated as he was on the three mice cowering in the next cage.

Now, driving down the turnpike, something smelled sour. On this stretch of road between the tidal marshes of Secaucus and the refineries of New Brunswick, you couldn't be sure if the bad smell came from inside or outside the car. Like the phenomenon of evil. The age-old question his professor of moral theology at Fordham had continually raised: is the source of evil inside us or is it a separate entity visited upon mankind? At one time Rowan would have put the blame solely on the world's shoulders. Now he wasn't so sure. Now he figured that maybe the evil force in the world was no more than the cumulative power of every individual act of malice and wrongdoing, and the consequences they spawned.

In terms of the smell, he wondered if it might be attributable to the mice in their fright having peed in the cage. Regina hadn't said anything about their excretory habits. Glancing back, he couldn't tell whether the cage floor had been soiled or not. He reached across the seat for his coat, holding the sleeve to his nose. That *certainly* stunk. Of that, at least, he could be sure.

He tossed it into the back seat and checked the rear view. Ten minutes now a black Town Car had been bringing up his rear: five, six car-lengths back. He squinted for a better look at the occupants—there were two of them in the front seat, that much he could see—but the tinted windshield and the glare obscured their faces.

He pulled into the center lane and eased off the accelerator. At first the Lincoln hung back; but after several miles it cruised ahead in the passing lane. An older man and woman. He breathed easier, though his heart was still racing. He'd been watching for the cars of guys he knew, but in fact whoever was coming after him could be in *any* car. That red Impala back there. Or that Bonneville coming up fast. He swung back into the left lane and gunned the Caddy, leaving the Bonneville in the dust. When he overtook the Lincoln he hit the horn hard because the old geezer at the wheel didn't pull over fast enough.

On the open stretch ahead he let the Caddy run. The sky had turned the same industrial grey as the landscape; wind tore

46

at the rubber stripping above the windows. When he crossed the Delaware Memorial Bridge and left Jersey behind he felt better. But as the afternoon wore on, the heavy greyness of the sky the color of his expectations, plus the flat characterless terrain, ate away at him. Think positive, he told himself. Focus on making time. It's really not that bad. You've got a plan, right?

Straight through to the South Carolina line, then ditch the interstate. That was the plan. Back roads through Georgia. Work his way into Florida via the Gulf Coast, heading for the southern tip of the state where this Dawson guy was supposed to be. Make his deal then get out of the country for a while. A year, maybe two. Enough for things to cool down. And then, what? He wasn't sure. Except that it wouldn't involve crime. Maybe he'd fall in love again. Maybe this time he'd make it work. Maybe, if he straightened out his life, Reggie would be willing to come live with him. Maybe. . . .

Some plan.

The *maybe* plan.

And maybe he'd make it to the Florida line without some car pulling alongside and blowing him away at the wheel.

THE motel, single-storied, flat-roofed, backed against a plowed field. A VACANCY sign blinked orange over the road; a row of tiny blue lights etched the porch-like overhang. Otherwise, night settled unbroken over this part of the world.

It took three hits on the bell to bring someone out, a man in his thirties, shirt open over a bare chest. He stood behind a metal cage, shook his head and rubbed his hand over his face to wake himself. "Not usually asleep this early. The kids, you know. Boys. They wear me out."

Rowan couldn't even imagine, didn't want to try. "Yeah."

The desk clerk read what Rowan had written on the registration card, said, "Your car. You forgot—"

"Caddy. '98." Rowan, too tired for details, had already moved toward the door. It was near midnight and he'd been awake the better part of forty straight hours. He figured if he kept driving into the night he wouldn't have to worry who was tailing him: he'd finish *himself* off in some ditch.

The shower, though, awakened him and he stepped outside for a smoke. Regression time again. How many times now had he given them up? A few hours back when he stopped at South of the Border for gas he'd bought a pack. Anything to blow off some tension.

Till then he'd avoided the obvious roadside rests and service areas, always driving a few miles off the Interstate for food and gas. So why did he stop at South of the Border with its carnival-like collection of curio shops, restaurants and amusement parks? He needed gas, yes. He was dying for a smoke, yes. But, if he were honest, he knew it was memory that prompted him to deviate from his plan. His honeymoon seven years back—Reggie and he had stopped there on the way to Miami.

She wanted to browse through the shops. So he'd wandered out back behind a fireworks store where he found a family graveyard in a field, a half-dozen stone markers from the 1800s. Something about the unlikely location of the grave-site there in the midst of an overgrown field tinged by the pink and green lights of the service area haunted him enough to read each of the inscriptions. Poor bastards. It wasn't bad enough they had to spend their lives tilling those desolate fields, they had to lie for all eternity next to some cheap-o, cornball, phony-Mexican roadside attraction.

When Reggie found him there she made a joke about how he shouldn't be having such dark thoughts on a day they were beginning their lives together. He'd kissed her, by way of brushing it off. Those days a kiss could do so much. So this time, too, he drove behind the fireworks store for a look. But he didn't get out of the car. A passing glance at the field was enough to bring it all back.

Now he drew on a Marlboro and stared down the walkway lit by the procession of porch lights. No lights in any of the units, not even a TV's flicker. Next to his room, an end-unit, a grassy yard housed a swing set, a see-saw and a gazebo. Beyond the yard a large pine stood on a rise and beyond that a field, small dark shoots in its furrows, that stretched away into a milky darkness. The air smelled of pine and newly-turned earth.

Before turning in, he checked on Freddy who lay coiled loosely in his back seat cage. He poked the cage until the reptile moved. Alive and well, thank the Lord.

He had trouble falling asleep. A plastic card on the bed table caught his eye and he read A SHORT HISTORY OF THE WHITE PINE MOTEL. The text explained that the motel, vintage 1955, had been run-down and abandoned for years before the present owners, Bill and Jenny Hatford, took it over in 1992. At the time they were recently married, had one child and were expecting another, and the motel was the answer to their dream of owning their own business. They invested their life savings and eight months of TLC into re-decorating the rooms, installing new fixtures and air-conditioners, re-doing *"every nook and cranny, inside and out."* The "history" ended with a plea from Jenny and Bill to treat the room and its furnishings with respect. Remember, the closing line read, this is our home as well as our investment. We ask you to love it as we and our boys do. Rowan didn't know whether to laugh at the paltry nature of their dreams or admire them. Like the family buried in the field behind South of the Border, they were either poor unfortunate slobs or luckier, far luckier, than he had been because at least in their adversity they had one another, the comfort of family. He tucked the card neatly between the phone and the alarm clock, the way he'd found it.

SOMETHING *was wrong.*

He woke to darkness. The porch lights were off and so was the VACANCY sign. He lay still, his body tense. He blinked to penetrate the blackness. Slowly a greyness settled along the upper window panes, became sky above the tree line. Shadows assumed the shapes of parked cars; a nearer shadow darkened the window, moved on. Whispers came from beyond the door.

Wide awake now, he strained to identify the voices. The door swung inward. Two figures stood in dark silhouette. One of them flicked the lights, the other leaned close to Rowan, squinting in the sudden brightness. Anthony La Grosa. AKA Gross Tony. Rowan groaned.

"Didn't wake you, did we?" La Grosa grinned, feigning apology. The man at the door, Mookie Wells, laughed.

"The hell outta bed," La Grosa said.

Like a tree he'd been growing rounder every year. Not quite tipping the scales at 300 yet, but not far away either. He dropped into a chair that strained under his weight. In the doorway, Mookie Wells glanced across the parking lot then pulled the door closed behind him. He was as skinny as La Grosa was fat. Rowan called them M&M, the deadly duo. La Grosa the *m*eat, Wells the *m*otion.

The big man studied him from the chair. "Once a screw-up, always a screw-up."

"That's me, a compound screw-up." Rowan grinned at him malevolently. "Why screw-up only once, when you can do it again and again?"

"You don't grow up, do you? You were a wise-ass when I met you, you're even more of a wise-ass now."

"I like to be consistent."

"I was in your position, I'd show a little more humility." He nodded to Wells. "Check him out, Mook. That bulge there in his pants."

Wells patted him down, pulling the wad of bills from his pocket. He held the money up for LaGrosa to see. "Big time spender."

The fat man motioned with his fingers. "Gimme."

Rowan sat hunched on the side of the bed, groaning inwardly. The money, Regina's money. That he'd screwed himself again was bad enough. But watching LaGrosa stuff the bills into his shirt hurt deeply. He thought about how hard she must have worked for that.

He'd let her down. Again.

He laughed at how pathetic he was. Though least he'd been smart enough to sleep with his pants on. He'd been spared the humiliation of having to get dressed in front of these goons. "How'd you find me?"

"Were you lost?" La Grosa broke into a belly laugh, Wells joining in. "What do you think, Mook? Needle in a haystack, right?"

"You're makin' me gotta pee here." Wells was doubled over by the door. "That was brilliant, Row. Shakin' them dogs like that to make them go. Real brilliant."

"Real touching with your ex, too," La Grosa said. "Real touching."

"So why'd you drive all this way? Coulda saved yourself gas money."

"Boss thought you should worry a little. A dose of anxiety, ya know, help you think straight."

"I'm thinking fine."

"Not the way he sees it." La Grosa, his triple chins jiggling against his shirt, hunched his weight forward in the chair. "Man's a double-crosser, he pays double, too. You know the rules."

"Hey, Tony, got to pee real bad," Wells said from the door.

"So, pee, already." He sucked in his gut to make room for

Wells to pass between his chair and the bed. In the moment when the man's eyes drifted toward the bathroom door, Rowan bolted.

Out the door, through the side yard, leap-frogging the see-saw, dodging between the swing set and the gazebo. He had reached the pine tree, the field opening beyond, when a hand grabbed his arm, yanked it back at an excruciating angle.

He cried out in pain. "All right, all right!"

He stopped struggling and the pressure eased. He was being pushed through the pine shadows toward the gazebo.

La Grosa, already inside, sprawled on the bench, watching Rowan being forced to his knees on the wood floor. "That's better. More appropriate for a man in your position."

Rowan turned to look at the man who had brought him to his knees. Not someone he knew. An over-sized greaser with a face blotchy as ground hamburger.

"Niccolo, piccolo." La Grosa was shaking his head, as if something really saddened him. "You're your own worst enemy, aren't you?"

Rowan stared back at him, offering nothing. He'd be damned if he'd give a punk like Gross Tony the satisfaction of analyzing him. Even if the guy *was* onto something.

"How many people you figure you hurt in your lifetime? I mean, not even counting your father, may he rest in peace, or your ex, or all them people put down money on a certain horse at Belmont last week, friends of yours, business associates like me or Mookie or Vincenzo here. How many, you figure?"

A wind off the field brought smells of earth and pine through the gazebo's open spaces. In the distance, growing louder, he heard a freight train's whistle. "Up yours, Tony."

"Up mine, huh? That's all you can say? Up *mine*?"

"That's all I can say."

"Listen up, you piece of trash." La Grosa's face flushed red, its color visible even in the dim light, the cords in his neck ready to pop. "Only reason you're not buried out in that field by now is the boss needs you to do something for him. Redeem yourself." He leaned so far forward Rowan thought the weight of his belly and his chins would pull him down to ground level. "Now here's the deal-eo. Listen close. Real close."

But Rowan never got to hear the deal. A car had pulled off the highway and stopped in the driveway, its high beams sending blinding white light into the gazebo. Later, Rowan would speculate that perhaps the driver was lost or was deciding whether the motel had shut down for the night. But as soon as the light struck them he was in motion again, slipping between Vincenzo and Mookie, jumping the railing and beating his way across the yard, up the rise.

The notion that he might race across the field and catch the freight offered itself to him but when he reached the pine tree and saw the wide field spread out before him, he stopped running. Beyond the wind-break the train traveled in a dark line like a promise withdrawn. He turned to face the man coming at him—it was Mookie—who ran with his gun held at his side. As he rushed across the top of the rise his foot struck a root, his body hurtling down into the field, his gun landing several feet ahead of him in the plowed earth.

Rowan reached the gun at the same time the train's whistle sounded again, an attenuated stabbing wail of a sound blown back across the empty farmland. Vincenzo had cleared the rise, stopping beneath the tree to raise his gun hand. Rowan fired at him first, the man's shoulder jerking back as if someone had pushed him. He was a wide target, hard to miss, and Rowan fired again, hitting his belly this time and Vincenzo, like an effigy dropped from the branches above, hung there a moment before collapsing. Rowan stepped back and shot point-blank at Mookie who had picked himself up—pine needles clinging to his cheeks—and was coming at him cat-like in a low crouch.

From the top of the rise LaGrosa, wheezing and wobbling, shot at him and missed. Rowan's shot missed as well. When the fat man emerged from the tree's shadow, Rowan took a step closer and fired again. Gross Tony, whose breathing troubles kept him from getting off his second shot quickly enough, seemed to hiccup when the bullet hit him, his mouth opening in an O as his cheeks went hollow.

WHEN Rowan came back down into the yard the train whistle had faded, sounding more like a dove cooing from the field's edge, and there was no sign of the car that had pulled into the driveway.

Only after he'd hit the road again, ten or twelve miles from the motel, was he struck by the bitter pain of remembrance. The money, the money.

No way could he go back.

Too risky now. His only hope was that the train whistle had muted the gunshots and that Bill and Jenny Hatford, worn out by their kids, were still in deep sleep. That would buy him a few hours at least. And thank god he hadn't written his license number on the registration card; Hatford had been too sleepy to catch it.

He reached for his wallet, held the billfold open with his thumb. A few hundred bucks, at best. He was really in dire straits now. In the rear view he caught a glimpse of the three mice, agitated and sleepless, eyeing their future in the cage beside theirs.

He'd never paid much attention to symbolism before, and he sure as hell didn't want to start now.

It was later in the night, sometime before four, when he passed a sign that read: *RIVER HOTEL, 40 Miles Ahead.* He drove for miles through scrub pine country and then, miles more, through lowland marsh with stick-like trees rising here and there at jagged angles. The entire time he brooded about this latest turn of events. Never had he killed a man before. Yet back there, within a span of seconds, he'd laid three of them to rest.

He'd wanted to make a clean start. Yeah right, he told himself. Real clean, Nicky. Real clean.

His moral theology teacher would have laughed at his naiveté. Virtue's an illusion, the old priest would have said. It means you haven't been tested properly yet. Only in moments of desperation is a man's true moral nature revealed.

So now he was a killer, too. One more thing to add to his list of sins. One more desperate move in a lifetime of desperate moves.

And the mob would be on him now with a full-court press.

Ahead of him a draw-bridge arched above a river and when he crossed it he saw lights a mile or so farther on. He stopped at a mini-mart and asked how far the road went.

"Don't go nowhere but into water and swamp," the clerk told him. "You done gone far as you can go."

PART TWO: FRIDAY

----*EIGHT*----

THE WHITE PANEL TRUCKS WERE registered to a man named Harlan Leach in the town of Jackson, Florida. Krebs had phoned Morrison the details early that morning. "What we have on Leach isn't much. Your basic redneck drifter. Lived all over South Florida. Odd jobs here and there—mostly unemployed, though. Half-dozen arrests for violating the state game laws. Didn't serve any time. Local judges tend to go easy on that kind of stuff. They figure it's a man's right to live off the land. The Cracker mentality."

A moment passed before Morrison asked: "Sunday night. What do you hear?"

"Something big's going down. You're right about that. It's in the air."

"Nothing hard? Nothing I can use?"

"Nobody's talking," Krebs said with genuine regret.

For years now Krebs had been his go-to man, someone who would talk to him without authorization. Repaying a favor Morrison had done for him a long time back. Thank God the fellow was the grateful sort, Morrison thought as he drove out of town in the direction of Jackson. Because for a man in his position, an agent who'd fallen out of favor, there was no one else who would talk to him without prior approval—which, of course, would never be granted now. What little the Division would offer him would be funneled through Caruso. And that, of course, would never be enough to save himself.

But Krebs—Krebs was a lifeline in the darkening sea.

THE road to Jackson angled south off Highway 41 into Big

Cypress National Preserve. Lowlands stretched away to dome-like stands of cypress, the overwhelming blue of the sky interlaced with strips of white clouds that cast drifting finger-thin shadows over the marsh. The town itself—no more than a cluster of wood frame houses built close to the road—stood on higher ground in a hardwood forest.

Past the houses a dirt road curled into the trees.

Morrison eased the Ford onto the hard-packed grooves of sand. The car bucked and dipped with the ridges, trees crowding close to the road on both sides, sunlight breaking in splinters across leaves and branch, touching the roadbed in splashes up ahead.

A half-mile farther on, the road dead-ended in a clearing where patches of brown grass sprouted from the sandy soil. At the clearing's far end, a small house stood near the tree line. The roof slanted back, lean-to style, and the wide planks of the siding had been weathered to a brittle grey. Nearby, a shed made of the same wood siding listed away from its stone foundation.

No one seemed to be around.

He left the car in the center of the clearing and walked toward the house. The front windows were boarded, the door padlocked. In red paint, across the door, someone had written KEEP OUT THIS MEANS U.

He knocked, louder than he had to for such a small house, and leaned close to the door. Nothing moved inside. He knocked again, then stepped back from the roof's overhang. All the windows had been boarded, save for a small side window with its curtain drawn. Between the folds of cloth, he glimpsed bed springs and a mattress, the room's darkness shot with thin lines of light that squeezed through the rotting plank walls.

The shed door was padlocked, too. No windows. He found a gap in the planks where he could smell more than he could see: hay, newly turned earth, and something sweet that he couldn't identify. A shaft of what might have been a pitchfork rested against the far wall.

Between the house and the shed a path ran into the woods. The narrow trail of dirt twisted downward at a slight grade between leafy, vine-draped trees. Partway down the hill he heard the murmur of water before he came upon a dark tea-colored trickle that meandered between muddy banks. The path continued on the far side winding farther downhill but he decided to turn back.

In the clearing he stood beside the Ford and stared across the empty yard. The day was clear, cooler than yesterday and for the first time in weeks he didn't feel overheated in his suit. It seemed, finally, the unseasonably warm weather pattern had broken.

Mosquitoes hummed in the forest's shade.

Time—all motion—ceased.

He had the prickly feeling of being watched.

He scanned the tree-line for hidden shapes, movement of any kind. Last night's image flashed before him: the dim and shadowed face, a rifle raised shoulder-high, holding him in its sights.

Slowly he backed toward the car, sliding in behind the wheel and cranking the engine.

HE parked outside the first of the town's clustered houses and took his briefcase from the trunk. On the porch he stood with a Bible in hand.

His knock went unanswered.

At the next house a car was parked alongside. The name hand-painted on the mailbox said LEACH. But again his knock went unanswered.

A curtain parted in an upstairs window. A pallid face, indistinguishable as male or female, stared down at him. He waved. The face that watched him showed no expression.

He walked to the door and knocked again. "Hello," he called out. "Hello up there."

His words hung in the air. When he looked again, the curtain had fallen back into place and the face was gone. He turned to see if he had roused anyone from the other houses, but his presence appeared to have gone unnoticed.

At the next house an elderly woman opened the door. She was shy of five feet, a brown shriveled face, bone-white hair. "Help you?"

"Yes, yes you can," he said in his smoothest down-home salesman's voice. "I have an appointment with one of your neighbors, a Mr. Harlan Leach, who was fortunate enough to win our annual Bible lottery. I'm here to present Mr. Leach with his prize." He held out the Bible. "But I'm afraid he doesn't seem to be at home at present. I was hoping you'd know where I might find him."

The woman's eyes, flat and glassy, fixed on the Bible. "He won him a contest, huh?"

"Yes, ma'am. You know where I might find him?"

"You can leave it here. Give it to him when I see him."

He forced a smile. "Well that's mighty kind of you, ma'am. Was up to me, I sure would leave it right here in your pretty little hands. But company policy says all lottery winners got to be handed their prize in person. That's the rules."

"I can't help you then, can I?" she said sweetly.

"You don't have any idea when Mr. Leach will be back?"

"No, sir, I sure don't."

"Do you know where he might be?"

"Anywhere." The woman stared past him as if she saw something but when he turned the street was as empty and still as before.

"Does he work anywhere nearby?"

"No place particular."

"I see," Morrison said, studying her to see whether she was being deliberately evasive. But her shriveled face and washed out blue eyes seemed innocent and guileless.

"Why not set a minute, take the load off?" She motioned to a bench farther down the porch.

He set down the briefcase and sat beside her on the bench, his eyes raking the street, the other yards, in hopes of finding someone more helpful. But it seemed, at the moment, this woman was his only option. "I noticed that second house there, the Leach name was on the mailbox."

"There's Leaches all through here. Thick as fleas. Married one myself." Her mouth tightened at the edges. "Thought he was so damn smart. Been gone to the earth near fifty years and *I'm* still here. That's how damn smart he was." She leaned forward and spat into the dirt. "Them Leaches has their ways," she said.

"How's that?"

"They just do, is all."

He waited for more, but she sat staring at the street, her mouth tight as a prune, her eyes vacant. He held out the Bible. "For your kindness."

"Thought that was Harlan's," she said, a note of suspicion creeping into her voice.

He patted the side of the briefcase. "Got his right here. All wrapped up, real pretty like." He stepped out into the sunlight and waved in the direction of the neighboring houses, in various stages of disrepair. "Anyone else nearby might know where Harlan is?"

"Not likely."

He again watched to see if she might be covering something up, but she was muttering and running her fingers over the embossed letters on the book's cover. "One more thing, ma'am. You mind telling me what Mr. Leach looks like, case I run into him on the street somewhere?"

"Kind of average-looking."

"Tall? Short?

"Kind of."

"Kind of what?"

She squinted her eyes and screwed up her chin, thinking hard. "Kind of average, I'd say."

"Thin? Fat?"

"Yup."

"Beg your pardon?"

"Kind of in-between, I'd say."

Morrison nodded, as if he understood. "Thank you, ma'am." He offered her his salesman's smile and turned toward the street.

"Praise Jesus," she said behind him.

"Praise Jesus," he said, with as much enthusiasm as he could muster. The last house in the cluster, a one-story sorry-looking affair, stood several hundred feet farther along the road. He heard a banging, metal on metal, coming from the back. When he came around the side of the house something lunged at him and he jumped back. The dog, black and huge, strained against the rope that held him, barking violently, teeth bared, drool foaming along the lower rim of its mouth.

Morrison stared back at the beast, the blind hatred in its eyes, and said, "Easy, boy." If his heart hadn't been pounding so wildly he might have laughed at the irony of that, the ineffectuality of his words, which, if anything, had only driven the mongrel to a deeper level of fury, straining so hard against his tether it looked as though he might choke himself to death.

Vicious master, vicious dog. That had usually been the case in Morrison's experience. He didn't blame the dog—at least not until he'd had a look at its owner. As he approached the truck parked in the back yard, its hood raised, he heard the cursing first, then saw the legs extending from beneath the truck.

He stood there, holding the briefcase, and cleared his throat. A voice from beneath the truck said, "What the—?"

The legs began to move, the body inching backward until a

wiry, hawk-eyed man sat there looking up. He pulled himself slowly to his feet and stared hard at Morrison.

"Name's—" Morrison began, holding out his hand.

"The hell outta here." He stepped past Morrison, reached into his back pocket for a screw driver and flung it at the dog who yelped and stopped barking immediately. Turning away he stared angrily, a sheen of sweat across his forehead, into the mouth of the truck. "Dumb asses," he muttered to himself then stepped onto the fender and leaned under the hood.

"Would you know where I might find Harlan Leach?" Morrison spoke to the back of the man's faded plaid shirt. "He's won a giveaway contest and I'm here to deliver his prize."

The man shifted his weight, grunting hard as he tried to loosen a bolt on the engine block.

"He's not home at the moment and I was wondering—"

"What'd he win?" The voice was flat, indifferent. He worked the wrench, without looking up.

"Five hundred dollar cash bonus."

"No way."

Morrison leaned close to the truck, added a calculated urgency to his words. "So you see that's why it's important I locate him. Because this offer expires—"

"What organization you say you was with?"

"The Holy Light Book Company. Memphis, Tennessee.

"Might as well leave it with me, cause you ain't gonna find Harlan."

"Why's that?"

The man raised his head, turned a sour look at Morrison. "Cause he don't wanta be found." He slid off the truck and approached him, eyes grey and raw and rimmed with red. At his side the wrench hung loosely from his fist. "And if you did find him you'd most likely be lookin' at the leave-me-the-hell-alone end of a double-barreled twin gauge."

The dog strained against his tether, barking violently again. "So you gonna leave that bonus money with me like I asked you to?"

"I'm afraid I can't do that."

"Then get the hell offa my property." He leaned aggressively toward Morrison, his grin crooked, breath smelling like something had died. "Before I let Satan here loose. Ain't had his breakfast yet."

---- NINE----

MEANNESS, DELIBERATE MEANNESS LIKE THAT, always disturbed Morrison and he stopped at the yard's edge to steady himself. He forced himself *not* to be judgmental. After all, he didn't live in the man's skin, had no idea of the forces that shaped him. He was coming to believe we were all worthy of compassion, if the facts were known. *If* the facts were known. They rarely were, of course. Instead we were merely passers-by, surfaces colliding and recoiling. Wary of each other from afar.

At least that had been *his* experience.

As a child he'd been afraid of such meanness, standing unarmed and defenseless in the face of it—the hoods, the punks, the gangs that roamed the housing project where he'd lived—but now he didn't have to cower. Now he had the means to stand his ground, inflict some damage of his own.

He'd worked hard to give himself that power. His stint in the army the first step. Hand to hand combat training where he learned to disarm a man, kill him if necessary, with his bare hands. The long hours on the firing ranges where he became proficient not only with high-powered rifles but with pistols, as well. His continued training with the F&W, then with Customs. And now, day by day, he kept up a personal training regimen to keep his body in shape, to maintain his marksmanship skills.

Yes, he had the means now to command respect. But as a reasonable man he used force only when necessary, and *only as much force as was necessary*. He knew when to pull back and re-group.

The vicious, near-hysterical barking followed him as he turned away. When he passed the mailbox, he checked for a name.

There was none. Like Harlan Leach, this guy didn't want to be found, either.

On the road out of Jackson he stopped at an old country store: uneven wood-plank floors, a visible layer of dust on the three aisles of shelves. He walked past the fishing and hardware supplies to the cash register in back.

Behind the counter, stacking packs of Marlboro Lights into a display case, a boy with pale-yellow hair turned to him with a half-smile, said, "Mack'll be right out."

A shadow appeared against the screen door behind him. The door made a twanging sound when it opened; a man, solemn-eyed and stoop-shouldered, came stiffly to the register.

"Howdy," Morrison said.

Mack was an older, more subdued version of the back yard mechanic. Same eyes, same body type. A brother or half-brother maybe, kin-folk of some sort, was Morrison's guess. "Sure is a fine day out there."

"Yep."

"Could use me a soda."

" 'Gainst the wall."

At the end of the counter, an old metal cooler hummed into the silence. Morrison pulled a Root Beer from the cold water. As he came back he took a box of Oreos off the shelf and set it on the counter. He reached for a dried-out looking donut in a glass display. "Real nice store you got here. Real historical."

"It's old," the boy chirped up. He was tearing open a carton of Camels with painstaking delicacy.

Morrison looked around for what else he might buy. He took two newspapers off a rack. "What do I owe you?"

Mack tallied the items as he bagged them. "$6.80."

"Say, you fellahs wouldn't happen to know a Harlan Leach, would you? Been tryin' to give him a big fat wad of prize money. Can't seem to find him noways. My boss is sure gonna be mad if I don't get Harlan his money. You wouldn't happen to know where I could find him right about now, do you?"

"No sir, I sure don't." Mack handed him his change and shut the register. His face had shut down, too, his lips locked tight. The boy kept tucking packs of Camels into the display case.

"Thought I'd ask one last time 'fore I give up. Sure is a damn shame he's got to lose out on that money, though." He handed him his HOLY LIGHT BOOKS card. Across the back, he'd written:

Harlan Leach—*contest winner*. "You happen to run into the man, give him this. Tell him call me soon as he can, so's he don't lose out on that prize."

On the way out he opened the door, the bell tinkled, and his eye caught a display of chewing gum. Instead of leaving he let the door slam and he leaned toward the wall for the gum. His mouth had been sour all morning.

Where he stood, the aisle blocked his view of the register. They must have thought he'd left, because he heard the boy saying, "You figure he's on the square or he's just another dumb-ass peddler tryin' to sell poor Harlan somethin' he don't need? "

"Smells fishy to me," Mack said, "Harlan being the way he is."

Morrison decided against the gum and opened the door again, the bell tinkling as it closed behind him. In the shade of the overhang he took the Root Beer out of the bag and dumped the rest of it—cookies, donut and newspapers—into a trash bin. The Root Beer burned his throat going down, the way he remembered it as a child.

AT a secluded stretch of the river, Emilio stood close to the water, lighting a cigarette. It took him several tries with the match, burning his fingers in the process, before he was satisfied with the draw. He blew on his fingers to cool them, then held the cigarette raised at arm's length to admire it.

Morrison left his car on the road and came toward him. "Since when did you take up smoking?"

"Since immediately." Emilio's smile was broad. He held the cigarette out for Morrison to see because it was a thing of beauty, long and sleek, smoke curling up from its tip. "Marlboro 100s. Very impressive, no?"

"I thought you were the clean-living type."

"Most certainly. But this helps to relieve stress, I am told. And we are under pressure at this moment, are we not?"

Morrison couldn't help but smile. "We are under pressure, yes. Most certainly."

"And this," Emilio held the cigarette at arm's length again, "this allows me to take smoke breaks, with the others. I am, how do you say it, one of the boys." He smiled as if he had made a joke, then his face turned serious. "Everyone on the evening shift smokes. One more occasion to see things, hear things. And today I am working a double shift, so I have even more time to observe."

"What have you heard?"

"Perhaps not very much." He shrugged. "But this, at least. Bobbie Dawson is meeting someone in Homestead today. I do not know who."

"No word on someone being shot in the swamp last night?"

"Nothing that I heard."

Morrison waited, hoping for more. "Is that it?" He couldn't hide the disappointment in his voice.

"No one is talking. No one is letting anything slip. But about the shipment coming in tonight. This time I have heard the word 'cats' used."

"What kind of cats?"

"Only the word 'cats' was used."

The big cats—lions, tigers, leopards—brought in hefty prices on the international market, Morrison knew. But there was a robust trade in the smaller ones, too. Lynx, bobcats, ocelots.

"All right," he said. "We'll talk again later. And there's one more name to listen for: *Leach*. Harlan Leach. He's connected in some way to Dawson and the others."

"Leech. Like the bloodsucker, no?"

"Like the bloodsucker. But spelled with an *a* rather than two *e*'s."

Emilio drew deeply on the cigarette, held the smoke in for several seconds, then bent over, coughing loudly.

"You'll have to do better than that if you want to be one of the boys."

"Yes, yes, I will practice," Emilio said when he recovered. "I have been practicing all this lunch hour." He looked at the cigarette as if it had betrayed him. He reached into his pocket for the box, holding it out to Morrison. "Perhaps you would like to join me?"

"Thank you, but no."

"You are—how did you put it?—a clean living man, as well. A holy man who has no religion. A man with no vices."

Morrison laughed. "No visible ones, at any rate."

"I do not think you have vices of any kind. Unlike your countrymen, who have so many, visible and not so visible."

"Now you've become a cultural critic, along with your other duties." Morrison found himself enjoying the friendly banter. If only they had more time.

"I had no vices either, before I came here." Emilio's smile was playful. He held up what was left of the cigarette as if it were a mirror. "But now I have been corrupted."

----*TEN*----

ROWAN, STILL GROGGY FROM SLEEP, sat on the bed and stared at the floor. It was mid-afternoon, which meant he'd been sleeping almost nine hours—a dead-to-the-world, dreamless sleep that left behind no memories. If only, he thought, it could be that easy to erase the past.

He blinked to clear his vision. The room was small, plain, with a slanted ceiling and a single dormer window. Other than the bed the only adornments were an oak dresser, a straight-backed wooden chair and a braided rug. Not much in the way of comfort. But at half past five in the morning, after having been on the road for the better part of a day and a night, he hadn't been particularly selective. He would have slept on the lobby couch, if it came to that. When the night clerk walked him to the third floor, showed him this room, he'd barely grumbled his assessment: "fine."

"Shall I get your bags from the car, sir?" the man had asked.

"No bags."

Just a snake. Which he'd left in its cage in the Caddy's back seat.

Moments after the clerk had closed the door, Rowan—his clothes and shoes still on—was asleep on the bed.

He smelled them now, his clothes, rank with the effects of two days' stress and sweat. That would be his first order of business, a new wardrobe, though from what he had seen of the town he would have to adjust his sense of fashion. He pushed himself up and stood unsteadily, riding out a wave of dizziness, surprised at how weak he felt.

That would have to be the second order of business: solid food, not the candy bars and chips he'd lived on in the car.

And then?

Find this Dawson guy. Make the deal. Blow this town. Keep moving. Figure a way, if he could—without a passport—to get out of the country. The final obstacle.

The floor boards creaked noisily as he crossed to the window. The place was old. A fire-trap, his old man would have called it. *Never catch me stayin' in a tinder box like this, third floor walk-up, nosirree. Someone smokin' in bed, kitchen fire, who the hell knows what, you're grilled hamburger.* The old man had been afraid of fires his whole life. So it figured, Rowan thought, given the twisted world we lived in, he'd die by fire.

He shook away the memory. It was life he had to focus on now, how to beat the odds, the way he had last night. Of course, now the stakes were higher, the odds even less in his favor.

Outside the window a fire escape in the guise of an iron ladder descended to the sloping roof of the porch. "Happy now, Dad?" he said aloud. It was the first time, since his death, he'd been able to joke about his father's obsession.

Beyond the building he could see a wide lawn, a row of bungalows and farther on the river curling past the wharves. Deadsville, he thought. If the boys don't get me, the silence will.

Over the sink in the bathroom he held his lighter to his credit cards, one by one, watched each of them soften and turn black until his name and account number melted away. He'd been living high on the hog of late: they were all maxed out. In any case, he was starting over. From here on, no paper trail.

He stripped off his clothes, let the steam from the shower wrap around him as he scrubbed away the remains of a long night behind the wheel. It disgusted him that he had to wear his soiled clothes again, but he'd take care of that soon.

In front of the mirror he combed back his wet hair. He'd lost some weight in his face, giving him a tauter, leaner-looking jaw-line. His blue eyes had regained their usual clarity. A good sign, he thought.

In the sink, as he wiped away the residue of his credit card meltdown, he felt surprised by the same uplift of spirits as when he'd left Regina. The bad news: he was on the lam from the mob and dead broke—a lethal, sorry-ass situation no matter how you cut it. The good news: he'd been given a second chance.

Who knew what he might become?

Maybe even the kind of son his old man had always wanted.

----*ELEVEN*----

FROM THE END OF THE STREET, Morrison watched Bobbie Dawson back the Camaro out of his yard. He waited until the car turned onto the Boulevard, heading north out of town, before he cranked the Ford's engine and followed.

Hemmed on both sides by dense stands of scrub pine, the road ran flat and straight to the highway, which allowed Morrison to keep a good distance back without losing sight of the silver sports car.

What he knew about Dawson he'd learned mostly from Krebs. The thirty-six year old man had been an employee of Blue Lagoon Fisheries, off and on since '97. No priors. In the past twelve months he'd made some heavy jewelry buys in Miami. For the night manager of a packing house, he had expensive taste in cars, as well. Besides the brand new Camaro, he'd bought a Cadillac back in June. Which was registered to the woman he lived with, Rayelle Williams, who waitressed and bartended at the River Hotel. She had served Morrison a number of times, both in the restaurant and at the bar. She was pretty, he thought, in a jaded way. A thin woman with dirty-blond hair dry and faded from too many chemicals, too much sun. Her face had the look of someone who'd seen what the world had to offer, and wasn't thrilled with any of it.

They were traveling east on Highway 41 toward Homestead when he caught sight of the pale-blue Cadillac behind him, coming up fast. He pulled his car to the right. The Cadillac came alongside. In the moment before it lurched ahead, he caught a glimpse of Rayelle, hands tight on the wheel, eyes locked on the road ahead.

70

It became clear when they approached Homestead that she, too, was tailing Dawson. As they wove through the streets of the city, she kept several blocks behind him, and Morrison kept close behind *her*. At one point, on the city's south side, traffic from US Route 1 spilled into the local streets, causing a jam-up. He found himself a number of cars behind them. Ahead, the light turned red. The Camaro had already made the turn. He was forced to stop and watch the Cadillac, the last of the cars to make the light, disappear around the corner.

When he finally made the turn, the street was empty ahead. He drove through several blocks of warehouses and truck terminals before spotting the Camaro parked in an alley between two older, nearly identical brick buildings. The one on the left, against which the Camaro was parked, had once housed a feed and grain supply company, according to the faded letters painted on its wall. Along that same wall, a few feet beyond Dawson's car, an iron staircase led to the second story.

He drove down the alley, past the car. When he reached the street he saw the blue Cadillac parked directly across from the feed and grain building, Rayelle's tight-lipped face raised toward whatever was on the second floor.

The alley picked up again on the far side of the street so he drove to the end of it and made a U-turn. Out of sight of the Cadillac, he parked with a dead-on view of the grain building.

The ground floor appeared unoccupied. The upstairs had been converted to what seemed to be living quarters of some kind, the stairs opening onto a wooden deck that ran the length of the building. Next to a metal door was a sliding glass door across which blinds had been drawn.

He watched Rayelle pace in the street several minutes before she crossed to the other side and climbed the stairs. She stood at the upstairs door, punching it with her fist until it opened. Bobbie Dawson stood there, shirtless, then a brown-skinned woman appeared behind him wearing a robe, pulling it tight across the front, Rayelle screaming something and lunging toward her but running into Dawson's arm which stretched like a gate across the door frame.

He came forward then, his thickset arms and muscular body forcing her back from the door, rocking her this way and that but she was still shouting and spitting at the woman. Dawson said something over his shoulder and the door slammed closed behind him as he kept backing Rayelle toward the staircase, lifting her finally and carrying her, despite her screams and kicking legs. In the alley he set her down and pulled her toward the street while she struggled, kicking and cursing, hanging back against the force of his arm.

Morrison had inched his car closer to the mouth of the alley in time to see him swing open the Cadillac's door and force her inside. He closed the door as if to lock her in and spoke to her through the window. "I can't come home now," Morrison heard him say. "I'm workin' with—" He thought the man said, "Lee" but he couldn't be sure.

Rayelle's head was bowed as if she might be listening to him, then suddenly the Cadillac leapt forward, spinning Dawson back away from it. He stood in the street watching the car drive away, tires squealing. When he turned around toward the stairs, Morrison saw the ragged lines of blood she had scratched across his back.

DAWSON was partway up the stairs when a white panel truck came down the alley behind him. The truck's horn stopped him and he came back to ground-level, standing close to the driver's side window, talking to the driver.

Crouched low in the Ford, Morrison verified the truck's plate numbers. A match with last night. From what he could tell the driver was the heavier of the two black men at the riverbank. He seemed to be talking non-stop. From time to time, Dawson nodded. Finally he stepped away from the truck and watched it move down the alley.

Minutes later, Morrison caught up with the truck as it turned onto a marginal road that led to Highway 41. Soon they were moving westbound in the direction of Mangrove Bay. Flat, marshy land dotted with occasional tree-laden hammocks stretched away to the south.

One car separated him from the panel truck which was keeping to the 55 mph speed limit. They passed two Indian villages, one on either side of the highway, an alligator farm that advertised GET SO CLOSE, YOU CAN PET 'EM, and an airboat tour operation called CAP'N WILL'S.

Finally, the panel truck made a left onto the remains of an unmarked dirt road that meandered south into the swamp. The roadbed, if it could be called that, was uneven and narrow, barely wide enough for the Ford. Morrison stopped at a point where the land crested enough for him to see the truck, apparently unattended at the moment, backed against the base of a wooded hill.

Coming down the hill, moving between the trees, the black man carried a cage. There was movement in the cage but at this distance, several hundred yards or more, he couldn't identify the animals.

The man descended the hill and loaded the cage into the back of the truck. Morrison followed as the truck headed north on 29 toward Immokalee and pulled into LAROO'S WILD ANIMAL PARK and PETTING ZOO, a few miles short of the city limits. He watched it bypass the parking lot and take a gravel road marked with a sign that read: *Service Entrance. Authorized Vehicles Only.*

Leaving his car in the lot, Morrison passed the park entrance with its two tiki huts and its oversized bright orange and yellow wooden sign depicting a leopard writhing in an anaconda's death grip. He followed the service road, stopping abruptly when he saw the truck parked inside a stockade fence-enclosed area with several sheds and a barn. The black man was dragging the cage from the back of the truck. Inside the cage was what appeared to be a pair of ring-tailed lemurs—extremely rare, critically endangered tree-dwelling primates, their wide and startled black-rimmed eyes staring, as if in expectation, in Morrison's direction.

And that, in an unexpected way, offered him an odd kind of hope. One more reason to push on.

----*TWELVE*----

WHAT MORRISON KNEW FROM EXPERIENCE was that smuggling operations had to be intercepted as close to the border, as close to the point of entry, as possible. Once the animals had been moved inland like this, they were harder to track, and it was harder to prove they'd been smuggled in. Which meant, because of an oddity in US law, that prosecuting their handlers was a near impossibility.

Under the Lacey Act, it was not a crime to own or possess exotic or endangered species, but only to sell them or their body parts for profit. And it was easy getting around that provision by simply "donating" or "giving away" the animals. So, in all practicality, prosecution became possible only for *the act of smuggling itself*, specifically for violations of the Smuggling Imports Contrary to Law Act.

He drove back to the unmarked dirt road. The area was deserted now. Nothing but the sun and shadow-streaked hill, and the high hissing sound of wind in the trees.

There was no path but he moved upward through a woodland of slash pine and oak where he had seen the black man carrying the cage. It was then he realized this was the wooded area below Harlan Leach's house. When he reached a stream he assumed it was a continuation of the one he had come upon, from the opposite direction, that morning.

He followed the stream eastward for a while but found nothing, only the undisturbed forest. Turning back and traveling westward, though, he found examples of human detritus: cigarette butts, candy wrappers, an occasional beer can. There were places where the ground was trodden into something of a makeshift trail, and in the sandy areas beneath the stands of slash pines he could see the occasional tire marks of a wheelbarrow.

He came upon the boiler first, its top a cone-shaped copper relic from the stills of Prohibition days. The base, though, had been reconstructed more recently. The area around it had been cleared, the ground looking as if it might have been swept with a broom. So was Leach a smuggler *and* a bootlegger?

A hundred feet deeper into the woods he spotted a shed: considerably larger than the one on Leach's property on top of the hill, though with the same kind of plank siding and a similar padlock—one that he could pick easily enough.

He smelled the animals before he saw them: the musky odor of fur and excrement and livestock feed. When he drew open the door he saw in the murky light that the crates and cages—a quick tally indicating there were twenty–four or twenty-five of them— had been stacked neatly against the right hand wall. Against the left wall were all the makings for home-grown whiskey: sacks of sugar and corn, a bag of oak chips, several gallons of maple syrup. And beyond that a series of oak barrels, the 55 gallon type he had seen on display in a Sears Roebuck catalog, lined the remainder of the wall. The barrels were air-tight but for a moment he imagined he could smell the sweet breath of the aging whiskey.

He stood there puzzled, watching the clouds of dust hanging in the mustard-colored light that slanted in from the high windows, and listening to the scuffling noises that came from the cages. What were these animals doing here? A second distribution point? If so, why here, so close to the fishery?

Or was this a separate enterprise? Something that Dawson and Leach and the black man were running on their own? And making bootleg whiskey, as well.

He moved across the room to inspect the wildlife. Once again, what he saw on display sickened him. The animals had been poorly cared for, to say the least. In the cages were ocelots and marmots, several pythons—including an extremely rare albino carpet Python— as well as iguanas, anteaters, brightly-colored toucans and a variety of monkeys: spider, dwarf and howler. Most, if not all, of the caged or crated captives looked malnourished and sluggish. Two of the ocelots had already died, lying flat and unmoving on their side amid a wasteland of excrement, and at least one or two more appeared to be about to expire.

More evidence of the unforgivable cruelty of this type of smuggling. What the traffickers called the "acceptable loss" factor. In their cold-eyed view, losing animals along the way was simply part of the cost of doing business.

Looking closely again at the surviving ocelots, looking into their dull, listless eyes, he was reminded of the look in his dog, Bucky's, eyes so many years ago, when he held him in his arms as the vet injected the drug that would put him to sleep. Morrison had insisted, despite his aunt's objection, that he be with Bucky when he died and, cradling him, had wondered then as he looked into his friend's still hopeful and expectant eyes, just as he wondered now looking at the dying ocelots, how people could doubt these creatures had souls, had feelings not unlike our own.

One thing he was sure of, as he closed the door and re-set the lock, was that this operation, judging by the range and array of animals it was importing, was even more extensive than he had imagined. Because, typically, smaller dealers specialized in only one class such as reptiles or fowl, or one section of the world, as a way of streamlining their network. But these people appeared to have set no limits. They were not only importing from Central and South America as he had at first assumed, but from Africa and Asia, as well.

He was standing outside considering this when he heard movement beyond the trees. Then he spotted the source, a small gnomish man not seventy-five feet away pushing a wheelbarrow down the hill, his narrow and bearded face bent low in strain. His wild hair, thick and densely matted, fell across his shoulders. Under the weight of his load he grunted, making guttural sounds that seemed to increase in intensity and volume every time he struck a rock or a root, every time he encountered an obstacle in his path.

He was moving in the direction of the still and when he reached it, he tipped the wheelbarrow forward, dislodging its cargo: two large sacks of what appeared to be—from where Morrison was standing—sugar. He bent low, dragging first one sack then the other closer to the copper boiler. Intent as he was on his task, he didn't hear Morrison's approach. When he turned finally from the boiler he was face to face with the barrel of a 9 mm.

He cried out and lurched away, eyes wide with terror, hair flaring out around his frightened face. In his panic he ran head-on into a tree, crying out again, turning with a red and bruised forehead to face his pursuer. He was pressed back against the trunk as if crucified there.

Morrison held the gun on him. "Who are you?"

Hands raised now in self-defense, the man cowered against the tree, making noises deep in his throat as if being choked. Up close he was even stranger looking than Morrison had thought. The man was hump-backed, a condition that contributed to the impression that his head was too big for his body, his eyes like two small holes drilled into his face above the dense foliage of his beard. His fingernails looked more like fangs than anything human.

"*Who are you?*"

The wild, nervous eyes looked everywhere but at Morrison.

"Who are you? What's your name?"

From the barrage of sounds issuing from the man's throat, certain syllables repeated themselves: "La. . . Le. . .La. . .Le. . . Lee. . . Leeeee."

"Leach? Are you Leach?"

The thin, narrow face bobbed convulsively, the sounds groaned forth like clogged breath, rising in pitch as he struggled to speak. "Leeeeee. . .Leeeeeeeeeee."

"*Harlan* Leach?"

"Leeeeee. . . .Leeeeeeeeeee!" A squealing, animal sound that came again and again.

His eyes, in constant motion, seemed to look everywhere at once.

Morrison understood now what the man in the country store meant when he had spoken about him. *Harlan being the way he is*.

He stood in a kind of paralysis before the deformed man. As if witnessing yet another wounded animal, he felt the air go out of him, his heart pounding ferociously, leaving him dull and sick in his gut.

He lowered the gun. In that moment, before the pistol had reached his side, the man bolted, leaping deer-like across the uneven ground, vanishing quickly into the thick underbrush.

Then Morrison was running too, though he was no match for the small, hunched fellow who was lightning-fast and unusually agile, dodging branches and plants, weaving between the broad trunks of oaks and the willowy stems of pines, leaping over fallen limbs and boggy depressions, moving more like an animal than a man. When Morrison reached the stream he had lost sight of him for good.

The forest, defiant in its stillness, seemed to mock him.

His face gone ashen, he stood rooted to the spot, struggling to regain his breath and staring at that point in the forest where he had last seen Harlan Leach.

So he had found him, finally. *But who was he?* An unearthly being, to be sure. A bootlegger who doubled as a guard, a gopher, a decoy? A crazed no-count who served as a front? Were they using him for cover—his name, his identity? Because if the trucks got traced back to him, if he was ever tracked down, he'd have nothing to reveal—mute that he presumably was.

Did that explain it?

He didn't know. When it came right down to it, he cautioned himself, he didn't know much at all about this situation he was caught in.

---- *THIRTEEN*----

ROWAN WAS FINISHING A BEER in the hotel lounge, getting the lay of the land. It had been a productive few hours since he'd hauled himself from bed. He'd found Dawson's number in the phone book and left a message. Then he'd prowled the town, what there was of it, and bought some cheap, touristy clothes. Now he figured he had some time to size up the place while he waited for Dawson to return his call.

He took a long look at his surroundings. Cypress walls, stained a rich reddish-brown, served as background for the mounted heads of wild boar, bear and deer. At the end of the L-shaped bar where he sat, a bobcat leapt from the polished surface of the wall. The aquatic world was equally well-represented: two swordfish posed as if in a duel, and several other large fish he couldn't identify swam toward the ceiling.

"Another beer?" the cocktail waitress named DeeDee asked him. She had a bounce to her walk, eyes bright and blue, a blond ponytail swinging free.

"Yeah, thanks."

She leaned below the bar, her short dress riding up on her thighs. When she set the beer down her face was flushed and she smiled brightly. It was a round, school-girl cute face that, like her body, had not yet lost its baby fat.

"So, what's there to do nights in a place like this?"

She set the bottle down. "You've got a choice, the video store or the video store. Or, if you want real excitement, you can hang out at the mini-mart."

"That's it?"

She laughed. "Except the Tiki. It's usually open till three."

He'd taken a short walk before, along the river, past the fishery. Checking things out. He was hoping he'd missed something.

"Sometimes folks go on up to Immokalee, the bars there. Or over to Homestead. But that's a drive."

"What's a pretty girl like you do to pass the time? If I might ask."

She blushed but quickly passed over the compliment. "Work, mostly. We don't close here till midnight."

"After that?"

"Hang out with my boyfriend, Lonnie. Watch TV." She glanced toward the dining room where two more tables had been occupied. Middle-aged couples, in for an early dinner. "Excuse me," she said.

He watched her glide between the tables, smiling brightly each time she took an order.

He finished off the beer and tapped his fingers on the bar in a restless rhythm. In the mirror he caught sight of himself. The only clothes available for purchase he'd found in the hardware store— mostly fishing and hunting outfits, mostly in camouflage colors. But tucked away in the back he'd come across a few sport shirts and a pair of khaki cargo pants. There were no shirts with flamingoes but the one he chose was close enough: white palm trees on a peacock-blue background. He admired it now in the mirror. Not bad, not bad. All he needed was a tan and he'd fit right in.

Through the French doors he watched a woman in a bikini climb out of the pool. For a moment she simply stood there, water beading on her skin, looking in his direction. Knockout body, dark hair that fell in waves to her shoulders. She reached down for a towel, showing off the fine curve of her back, her lovely legs.

"Aggie," a voice called behind her.

Taken, Rowan thought. *Just my luck.*

She turned and went to the man, slumped in his lounge chair. His shirt was open to the waist, but otherwise he was fully dressed, shoes and all. Rowan sized him up quickly: the way he slouched there, the way he looked at her. A blond-haired hillbilly version of the guys he knew in New York. Face in a perpetual smirk, like they had one up on you. All balls and no brains.

She finished patting herself dry and settled in the chair beside him.

It never failed, Rowan thought. Dynamite girl, lame-ass guy. What a waste.

Around her now, the deck had emptied out, the pale blue tiles gleaming brightly in the evening sun.

He drank some beer, rapped his knuckles impatiently on the bar. On the wall, the bobcat lunged toward him, mouth open, teeth bared. "Hey," he said. "I'm not looking for any trouble." He laughed. The bobcat still looked pissed.

He thought maybe he should go out to check on Freddy. He'd left him in the back of the Caddy, a sheet over the cage, the car windows open enough for air.

He checked his phone to be sure he hadn't missed Dawson's call.

He checked the time. 6:55.

Night. It was going to be a long one.

WHEN Rayelle had come through the dining room, later than she'd ever been, there were already five or six tables seated for dinner but she didn't hurry. Mrs. Lowry had scowled at her from behind the registration desk—so what?—and she had sashayed past her, paying no attention. The way she was feeling, they were lucky she came in at all. Damn lucky. What she wanted to do most in the world was sit home with a full glass of gin and cry her eyes out. Instead she had forced herself here, though not from a sense of duty to the hotel so much as to herself. She wouldn't let Bobbie defeat her.

She stood in the doorway of the bar, listened to the song coming from the jukebox. Something catchy and hopeful in its rhythm. Sinatra. *The Shape of Things to Come.* Mrs. Lowry wouldn't allow anything that wasn't from the 40s or early 50s. It complemented the character of the hotel, she liked to say. It contributed to the atmosphere.

DeeDee was at the register, ringing up a dinner tab. "Hey," she said.

"Hey."

"You okay?"

"Yeah, I'm fine."

"You're *never* late."

"Yeah, well—"

DeeDee's large calf-eyes watched her doubtfully. "You look"

"—what?"

"Upset. I don't know—"

"I'm okay." She forced a smile, glanced around the room. "Things picking up?"

"Mostly the dining room. Mrs. Lowry says there's a tour bus down from Miami."

Rayelle rolled her eyes. "Lucky us."

DeeDee gave her a sideward glance—something in her friend's tone was different, wasn't right—then she hurried out to the dining room.

Standing at the register Rayelle spaced out for a minute, staring through the French doors, not at the pool but the sky above it, the brilliant blue of day beginning to soften. Someone was motioning to her. She turned to see the man at the end of the bar holding up an empty Miller Lite bottle.

She brought him a new one, reached for his glass.

"I'll pour it, thanks."

"Suit yourself." She set the bottle down, already turning away.

"I'm Nicky." He held out his hand.

She didn't want to take it, but he held it there, and his smile was so broad she gave in.

"Rayelle," she said.

"First night here, you know. Tryin' to get the lay of the land."

She laughed at that. "What you see is what you get."

"Maybe you could give me a guided tour. Who's who here at the bar."

"You're kidding, right?" She couldn't tell. He had a quirky light in his eye, a smile that seemed to be playing with her.

"Yeah," he said, "kind of. But I'm curious. The guy at the other end there, near the register. With the white cap and beard."

She looked down the bar but knew who he meant. "That's Hank. One of our local air boat captains."

"An old salt."

"As salty as they get, I guess."

He waited a moment before asking about the man he was most interested in. He'd been watching him through the door to the restaurant since the man arrived, sitting alone now at a table that overlooked the river. That, in itself, had caught Rowan's eye immediately. Of all the patrons, both at the bar and in the restaurant, he was—except for Rowan—the only person unaccompanied. "The fellow with the suit and tie. By the window."

Again, she knew exactly whom he meant. She didn't even have to look. "That's Mr. Morrison. One of our hotel guests."

"Overdressed, isn't he?"

"Some folks like to dress for dinner. It's a sign of good breeding."

"What, you don't think my palm tree shirt shows good breeding?" He laughed, and she laughed with him.

"Doesn't suit you," she said. "With your New York accent and all. Your hip style. On you, it's like a costume."

"So you think I'm hip, huh?"

"Not *that* hip." She said it flatly, then offered her jaded half-smile.

But Rowan was barely listening. He was watching the man at the window table. Earlier he had seen him hurrying along the path from the parking lot, going somewhere fast. There *was* something remarkable about him. The meticulous way he carried himself, the way he sat primly now in his chair and carefully folded his napkin on his lap. Every gesture precise, measured, as if driven by a single-minded intensity. A man of purpose and determination, who knew exactly what he wanted out of each moment. Not unlike the way, Rowan recalled with a longing sharp as pain, he himself had once been.

He turned his attention back to Rayelle and flashed his broad smile. He wanted to ask what else she knew about this man, but thought that unwise at the moment. So instead he asked: "What about these others here at the bar? What can you tell me about *them*?"

"These others," she said, "I don't know. Tourists, probably. Down from Miami or Naples. They last one night, maybe two. You got to like the quiet, you come down here."

"What about you?"

She raised her eyebrows. "What about me?"

"You like the quiet?"

"I handle it."

"Don't think I'm gonna be so lucky."

"Luck's got nothin' to do with it." Her eyes were blue-grey steel, unflinching. "Friendly tip, though." She gave him a pointed look. "Most folks down here value their privacy. Don't like to answer a lot of questions."

He tipped his glass toward her. "Thanks for the advice."

"Comes with the service," she said, moving away.

DeeDee had returned with drink orders from the dining room. They worked side by side making them, Rayelle doing the whiskies, DeeDee the gins and vodkas. She kept glancing over at Rayelle, eyes bright and eager. Rayelle *knew* she was dying to tell her something, but the way she felt right now she wasn't going to make it easy for her. She waited until the drinks were made, until DeeDee had served them and returned to the bar with the empty tray, until she looked like she might burst if she didn't get whatever it was off her chest. "Okay, what is it, honey?"

DeeDee, face beaming, looked as if she might jump up and down. "I been thinkin'."

"There you go again," Rayelle said deadpan, but her friend was too excited to catch the sarcasm.

"Me and Lonnie, we're thinkin' about moving the wedding up to early spring. We're wondering if maybe you and Bobbie, I mean, wouldn't it be wonderful, a double wedding?" She leaned closer to the cash register, reached across to take Rayelle's hands in her own.

Her eyes were so wide and hopeful Rayelle forced a smile, squeezed her hand before disengaging herself. She looked out toward the pool. "It would be, yes."

"Uh-oh. You and Bobbie have another fight?"

"Sort of, yeah."

"What about, this time?" She came around to stand in front of her, face to face, see how bad she felt.

"Too long to go into. Now, anyway." She glanced down the bar. The New York type who couldn't stand the quiet was motioning to her with his beer glass.

----*FOURTEEN*----

IN THE DINING ROOM, MORRISON sat impatiently by the window, waiting for someone to take his order. Dinner had long since ceased to be a social occasion but tonight the fingers of loneliness had once again crept inside his armor, left him vulnerable. So much so that he found even the senseless chatter of the piano bar with its endless coterie of party-goers, and the bustle of waitresses and busboys moving among the surrounding tables a source of comfort. He had to laugh at himself. In the eleventh hour, he was going soft.

The perky blond appeared beside him, smile so bright it could light a blind man's darkness. If he ever had a daughter, he would want her to possess a smile like that.

"Evening, Mr. M. Your usual?"

"Not tonight, thanks. Just water. Lemon, no ice."

"Coming right up."

She swirled away, pony tail bobbing. Several minutes later he was disappointed when a busboy brought his water, and then a second time when it was not the perky blond but another waitress named Anne who took his dinner order.

Despite not having eaten all day, he ate without much appetite and paid more attention to the slow drift of the river outside the window than the food on his plate. When he wasn't worrying about Emilio, worrying that in the boy's persistent quest for information he was elevating the suspicions of his co-workers, Morrison would glance around to look for DeeDee who seemed always in motion, moving ballerina-like, between the tables. On one occasion his glance carried into the bar where he saw a man in a bright blue tropical shirt looking toward him. He was in conversation with

Rayelle Williams. There was something in the way they leaned together and looked toward him that told Morrison they were talking about him.

For all his effort to remain incognito, he mused, lately he sure drew his share of attention. Another one of his life's ironies that, in this instance, amused him. The man looked harmless enough, though in undercover work you learned fast not to trust appearances.

He wondered about Rayelle. How much did she know about her boyfriend's animal peddling? Plenty, he figured. She was a country girl but, from what he could see, she was far from dumb.

On the way out he noticed the man in the bright shirt was gone. In the bar's doorway he stopped and looked toward the pool. Never once had he gone swimming there. He felt a moment's regret, again, for lost opportunities—big *and* small. Then he noticed Johnny-O sprawled in a deck chair, his face in shadow. Beside him in a chair in the late sunlight lay Aggie, revealing in her minimal swimsuit even more flesh than she had shown him last night in her robe.

In that moment Johnny turned in Morrison's direction, a grin breaking across his lips, his right hand shaped as a pistol rising slowly, pointing his way.

Good thing I'm paranoid already, Morrison thought, or I'd be even more beside myself, with everyone and his damn uncle pointing their guns at me.

In the lobby he stopped at the desk to book a room in the hotel. "For a business associate," he explained to the clerk. "He'll be arriving tomorrow or possibly tonight. I'd like to have the room waiting for him."

He asked for the top floor, a corner or an end of the hall room. The clerk himself, because the hotel didn't employ bell boys, walked with him up the wide staircase to the third floor. The room was at the end of the hall nearest the river.

"I'll hold the key for him," he said once the clerk had opened the door.

He was a thin, nervous man with round, wire-rimmed glasses—not your typical redneck local. He seemed reluctant to hand over the key. "Front desk is staffed through the night tonight and tomorrow, and until midnight on Sunday."

"I understand but I'd like to hold the key, in any case." Morrison smiled graciously. " I'm sure to see him before he stops at the desk."

"As you wish."

Alone in the room Morrison went to the window to verify access to the fire escape. In the hall he walked from one end to the other. From the emergency door nearest his room, there was another access to the fire escape. He would sleep here tonight and tomorrow night. In case he had miscalculated. In case they came for him instead of waiting until Sunday. He would be safer here than in the bungalow. He would hear their footsteps on the stairs and in the hall.

The door next to his opened. The man in the bright blue shirt leaned into the hall and said, "Heard footsteps. Had to see who's up here with me." He offered his hand. "Nicky Roberts."

Up close like this, there was something unnatural about the guy—his clothes, for one thing. The bright shirt, the spanking white tennis sneakers. Something uneasy in his manner. He looked like a caricature of the Sunshine State tourist. "Morrison," he said, shaking the man's hand.

"Yes, yes, I know. Been askin' about you."

"Why's that?"

Rowan shrugged. "Curious, I guess. You seem a cut above the rest. Man with a purpose, man on the go. Said that to myself soon as I saw you." He looked at Morrison appraisingly. "No sense us standing out here in the hall. I'm just about to open a bottle of Jack Daniels."

"I don't have much time." His standard line. He'd lived behind it for years. But saying it now he couldn't even convince *himself*. At the moment he had nothing but time, waiting for darkness to fall, waiting for the hours after midnight when the shipment of "cats" was most likely to arrive.

"One drink," Rowan was saying. "First night in town, you know, hate drinking alone. And, from the looks of things, you could use some company yourself." He went to the bedside table and poured two drinks, generous ones, into the water tumblers. "Okay to come in," he called to Morrison who had remained at the door.

He had been taking in the room, reading what it revealed about this man who had invited him in. The fellow traveled light, to be sure. No suitcases, no personal items—other than the whiskey—nothing, in fact, to show the room was inhabited. A man on the run, was Morrison's guess.

"Cheaper than buying them at the bar," his host was saying. "Gives the wallet a break, especially when you start this early." He raised his glass. "Here's to the night ahead."

Morrison sipped the bourbon. He'd promised himself to hold back on the booze but his nerves were on edge. "So, what did you find out about me?"

"Not much." He had settled himself on the bed, sitting back against the pillows. "You're a private guy, keep to yourself. You don't bother anybody."

"I daresay I've bothered a few people," Morrison said, attempting a joke. He had moved to the window, staring upriver toward the fish house, wondering when he would hear again from Emilio.

"They don't know what to make of you." He said it in an amused, rather than a probing way.

"Who doesn't?"

"The restaurant staff. The folks at the front desk."

Morrison took some consolation in that. As long as they didn't know what to make of him, it meant they didn't know the truth. And hiding the truth was the *sine qua non*. It's what had kept him alive these past years.

"One theory is maybe you're a Fed, but nobody's sure what kind. Homeland Security, maybe. Definitely not DEA. These folks seem to know the DEA types. Another line of thinking is maybe your story is true, that you really are a Bible salesman, semi-retired."

"What does the waitress think?"

"Rayelle?"

"How many waitresses did you talk to?"

"Only Rayelle."

Morrison sipped the whiskey, wondered why he was asking. Other than for concealing his identity, he had rarely concerned himself with what people thought of him. For some reason, now it seemed to matter.

Rowan laughed and stretched his legs out on the bed. "She thinks you're an odd duck."

"That's me. Oddest duck in the raft." He saw again the toughs circling him in the dingy light of the projects, calling him "weird," "strange," a " faggot coward," getting ready to beat it out of him, his oddity.

He set his glass on the window ledge and smoothed his moustache with his fingers. "What do people say about *you*?"

Rowan laughed again. "I'm too new. They haven't had time to form any theories yet."

"Prior to this, then. Where you came from."

With a flick of his wrist Rowan held the glass against his lips, finished off the whiskey. He sat on the edge of the bed, looking up at Morrison. "Like everybody, I've got a past." He reached for the bottle, held it out to Morrison who waved it away. "Right now, I'm looking to make connections. Meet the right kind of people, that sort of thing. I'm looking to make a deal."

Normally he would have let it go at that. As an undercover agent, it wasn't in his best interest to get involved with other people's needs. But it might have been the isolation he was feeling, the danger of the situation he was up against, that made him recognize a kindred spirit in the man sitting opposite him. A man who, like Morrison himself, seemed to be fighting hard to conceal the gravity of his desperation. "What kind of deal?"

"Well, I—"

At that moment Morrison's cell phone rang.

Emilio.

"I've got to take this," he said.

Rowan sighed in resignation and poured himself another drink. "Like I said, a man with a purpose."

HE took the call in his room, standing near the window that faced the river, speaking in whispers. The shipment was due in tonight as scheduled, Emilio reported. He did not know the time.

"Gun Rock Bay? Same as last night?"

"I do not know that for sure. But I do not think so. Earlier tonight I overheard Dawson telling someone he was 'going fishing at Osprey Creek.' I have heard that expression before: *going fishing at* such and such a place. I think it is their code."

That made sense, Morrison thought. Why not vary your route when the swamp offered hundreds to choose from? "Do you have anything else for me?"

"I wish I could say yes. I am truly sorry."

"All right. Keep your eyes and ears pulled."

Emilio laughed. "Always."

----*FIFTEEN*----

OSPREY CREEK CROSSED UNDER HIGHWAY 41 six miles east of Gun Rock Bay. Parked on the road's shoulder, sheltered by a tree's deep shadow, Morrison had been waiting nearly two hours. Nothing but darkness around him, broken every so often by the pin-prick stab of headlights far away on the highway, the white orbs growing larger and rounder, finally spinning past him in a rush of wind and engine noise, leaving behind a milky, fog-like after-image that quickly evaporated.

Across the two-lane highway a narrow band of scrub oak separated the higher ground of the pavement from the sloping lowland of the mangrove swamp. The moonless sky did little to illuminate the tangled web of streams and tributaries that meandered to the Gulf. Somewhere in that elusive wilderness, boats were moving toward him this very minute bearing their contraband.

It was the unyielding darkness beyond the windshield, the deadening silence of this part of the world, the seemingly endless waiting, that turned his thoughts again to death: how the imminence of it framed the life he'd led, how it rendered that life both meaningless and all-important.

But what kind of a life had it been? How had he become the man he was now?

There seemed no easy description. What came to him instead were random images, too isolated and incomplete, it appeared, to make a whole:

The mother he knew only from pictures in a photo album, her death coming before he'd learned to walk.

A fire truck running a red light when he was eleven, striking his father's car as it turned into their driveway, Morrison watching from the front yard, waving to his father before he made the turn, his hand still raised, frozen in the air, even after the car was gone from view, replaced by the fire truck's gleaming red panels, the tinkle of shattered glass and the crunch of staved-in metal.

The suffocating darkness of his bedroom in the house of the aunt who had taken him in. The night interminable with hours, the sound of his tears the lullaby that carried him into sleep.

The morning of his twelfth birthday when he found Bucky, the Airedale stray with the brooding eyes, in the alley behind his aunt's apartment. The beginning of his abiding love for animals.

Those were, he thought, defining moments. And this, too, that came later.

A chilly night in June when he was fourteen. Walking Bucky later than usual. Not seeing the gang of boys approaching until it was too late, until they had him cornered in a remote section of the park, coming at him with sticks and fists, and coming at Bucky too, kicking him with their black and pointed boots, batting him with their sticks so that it wasn't his own pain that he felt so much as his dog's, the high-pitched and agonized yelps that issued from him each time he was struck, the wounded and uncomprehending look in his eyes afterward as he whimpered in Morrison's arms.

His dog didn't die then, he was like Morrison himself too tough to succumb to a gang of punks, but the effects of the attack weakened him, left him with a permanent limp, until finally his kidneys stopped functioning and his legs gave out altogether.

It was pain, he thought, that teaches us who we are, who we will become.

And then he was thinking of a time years after that, in college, when he spent the night in a van in the Minnesota woods as part of a field study program he'd volunteered for: tracking the movement of radio-collared wolves. It was a study to measure the range of a pack's territory so that the state's Fish & Wildlife Service might better insure their survival as they were being re-introduced into the lower forty-eight. Faithfully, through the night's black hours with only the wind and trees for company, he'd recorded every beep that came through his ear phones, he'd made a notation on the map grid every time the needle on the telemetry machine quivered. He had found it thrilling knowing they were out there in the dark, the wolves, unseen and unhampered by man, hunting as they had hunted throughout the ages.

And now, thirty years later, he had come full-circle: sitting alone in the dark, tracking the movement of wild things in nature. Only this time their movement was in cages.

So what did all those moments add up to? Had he accomplished what he set out to do—make the world, in some small way, a better place for his having passed through it?

Possibly, he'd made a *marginal* difference but, to his way of thinking, not *enough* of a difference.

At least not yet.

IT was nearly two in the morning when he watched yet another set of headlights appear on the highway, coming toward him, this time slowing several hundred yards from where he was parked, the familiar white panel truck turning onto a dirt road that led into the swamp, the lights slashing across the tree line before dropping out of sight, the truck gone too, swallowed by the low-land darkness. A few minutes later the second white panel truck made the same turn, cut its lights almost immediately, and jounced noisily on the uneven road until the night closed over it and it too was no longer visible, no longer heard.

Thirty-five minutes later the two trucks, in tandem, re-appeared and headed west, the way they had come. This late there was virtually no traffic so it was possible for Morrison to keep back quite a distance without fear of losing them. They were traveling north on 29, past LAROO'S WILD ANIMAL PARK, through a section of the Big Cypress Preserve on a dark and lonesome stretch of road, then on a wider road that skirted the edge of the Miccosukee Reservation and finally into a desolate area of the South Florida peninsula, no light of any kind save the tail lights of the two trucks ahead of him. Slash pine rose in shadow on both sides of the road, fronting the endless acres of thick and unbroken forest.

Other than the roadway itself, there was no sign of human intervention for miles until a high tensile fence appeared off the left shoulder. Like the forest, the fence seemed to go on forever, three or four miles at least, by Morrison's calculation, with an occasional sign nailed to it announcing PRIVATE PROPERTY NO TRESPASSING.

Finally, the trucks slowed to a stop ahead of him, turning one after the other into a break in the wall of trees. As he approached he saw there was a white-sand road curling into the dense woods, a man in some sort of paramilitary security uniform drawing back a gate for the trucks to enter. The timbered sign that arched above the gate read *Indian Point Hunt Club.*

Morrison drove on for another mile, then turned and came back slowly. The gate had been closed. No sign of the gatekeeper or the trucks, only the glint of white sand winding through the trees.

Shy of the gate he pulled the car onto the shoulder and let the motor idle.

Another segment of the network, he mused. Was it way station or final destination? His guess, judging by the size of the club, its road frontage alone, was that the animals in the trucks, if in fact they were cats, were most likely cub versions of *big* cats— lions or tigers or some variety of leopard—and here to stay. There had to be considerable money behind a spread this extensive. Its members would demand the best in big game hunting.

He had already asked Krebs to check on LAROO'S. He'd leave a message for him now to check on this hunt club, as well. Were they connected in some way, or simply two discrete clients of the Blue Lagoon operation?

For a moment he considered leaving the car and making his way in on foot. But there was too great a chance he'd be spotted by the drivers of the trucks on their way out or by the security force. And then there was the chance he might encounter one or more of the imported prey roaming that dark land.

Either way, he didn't like his odds.

PART THREE: SATURDAY

----*SIXTEEN*----

AT THEIR RENDEZVOUS POINT ON the river, Emilio was waiting near the sea wall in the early morning light, working on his smoking technique. "Look," he said when Morrison arrived. "I have learned the proper way." He held the Marlboro pinched between his thumb and first finger, brought it to his mouth and drew in with deliberate intensity. The smoke came shooting out the corner of his mouth. With exaggerated indifference, he held the cigarette down at his side and flicked the ash. "How do I look?"

"Tough as Bogart."

"He is a movie star, no?"

"He is a movie star, yes."

"You are playing with my English."

"I'm joking with you."

Emilio lowered his eyes. "I appear foolish, do I not?"

"I'm laughing *with* you, not *at* you."

"There is—how do you say it—a *fine line* between the two, no?"

Morrison laughed. "Yes, there is."

Emilio grinned and took another drag with the same over-stated flourish. "I bear no hard feelings then."

"That's good."

"Mr. Bogart will become my mentor. I will carefully review his films."

"You'll be the hippest Guatemalan in Mangrove Bay."

Emilio was amused by that. Morrison took pleasure in making the boy laugh. He would have liked to dawdle there, prolong the banter. It was time, though, to push aside the affection he felt. "What do you have for me?"

Emilio's eyes narrowed. He looked away at the river. "Perhaps not much, but *some*thing." He turned back to Morrison and drew on his cigarette. "Tonight there is a meeting."

"Where?"

"The Blue Lagoon. Somewhere on the property. That's all I know."

"*Who?*"

Emilio shrugged. "I overheard Mr. Dawson tell Mr. Connors about it. No names were given. Later I overheard Mr. Conners ask Mr. Dawson if the boss was coming. Mr. Dawson nodded his head."

"No name mentioned?"

"I did not hear a name mentioned. And I do not know if the question about the boss was related to the meeting."

"All right, all right," Morrison said. "That's something, at least."

"There was mention of someone being shot the other night. Mr. Dawson made reference to it when speaking to Mr. Connors."

"Do they know I was involved?"

"They did not mention you by name."

"But—?"

"It is not clear what they know and do not know."

Morrison studied the boy, wondering if he was holding something back. "But they *suspect* it is me?"

"They are curious about you. They do not know why you are here. Or why you have stayed so long." Emilio lowered his eyes in apology. "I did not find out anything about this man, Mr. Leach."

"He's not important anymore."

"No?" Emilio watched him, waiting for more.

"He's slow-witted. A sad case. My guess is they're using him as a shield."

"The village idiot?"

Morrison smiled at the boy's use of the term. He thought: we hide the pain behind such phrases. "Yes. Something like that." He watched the curious, open face. "Have you ever seen Dawson with a heavy-set black man?"

"No black men work at the Blue Lagoon. I am the darkest."

"Has Dawson ever hinted that he might be involved with a second smuggling operation, something on his own perhaps?"

"Nothing that I have heard." Emilio checked his watch. "I must work soon. They are closing early tonight. Perhaps because of the meeting, but I do not know that for certain." There was a glint of triumph in his eyes when he added: "I believe they will ask me very soon to be part of their team. Mr. Dawson asked me last night if I wished to earn more money. He said he had a special opportunity for me."

"Good. That's good. But watch out. You can't be too careful now, do you understand? The situation is critical. These men are dangerous."

"I understand that, of course. It is why I am a part of this. To stop them from being dangerous."

"If anything—" He searched for the words to say what he needed to. "If anything happens to me, I want you to go away from here. Immediately. Don't tell anyone where you're going. Not even anyone in the Division. No one at all." He watched the boy's eyes as he processed this. He thought he should tell him to flee now, before things got worse. But he needed him too much. At least until tonight, until after the meeting. "It won't be safe for you. Do you understand?"

"I understand, yes."

"Good. Good."

A heaviness filled the boy's eyes. "It will harm my heart forever, should that happen."

"It will harm mine, should anything happen to *you*."

"I am not worried about myself." He arched his shoulders with renewed confidence and gave Morrison a wide grin. "It is not so healthy to dwell on the black side, no?"

Morrison laughed. "The *dark* side."

"Black or dark, they mean the same, no?"

"Yes, just about."

Emilio hung the cigarette from the corner of his mouth and began moving his lips, talking like a gangster in one of the American movies he'd seen. The Marlboro popped from his mouth and fell to the ground. He stared down at it in dismay. "That is my next accomplishment. To talk and smoke at the same time."

It was after noon before Morrison heard from Krebs. The man's voice over the phone sounded rushed, anxious.

"Yeah, Walter, sorry for not getting back. Had to leave the office for awhile. My daughter got hit by a swing in the playground. Nothing real serious, but I had to check it out. I'm on my way back now."

"She's all right?"

"Yeah, yeah, she's fine. Shaken up a little is all. Daddy had to reassure her everything was going to be okay."

"I don't suppose you have anything to reassure *me*."

"Whether you'll find it reassuring or not I can't say." Krebs paused to clear his throat. In the background Morrison heard the sound of traffic. The Beltway, he figured, where it was always rush hour.

"The word around here is that Christophe LaRoo Sr.'s been bringing in African Greys by the boatload. His son, Christophe Jr.'s been smuggling them out of Zaire and the Congo, where exporting them is illegal, into Senegal where there's no export restrictions. From Senegal he ships them here. Supposedly, they're supplying pet stores throughout the Southeast."

Morrison was familiar with the appeal of the African Grey. Of all the parrot varieties, it was the best talker. Also in its favor was the fact that it was a robust and healthy bird, not susceptible to disease or premature death and, best of all, usually friendly. Which made it a huge hit with the pet-loving public. And the economics were advantageous, as well. A poacher might get fifty bucks per bird. Retail, the Grey was worth in excess of a thousand dollars.

"Apparently, they're into lemurs, as well."

"I don't have anything on that," Krebs said, his voice fading out briefly. "But it turns out both LaRoos, father and son, are charter members at Indian Point. And the club is owned by a guy named Henry Wallace, who just happens to be the brother-in-law of your buddy, Alex Crimmins. The speculation is it's really Crimmins' money behind it all, the brother-in-law's just a front man. Which is, as you already know, Crimmins' *modus operandi*. Supposedly, the big guy uses the club as his private hunting grounds whenever he's not in the mood to fly to Africa for one of his frequent safaris." Krebs waited a moment before adding: "Word I hear from one of our men in Texas is he's headed down your way tonight for a weekend getaway."

"His island? Or the club?"

"Nothing on that yet. I'll keep you updated, if I hear anything."

Did that make it more likely now, Morrison wondered, that Crimmins was in fact "the boss" Dawson had alluded to, the man who might or might not be attending tonight's meeting? One big question still nagged at him. "Why do you suppose a man

100

with Texas oil money behind him might want to traffic in illegal wildlife?"

"Most of his money is family money. Maybe he wanted to make his mark on his own, prove himself and all that. Or maybe it's just a hobby with him, keep himself entertained while he's waiting for his next oil rig to go up." His voice broke up. When it came back clear and intelligible again he was saying, "Maybe he's not heavily involved, at all. Maybe all this stuff is coincidence and we're barking up the wrong tree."

Maybe, Morrison thought, but he had never been a big believer in coincidence. To his way of thinking, it was design and intention that governed the activities of man, not happenstance. Case in point: his own life. Tragedies and disappointments aside, he knew he had only himself to blame for what he had become, or not become. So, too, with Crimmins. A pattern was emerging. It was most likely leading *some*where.

At the very least, he figured, the possibility that Crimmins was not only a hunter of big game but a purveyor of it, as well, was beginning to take on new life.

ALEXANDER Crimmins' big-game hunting exploits around the world had been written about in any number of men's magazines, as had his penchant for beautiful wives—he was on number four, at last count. Over the years there had been an abundance of news photos depicting his endeavors in both arenas. Typically, they would feature Crimmins in safari garb standing with his shoulders hiked in a proud, overbearing way, a rifle in his hands, his current wife (he preferred thin, statuesque blondes) standing beside him as he stared triumphantly above the carcass of whatever large creature—lion, tiger or boar—that he had felled. At fifty, he was a heavy-set man with a pock-marked face and in these photos his dark, pugnacious eyes seemed particularly aggressive, daring the world to cross him. In the photos taken of him at various high-flying social functions in and around the Houston area, however, he appeared less threatening, offering to the camera one of a variety of smiles ranging from reserved to sardonic.

Otherwise the man kept his life to himself. He ran the family business, Texas Star Energy, from his 2500 acre ranch north of Houston and spent most of his time there. The island off the Florida coast had been a recent acquisition, though apparently from what Morrison had read, he'd been looking to buy property in South Florida for some time.

Morrison was pondering whether it was a base from which the man could monitor his importing ventures or simply a vacation getaway as the plane he sat in, a twin-engine Cessna, lifted off the Mangrove Bay airport runway and leveled its course, moving southwestward toward Hells Island. He wanted to see the place up-close, get the lay of the land, because he was pretty sure he'd be making a trip out here before the weekend was through. If not to see Crimmins himself, then at the very least to look for evidence that might link him to what was going on at Blue Lagoon.

"So you're interested in buyin' some island property down here," the pilot, RoyBoy, said beside him over the roar of the craft's twin engines. It was the ruse Morrison used when he arranged this flight several hours earlier.

"Yes, possibly. With some business partners."

"Can't think of a prettier place in the world."

"Yes, it is, isn't it?"

"God's gift of paradise." He was a small, grizzled man who hunkered low in his seat, talked to Morrison out of the side of his mouth. They'd flown together once before, when Morrison first arrived. At that time he'd wanted to get an overview of the place: land, bays, islands. The Admiral had set it up. He and RoyBoy were fishing buddies.

They were crossing open water. On the horizon, the dark green mangrove islands wavered in the blinding mid-afternoon light. Royboy was talking about the kind of planes he'd flown in Vietnam. "Cargo mostly, big mothers, C-130s." He gave a self-deprecating laugh that turned into a cough. "Look at me now. I'm strictly a tour guide."

"There are worse things."

"I suppose."

In the way the man's voice trailed off, Morrison heard a note of regret. Like the Admiral, a longing perhaps for more blood-pumping times. He could see why they were good friends.

They were approaching the dome-shaped rise of Hells Island. It was the hilliest of the "real" islands between here and Florida Bay and as the plane made a slow arc to circle it, Morrison noted again how nearly perfect a stronghold it was, the house securely perched on top, the sloping land around it open on three sides. Only on the southeast side was the hill wooded and even there it looked as if trees had been cut down near the top to provide greater visibility, greater protection against trespassers.

At first glance there appeared to be no activity of any kind. The helicopter pad, built below the house, appeared large enough to accommodate two choppers. In Morrison's reckoning, this was how Crimmins would travel to and from the island, though the boat dock provided water access as well.

"It's got everything," RoyBoy was saying on their second pass, " 'cept a pool. I'd want a pool, if it was me."

"You like to swim, do you?" Morrison said absently. He had his glasses trained on the house. From above, it seemed larger than it had from his vantage point at sea level the other night.

"Seems a place like this should have a pool. Kind of like if you own a Bentley you should have a chauffeur, know what I mean?" He glanced over at his passenger. "You want me to get in closer?"

"Close as you can."

This time, as they came in for the third pass, Morrison picked up movement on the helicopter pad. A man was bent low at the edge of the pad, wielding something in his hand. The thing shimmered in the light and Morrison saw that it was a machete the man held. He was cutting back the vines or brambles that were encroaching upon the landing pad. A second man was doing the same thing at the opposite end of the pad.

"You got some maintenance folks out there today," Royboy said.

Morrison grunted in affirmation. He had found a third worker sweeping the cut-stone deck that bordered the front porch. None of the men were recognizable at this distance. The one sweeping the deck shielded his eyes and looked up to follow the path of the Cessna as it passed overhead.

As a precaution, Morrison drew back from the window and instructed Royboy to head out toward sea.

"The dock's good-sized," RoyBoy was saying. "Looks real sturdy. You could tie up a yacht or two there. If it was my place I'd want a yacht, one of them ones they hand-make in Maine with the natural wood, you know." His cough kicked up again, deeper and throatier this time, a loud retching sound. He leaned forward, then back, still coughing—the plane swerving left then right like a car in a skid—and Morrison, bracing himself with his arm against the door, had the uncomfortable thought that his pilot might be having a heart attack.

"I'm fine. Fine." He spoke between coughing spasms. "Just gets to me sometimes."

Morrison was afraid to ask just what it was that was getting to him.

When Royboy recovered he leaned back in the seat and sighed. "Damn lungs. What the hell good are they?" He struggled to compose himself and offered a weak smile by way of reassurance. "One thing you got to think about, though, with that place down there. Hurricane'll rip that island apart."

"That's the way of the world, isn't it? You find paradise and there's always something to muck it up, mosquitoes or hurricanes, or some damn thing." Morrison had said it as a joke, but when he looked over at his pilot the man was nodding, his face sober and intent, as if that were the truest thing he'd ever heard.

"That's good enough for now, Roy. We can head back."

The plane banked away from the island, blue sky and clouds falling beyond the windows, the engines revving at deafening levels.

Morrison turned back to watch the island growing smaller, settling back into the turquoise waters of the Gulf. He wondered if the presence of the maintenance workers was yet another confirmation that Crimmins was on his way.

---- *SEVENTEEN*----

A VULTURE PERCHED ON THE roof of Rowan's Caddy and stared flat-eyed at him as he crossed the parking lot. Half a dozen of its brethren roosted or paced on the pavement nearby. Rowan took this as a bad sign. The unpleasant smell emanating from the half-open car windows only added to his misgivings.

The birds scattered at his approach, taking refuge in the branches of the tree overhead.

It was Freddy's feeding time but it was clear, once he removed the perforated sheet from the cage, that Freddy wasn't hungry, would never feel hunger again. On the cage floor, he lay unraveled and limp, his yellow markings looking decidedly more orange than when Rowan had last fed him.

It felt as if he'd been sucker-punched below the belt. He leaned against the car and breathed deeply. Bad luck. Bad luck. Bad luck. Would it ever let him go?

His shock turned quickly to anger. At Bobbie Dawson, first and foremost, for not meeting with him, for not even returning his calls. And at fate for its perpetual curse. He'd done what he was supposed to, hadn't he? He'd followed Regina's instructions to a *T:* fed the thing its mouse, gave it water, air, kept the car windows open, parked in the shade. What more could he have done? It wasn't his fault Dawson didn't get back to him. It wasn't his fault. He stopped his lament. No sniveling, remember, he reminded himself. Get a hold of yourself. So, it's another bad break. This one won't be the last. You can be sure of that. You can bet your life on that.

He rubbed his eyes and stared across the bright glare of the parking lot toward the hotel and the river beyond it. Now what would he do? The clock was ticking. He was playing in overtime now. They'd find him here, just as they had found him in Georgia. A matter of time, that's all it was. He'd be dead meat, like Freddy. Unless he could find another way to make some quick money. Enough, at least, to get him out of here, keep him moving and, if he was really lucky, maybe hold him over a while in whatever foreign land he escaped to. *If* he escaped.

Above him, the vultures brooded over the Caddy from their perch in the tree. He pushed himself away from the car and carried the two cages into the woods behind him. The python he left locked in its cage. Let the buzzards find a way to get at him, if they wanted him that badly. The two remaining mice, he let loose. Freed from death row, they seemed startled. They hesitated inside the cage before bolting. He watched them scamper through the underbrush, joyous at their new-found freedom.

"You're on your own now, guys. Make the most of it."

He was walking back toward the hotel when he heard a car pull in behind him. He jerked around in panic but it was only Morrison's car, the bland grey sedan. Rowan had been checking up on the guy: knew his car, knew he was renting two different rooms. The one on the third floor of the hotel next to his own, and one out in the cottages—number 16. *Why* he had two rooms, he couldn't figure. The desk clerk had said he was holding one for a friend, an explanation Rowan didn't buy. He didn't believe the guy *had* friends.

When Morrison spotted him he swerved the car, drove to a far corner of the lot. In a matter of moments he was out of the car and walking quickly across the lawn. Rowan had moved quickly too, running to catch up, intercepting him on the grass halfway between the hotel and the bungalows. "Mr. Morrison. Walter," Rowan called behind him.

Morrison stopped and turned slowly with a pained look of resignation. "Yes? What is it?"

"Could I have a word—?"

"I'm busy right now. I've got—"

"Only a minute. I'll buy you a drink over at that tiki place."

"Out of the question. I've got—do you need something?"

Rowan cleared his throat. "Well, I—I'm in a bit of a jam."

"What kind of jam?"

Rowan hesitated. The role of beggar didn't suit him, certainly not twice in the same week, and certainly not with a stranger. In the past he'd always been able to wiggle out of trouble by using his wits. But now—now what? "Right now, I'm a little short of cash—"

Morrison reached for his wallet. His expression said: he would pay the man off and go about his business. "How much do you need?"

"No, no. I'm not asking for a handout."

Morrison seemed confused. "What then?"

"I thought you might know, busy man like yourself—" Rowan chose his words carefully, "how I might make some quick cash down here."

"I'm afraid I can't help you out there." Morrison had regained his composure. He would soon be free to go on his way. "You see, I'm only a Bible peddler."

"Yes, yes, I know but I'm willing to do any—" The man was turning away from Rowan. He was speaking to the dark suit as it moved away. "If you hear of anything, if you think of anything—"

He hated the sound of desperation in his own voice. He hated that he had to be so direct. He was much better at finagling his way, manipulating, insinuating. But that's what happens, he told himself, when the road dead ends ahead of you. Still, he was sure his instincts were right. This guy was into something way beyond hawking Bibles.

He stood there watching him hurry away. When Morrison reached the bungalows, Rowan decided to set out after him.

The row of bungalows faced north, upriver, and when Rowan came to them the man was nowhere in sight. In the shadow of a willow tree, he waited. Several minutes later, Morrison emerged from the far bungalow and walked with determination along a path that paralleled the river.

Rowan followed at a safe distance.

AT a bend in the river Morrison stood by a mooring post and made a call on his cell phone, glancing behind him, as if he knew he was being watched.

"Anything new?" Morrison asked when Emilio answered.

"I am only now finishing my shift," the boy said. "I will call you once I leave."

Morrison paced from mooring post to mooring post. The river was still, barely moving in the hot, windless air. On the far side, the trees were bathed in a rich golden light, a brightness that was unique to this time of night, an hour or so before dusk. He would have preferred to see the boy in person, his presence might have soothed the loneliness he felt, but meeting him now was simply too dangerous. He wouldn't place him at greater risk.

He was watching a pelican skimming above the water as it flew upriver when Emilio returned his call. "The meeting is set for ten o'clock," the boy told him. Somewhere on the Blue Lagoon property. I don't know where."

"All right," Morrison said. "All right." He stared at the bright gold light on the trees. "Stay away from there tonight. I don't want you getting hurt."

"It is not me I am worried about, but I will keep away." Before hanging up, he added:

"I will be praying for you."

Morrison put a call through to Krebs. His friend's voice was crisp and clear, but recorded: "Hey, it's me, Gene. Shoot."

Rowan, watching from the cluster of willow trees, tried without success to read Morrison's lips. But the feeling he had when he first met the man had now become a conviction: something big was going down. Walter Morrison, one way or another, would be his ticket out of here.

----*EIGHTEEN*----

AT DARK, NINETY MINUTES BEFORE the meeting was to take place, Morrison walked the half-mile upriver from the hotel. The Blue Lagoon's early closing left the piers unnaturally quiet, motionless except for the flutter of pelican wings. The long-beaked birds had taken over the riverfront. It was on the inland side of the buildings, around the dumpsters, where the vultures held sway.

The complex of buildings, white paint chipped and flaking, extended several hundred feet along the river and even farther than that inland. On working nights, the entire length of the pier would be lit with an artificial brightness. Tonight only a single light shone from a window of the riverfront building.

He stepped into the dark shadow of a porch. From there he had an unobstructed view of the pier: the long façade of the building with its loading gates shuttered tight and the ramps that led down to a network of docks on the river.

For the moment all he had to do was listen to water sucking the pilings and watch pelicans perform their sky dives.

And wonder how much headquarters and Pendleton knew about Crimmins that they weren't telling him.

And wait.

THE sound of human voices brought him abruptly to his senses, as if an alarm had rung. Two men came out from a door beyond the loading gates.

Even without the light from the window he would have known it was Emilio. He knew the boy's posture, the barest hint of slouch he'd adopted, especially since taking up smoking. He stood there now lighting a cigarette, nodding his head as the other man—Bobbie Dawson—talked to him in low-voiced confidence.

Something in the scene disturbed Morrison. Not that Emilio was *with* Dawson—they were co-workers, after all, and it was Emilio's job to garner information, so of course he would be friendly, chatty. It was the shock of seeing him here—after he'd told him to stay away—emerging from the shut-down building, as if conspiring with Dawson.

But that was his job, wasn't it? To infiltrate the inner circle of this operation, to do whatever was necessary to earn the enemy's trust. Morrison tried to reason away the unease he felt.

The two of them were laughing, sharing a private joke. Emilio had assumed his best Bogart stance, cigarette dangling from his lips, shoulder tipped forward as he listened to Dawson who leaned close, seeming to whisper into the boy's ear. Earlier in the day Emilio's simulated tough guy-with-the-cigarette routine Morrison had found endearing; now it seemed a betrayal.

Dawson patted the boy's shoulder, added a friendly squeeze, then turned to lock the door behind him. Emilio came toward the end of the building where Morrison hid. Walking the opposite way, Dawson vanished in the shadows.

For a moment Morrison considered not revealing himself, letting the boy walk right on past him, as if he had seen something he shouldn't have and didn't want the boy to know. But when Emilio reached the end of the building he called to him softly. The boy turned quickly.

Was it his imagination that made him believe Emilio was unpleasantly surprised, that in the moment before he stepped into the shadow of the overhang there was something in his eyes that should be a warning: guilt perhaps, the shock of being caught red-handed? The darkness took away the subtleties in the boy's eyes and Morrison was trying to hear in his voice confirmation of his worst fears.

"Everything is going along according to plan," the voice said. It was the soft, unruffled voice that Morrison had grown accustomed to. "The meeting is in the office at the far end of the pier. If you take the alley behind this building you will approach the back windows without being seen. We will talk later," he said before turning away, slipping into the darkness of the pier.

Morrison stared after him, half-wanting to call him back so

that the boy could explain himself, defend his actions.

But he said nothing. He let him walk way.

FOR a short while Morrison stood there uncertainly before turning to search the opposite end of the pier. Dawson was nowhere in sight. It would be foolish, he thought, to walk in the alley as the boy had suggested. He could be trapped too easily there, sealed off at each end, and it was darker than here on the pier, that much easier to be taken by surprise.

He stayed under the overhang until the porch ended and he was forced into the open. Quickly he moved along the pier, past the loading gates and through the window's fan of yellow light. At the corner of the building, the office windows were dark. He stopped to listen for voices above the soft lapping of water against the pilings. No voices, no movement. He checked his watch: it was past 10:30.

There in the building's shadow he waited.

His gun, he decided, was best kept holstered. If he was discovered, well, he was only out for an evening stroll. Unless Emilio had betrayed him, no one could be sure of his identity. Whatever their suspicions, they could be certain of nothing. *Unless. . .* but he could not bring himself to accept—not yet, not yet—that the boy he had come to consider his friend, *more than a friend, a son*, had betrayed him.

He stepped around the corner of the building. From high on the wall a single bulb cast a blue light across the wooden deck. At the mouth of the alley, he stopped again and listened. Rats skittered along the base of the walls. Overhead, on the roof of the secondary building, three vultures perched in a line like grotesque gargoyles.

Long and narrow, the alley stretched away into obscurity. Crossing it, moving deeper into the labyrinth of sheds and storage shops, he was struck by a massive weight. He felt himself leave the ground, his breath sucked out of him, and he was struck a second time, this force coming from behind, the hard rough wood of the packing house.

Something hurt bad in his neck or shoulders, he couldn't tell which, and light spun across his eyes: the blue-white light of the overhead bulb. Into it was thrust a dark face, hot breath coming at him, two yellowed eyes flecked with blood and meanness. It was the black man he had followed from the feed and grain warehouse to Laroo's, the same man he had first seen two nights ago on the banks of the creek and probably the same man, though he couldn't be certain, that he had followed last night to the hunt club.

A brightness seared Morrison's eyes again before he felt a cold steel gun barrel against his neck.

Another face appeared behind the black man. The driver of the second panel truck. A big man as well, but the slimmer of the two. The second face said, "He the one?"

"Yeah."

"Then do him."

Morrison felt a twitch in the man's arm, a split second delay between the intention and the act, then a voice spoke from the alley's darkness: "Hey, what's going on?"

The man holding him froze before jerking suddenly to fire in the direction of the voice, precipitating a volley of gunshots that blew apart the stillness. The large black man stiffened, a slow-motion freeze, his gun hitting the floor boards, the hulk of black flesh forcing itself against Morrison in a macabre dance-like motion before falling sideways to the deck.

The thinner man had backed away, turning now and bolting toward the river, his footfalls striking hard against the wooden planks of the pier.

From the mouth of the alley, a figure emerged. It took Morrison a moment to realize it was the man who had introduced himself as Nicky Roberts.

THE footsteps of the fleeing driver had faded but Morrison, his skin slick with sweat, kept running in pursuit. He followed the sea wall north until he reached the trailer park. His shoulder aching badly, he moved quickly up one street and down another, peering into shadowy spaces beyond the lighted windows.

A group of Guatemalan men, drinking beer in an alley between two trailers, eyed him warily. When he asked if they'd seen a black man on foot, one of them shook his head no; another grumbled in Spanish. He moved on until he had passed through each of the small streets and found himself in front of the Shack.

Saturday night and inside the building everyone had a paycheck to burn. Bodies jammed three deep at the bar. A woman danced on a table to the concerted clapping of the men seated around her.

He did not see Emilio in the crowd.

From the back deck, his eyes searched the riverfront: uninterrupted blackness to the north, to the south the dark shoreline broken by the pier's single, wavering light. For a second time he prowled the streets of the trailer park, refusing to give up. Information—he needed it badly and the man lying on the deck in a pool of his own blood was beyond answering questions.

At the north end he found Emilio's trailer dark, the door locked. On each of the windows the curtain was drawn tight.

From the door of an adjacent trailer a woman watched him. "No see tonight," she said.

"His compadres?" He tried to describe the two boys from Santiago Atitlan.

"No here," she said.

Reluctantly he walked back along the river.

THE dead man, lying face down against the boards, had begun collecting flies. Blood oozed behind his ear, staining the collar of his white shirt. As Morrison had expected, the man who saved him was nowhere in sight. He'd been savvy enough to realize it wasn't a healthy idea to hang around in the vicinity of a corpse, particularly one of his own making.

In the dead man's wallet he found what must have been six or seven hundred dollars in cash. His driver's license identified him as Ned Turner, age 31, from Myrtle Beach, South Carolina. Otherwise the wallet was bare: no credit cards, no phone numbers scribbled on scraps of paper, no photos.

He stuffed it back into the dead man's pants. On the roof above the alley a vulture flapped its wings. There were six of them now, beady-eyed and restless, waiting their turn.

From the pay phone on the pier he called Krebs. His machine gave its brief instructions. Morrison's message was equally brief: "Call me ASAP."

Out of desperation he tried him at headquarters.

Again, he got a machine. In despair he tried yet again, hoping by some miracle the man might suddenly pick up.

He called Emilio but had even worse luck. The boy's phone would not ring: nothing but a dull buzz. Before he could try again, his government–issued phone rang, Caruso's voice telling him,

"We have to talk. Meet me in thirty minutes."

Morrison wanted to talk right then but the man had already hung up. He looked at the phone in dread. For the next few minutes he stared at the river. Waiting. Hoping both Krebs and Emilio would call.

----NINETEEN----

WHEN HE REACHED THE TURNOFF south of town, he set his gun on the seat. In case.

At the dead end, Caruso waited in his car. Morrison pulled next to him so they could talk window to window.

"I'm supposed to give you this." Caruso handed a manila envelope through the window.

"What is it?"

"Open it."

Morrison undid the clasp. There was an aerial photograph of the river and the Blue Lagoon, and a sheaf of papers detailed with text and illustrations of the pier and the interior space of the fishery's primary buildings.

"Everything you need's in there."

Morrison scanned each of the sheets. It looked to be the usual Division maneuver: hit them hard and heavy from every entrance.

"You'll find yourself there under the usual codes," Caruso was saying. "Tomorrow after midnight, the state police'll start sealing off the town. Roadblocks on the bridge and up on 41. Coast Guard at the mouth of the river, both forks. They'll be dogs and choppers covering the swamps, if anyone's crazy enough to try to make it out on foot. Zero hour's soon as the shipment arrives, most likely sometime between one and four a.m." He sat back in the seat, his hand draped loosely over the wheel. He'd gotten a haircut since Morrison had last seen him, more of a buzz cut than the flat top he'd been wearing. If anything it added to the smugness of his look.

"I was hoping—"

"This isn't about your hopes."

"I was hoping he'd change his mind."

Caruso was smiling faintly, as if Morrison had amused him in some way.

Mosquitoes hummed in the space between the windows. "A few weeks, a few days maybe. I can get something on Crimmins, or whoever's running this."

Caruso stared at him blankly, scratching a bite on his chin. "You think you work for Disney? You think you're some kind of clown hired to entertain folks on the midway? We're going to shut these flesh peddlers down. *Now.*"

"Pendleton doesn't know—"

"Pendleton knows more than God." Caruso sighed, as if he'd been talking to a child and his patience had run out. "You're wasting your time. You don't have anything hard."

"I know that Crimmins—" Morrison choked on what he wanted to say. What was the use? It was like the newly departed begging the undertaker to turn back the clock. To steady himself he listened to the drone of mosquitoes before he spoke again. "There was some trouble tonight."

"There was some trouble tonight," Caruso said, mimicking him.

"You already know?"

Caruso smirked at him in the dark. "Yeah, I know."

"You also know who set me up?"

"Why don't you ask that kid you're using as a mole?"

He didn't like the man's tone, his insinuation. "What are you saying?"

"It ever occur to you maybe you were being played?"

Morrison's instinct was to protect the boy. But why, he asked himself, should he trust him now anymore than he should trust Caruso or Pendleton?

He saw again the boy and Dawson consorting on the pier, Dawson's hand rubbing the boy's shoulder. Maybe Dawson had made him an offer too grand to be refused. After all, the boy needed money not only for himself but for his family back home.

And from what Morrison had seen of the world, money sooner or later trumped all other considerations. It was always money that people sold their soul for.

And wasn't it true Dawson and his crew were a congenial bunch of guys, more fun-loving and appealing in terms of companionship than he himself was with his decidedly serious view of the world,

116

his loner mentality?

And hadn't the boy's information led him directly into a trap? There was no meeting in the office, only the two men in the alley waiting to pounce.

And, most telling of all, hadn't he seen the hint of deceit in the boy's eyes when they spoke on the pier?

There were a hundred reasons suggesting the boy might have betrayed him.

Yet he immediately regretted not coming to Emilio's defense. By his silence he acknowledged his doubts, his suspicions.

"It's a sad business," Caruso was saying, "when a man can't tell his friends from his enemies."

"What's that supposed to mean?"

"Ned Turner was F&W. Working undercover. Just so you know."

Morrison stared past him. Beyond dark branches, the moon hung its arc of light above the bay. "Why wasn't I informed?"

"You go where you don't belong, bad things happen." Caruso's words were matter of fact but a tightness had settled in around his eyes and mouth.

"I'm doing my job."

"Your job is to take us in tomorrow night. Nothing else."

For a moment he thought Caruso was going to quote from the Pendleton bible: *the Division has zero tolerance for deviation of any kind.* But the man, deep in thought, was staring at the dark forest beyond the windshield. "You better tell that mole of yours to watch his back. He's in way over his head."

Again Morrison thought he should defend the boy, but he remained silent.

A mosquito had gotten inside the car and Morrison swatted it in the dark. The annoying buzz ceased momentarily, then resumed. He couldn't stop himself from trying one more time. "These animals are coming in from all over the world. Blue Lagoon's only the tip of the—"

Caruso's head jerked toward him, eyes flashing. "Nobody, and I stress nobody, is interested in your conspiracy theories." He seemed to relax then, his lips slackening to a smile. "We've all got a part to play, Walty. Big or small, major or minor. It's already been arranged. It's the one that's got our name on it." The smile oozed to the corners of his mouth. "So why fight it? Because when all is said and done, you don't really have any choice in the matter, do you?"

----*TWENTY*----

ROWAN SAT AT THE HOTEL bar downing another in a long night of beers, trying not to get sentimental. He'd done it again: one more killing on his hands. And he was still no closer to finding his way out of here; if anything he'd dug his hole deeper. What was it Tony LaGrosa had said about him? *Once a screw-up, always a screw-up.* His only defense: he hadn't meant for things to turn out this way. He'd been tailing Morrison, that's all. Following his hunch. Seeing what the guy was up to. Hoping there was a way to use him.

Faced again with the barrel of a gun, he'd responded like the big shot he'd always wanted to be. Now, as if it wasn't enough to have the mob hot on his tail, he had to worry about who else would be coming after him. If he could only get a hold of Morrison, maybe he'd find out. He'd checked his rooms, the hotel and the bungalow, but the guy had disappeared, or seemed to. In the meantime he had to make do with what he heard at the bar: *some fellah shot on the pier . . . nobody local . . . colored dude . . . no witnesses so far . . . first murder here in town in . . . the sheriff ain't saying much. . . .*

Stay cool, he told himself. Nobody saw what happened but the other black dude and Morrison. It wasn't likely either of them would be going to the police anytime soon. At the least, at the very least, the guy owed him big time. Maybe he'd find a way to repay the favor.

So Rowan ordered another beer in hopes of taking the edge off.

Like a man on Death Row his life had begun assaulting him in flashes; each beer carried on its shoulders memories he would have preferred to ignore. Even the good ones, gathered from the period when he and Regina discovered love—such a startling time, as if *they* were the pioneers, as if no one had reveled in its pleasures before them—had, at this point in his life, turned hurtful.

He remembered something from those days that Regina had told him. Once a year on her birthday, she spent a few minutes examining the past twelve months, what it had brought her and what it had taken away. It made her feel better, she said, let her know where she stood.

"I *know* where I stand," he had declared, flexing his feet, reducing her comment to its most literal and mundane level. "I'm standing right here. On our living room rug." Those days he had no time for reflection. Things were moving too fast. Only the future mattered and the steps he would take to get there.

Now the future existed only as a dead end, approaching fast. The present moment was all he owned and, of course, his past. But even these things seemed less his than objects on loan. Anytime now the Re-Po men were coming to reclaim them, part of what he owed, along with his body and blood. Because who was he kidding? Years ago he'd made a pact with the Devil, and hell offered no place to hide. The White Pine Motel had proved that: LaGrosa and the boys laughing at him because he'd been in their sights the entire time. Cat and mouse—they were playing with him. *They had his number.*

What does it say about a man if his enemies know him better than he knows himself?

It seemed to him that what he'd lived was not so much a life as a series of mistakes. Fast-track friends, fast-track lifestyle. The track led here.

"Bad influences," his old man would have said, "me among them." He could see the old man's scowl, the way one side of his face shriveled in disgust. "But don't say I didn't warn you. Hell, *I'm* the warning. Look at what it's got me. Fifty years old and I'm still running numbers. Your old man's a joke. A two-bit player in a game of high rollers."

He could still see the disappointment in his father's face when he found out his son was running with Tony LaGrosa's crowd. "You think that's why I sent you to Fordham? You think that's why I busted my ass all these years?" The old man, small though he was, swung at him, put all the wiry strength of his 5' 8" frame behind it. But it wasn't the punch that hurt Rowan. That was nothing compared to the look on the old man's face.

He sipped his beer dolefully, thinking yes, he'd been a victim of his mistakes. But it wasn't as simple as that, was it? What did his prof at Fordham always say? *Look at the result and you'll see the intention.* According to that line of thought he'd *wanted* to end up here—with nothing and no one. A self-inflicted punishment. For leaving Regina? Betraying their love? Betraying the old man's expectations of him?

Ah, the realization.

Now, the detour.

Because whenever he'd come close to understanding something about his life, sure as hell a distraction would present itself. He'd be sidetracked for days or weeks or maybe only minutes but long enough for the insight to fade, to preserve him from change. This night was no exception.

She arrived via the back door, accompanied by her boyfriend, the guy he'd seen with her earlier at the pool. Aggie and Johnny-O. He'd asked Rayelle about them.

"Who knows what their scam is?" she'd said.

Rowan laughed. "Whatever it is, though, you're sure it's a scam, right?"

She gave him a world-weary look. She'd seen it all.

Rowan watched them at the door: the moment's hesitation, Johnny-O's eyes working the room, then his hands on her bare midriff, guiding her to the empty seat next to him.

"This taken?" Her fingers touched the high-back seat of the stool. Long, thin fingers.

A long, stroking touch.

Rowan spun the seat around for her. "Not until now."

"Thanks, man." Johnny-O waved for the waitress, then reached to shake Rowan's hand. "Haven't seen you around."

Rowan forced a smile. The kid didn't improve up close. He'd pegged him right the first time. A hick version, complete with the makings of a billy-goat beard, of the guys who worked with Fat Tony. Brass balls, baloney for brains, as his old man would have said. Rowan knew they could make your life miserable, though. They were pros at that.

Rayelle stood behind the bar, waiting.

"Vodka Collins for the lady," Johnny-O said before turning to Rowan. "And whatever you're drinking, man."

"Just a beer." He really didn't want to drink on the kid's dime but desperation was a great equalizer. When you're down to a few bucks and a few hours, you feel more kindly toward your fellow man. Who knew? Even a kid like this might be of use. "You guys been down here a while?" he offered for starters.

"Years," Aggie said.

"Don't listen to this one." Johnny-O flicked his eyes at her in disapproval. "Two minutes go by, something earth-shattering don't happen, she's bored out of her skull."

"Keep me here much longer, I'm gonna look like *them*." She tilted her chin in the direction of the locals at the bar: the women, over-sized and sloppy-looking, in baggy shirts and grungy jeans; the men, old before their time, in overalls and work boots.

Johnny-O snickered. "You ain't never gonna look like them, honey. Not in a million years."

Rayelle brought the drinks. Rowan flashed her a smile but she was focused on taking the kid's money.

"Business or pleasure?" Johnny-O was saying.

"What's that?" Rowan said, thinking he'd missed something.

"What brings you down here?"

"Pleasure, I guess."

The kid guffawed. "You ain't sure?"

"Can't say I've had much fun yet."

"Then get to it, man." He motioned toward DeeDee who had just come in from the dining room, carrying a tray of used bar glasses. "There's a cutie for you. Or even that one's not bad." He nodded at Rayelle who was serving drinks at the far end of the bar. "In that worn-out kinda way."

"Thanks for the tip."

"Anytime." He had turned slightly, staring at his girlfriend who watched him as she sipped her Vodka Collins through a straw.

Something passed between them, Rowan thought. The secret code of couples. "What about *you*? Business or pleasure?"

Johnny-O ran his hand along Aggie's leg, cupping her knee, rubbing it slowly with his thumb and forefinger, grinning at her all the while. "Little a both, little a both. Ain't that right, baby?"

"Whatever you say, Johnny." Her blank eyes focused on her drink, her lips wrapped with determination around the straw.

Johnny-O checked his watch. "Got to make a call." He turned to Rowan. "Keep her company, will you? Wouldn't want her bored to tears while I'm gone." He patted Rowan's shoulder but his eyes, milky blue and opaque, were harder to read. Threat or encouragement? Or both? Then the kid was threading his way between the cocktail tables on his way toward the pool.

Aggie lowered her glass and smiled. "Don't mind him. He's just upset."

There was a vacant look to her face not unlike the bar girls he'd known in New York; but there was no denying her beauty. Her eyes, shimmery as translucent glass, dared him to look away. "What's he upset about?"

"He gets moody when things don't go his way. Right now he's pissed. His business partner didn't show up."

She seemed more than willing to talk, so he pressed on. "What kind of business?"

"Importing." She bit her lip as if she'd maybe said too much.

He figured from the way she said the word that his imports were of dubious legality.

"You mean, like what?"

"Nature stuff, mostly. Whatever. He'd import tree frogs if he could find somebody willing to buy them."

Rowan winced at the irony. The kid was into wildlife. If they'd met yesterday, he wouldn't have needed Dawson. He would have unloaded Freddy, been on his way. Perverse fate sending him another of its messages: *Up yours, Mack.*

She sipped her gin and swiveled head-on to him so he could see between her legs, her skirt short enough to reveal her pink panties. "He's always running off, leaving me by my lonesome."

Just like the movies, he thought. Disgruntled wife/girlfriend solicits love-struck nice guy to bump off her man. Except he was no nice guy, and he hadn't quite figured exactly what her game was. "What about *you*?"

She smiled sweetly. "What *about* me?"

"While he's off importing and you're by your lonesome."

"I always find *some*thing to do." She smiled again, keeping her eyes on him, opening and closing her legs slowly as she swiveled her stool side to side. "Mostly, though, I do whatever he wants me to."

"That's all right with you?"

"Why wouldn't it be?"

He shrugged. "Doesn't sound like much fun."

"I get by," she said. "What about *you*?"

"You could say I'm changing careers. Looking for new opportunities."

She laughed. "You and Johnny should get together. He's *always* looking for new opportunities."

Open the door a little wider, he thought. Why not? He raised his beer in a mock toast.

"Who knows? Maybe we will."

"I think about changing careers all the time," she said dreamily, poking her straw between ice cubes to spear the cherry. "But I never do. Change, I mean. You get stuck, you know? You get scared you're gonna lose what you have. Then where you gonna be?"

She looked at him steadily, as if she really did want him to answer. What he thought he saw in her shimmering green-gold depths was the dull glint of regret. Then she was leaning close to him, her smooth tanned knees touching his, her panties a pink bulls-eye in the gap between her thighs.

"This stuff is lame." She set her glass on the bar and looked at him hopefully. "You know where I can get something to *really* get me off?"

----*TWENTY-ONE*----

MORRISON STOOD AGAINST THE BACK wall of the Shack. From there he could view the entire room, watch the movement through both doors, front and rear. The usual weekend crowd, raucous and colorful and well past tipsy. A few tourists thrown into the mix of Crackers and Guatemalans.

Where had the boy gone?

Surely this was a sign of Emilio's duplicity. How else to explain his disappearance?

Obviously he didn't want to answer questions, wouldn't offer Morrison the chance to read again the deceit in his eyes.

Truth was, he missed the boy terribly—if he only could see him again he would forgive him anything. That, he thought, must be what love was: your need for it exceeds any hurt or pain your loved one might cause you.

He thought of the aunt who had raised him, as a case in point. Aunt Tara.

She met a man who came to live with them when Morrison was fourteen. "Tango" was the nickname she gave him because he took her dancing on weekends, but he disliked Morrison from the start and imposed a Draconian system of punishment whenever Morrison strayed from the man's narrow definition of permissible teenage behavior.

The beatings involved a variety of instruments: straps, paddles, broomsticks, bare hands and, on two occasions, fists. The man turned his rage on Aunt Tara as well, though less frequently and only when he was drunk.

When Morrison complained, she would break down and say she knew Tango wasn't perfect but he loved her and she needed

124

that love, the love of a man, she'd lived too long without it, and that the two of them—both she and Morrison—would have to learn to accept the bad with the good. That's the way it is in this world. You have to make adjustments.

Once, in the midst of her tears, she'd fallen to her knees and clung to Morrison.

"I know I'm making it hard for you," she sobbed. "I know life was better for you before he came here. I know that. But I'm not pretty anymore and I might never have this chance again. Someday I hope you'll understand. Maybe you'll even forgive me."

He thought now, yes, he did understand. It had taken him this long.

The boy was someone he could not bear to lose.

Standing in the crowded bar he had the same feeling he had in his youth. Tremors of hurt shook through him. He felt himself unraveling: a loosening of bone and tissue, as if his body, his will, were beyond his control.

He would find the boy, and they would talk, and things would return to the way they had been before this terrible night.

Finally, the tremors eased.

A fight had broken out midway down the bar. Arms flailed and someone cursed loudly. The back and forth motion rippled through the crowd. Bodies pushed and shoved.

Morrison slipped out onto the porch. It was cooler there and, through the doorway, he watched arms swinging wildly and heads butting heads. He turned away to phone Krebs. The cell phone message, as usual, asked him to leave his name, his number. As did his office phone.

Had they gotten to Krebs? Had his longtime friend forsaken him, as well?

He held the useless phone at his side and stared at the slow curl of the river. In the bar the shouting and screaming had diminished, giving way to the familiar din of good cheer and fellowship, a world far away from his own.

Solitude was the nature of the undercover investigations he specialized in. That was nothing new. But now he was totally cut off. There was no one in the Division—not a soul left in the world, really—that he knew well enough to trust.

Once he moved away from the Shack the silence of the streets enveloped him. No light in the windows of the boy's trailer, though now the door was open several inches. He pulled back the screen and stepped inside.

He called out in the darkness.

There was barely enough window light for him to find his way through the kitchen and down the short hall. In the bedroom he switched on the overhead lamp. The brightness made him squint, the empty room with its paneled walls a disappointment. The bed, its floral spread unruffled, had not been slept in that night.

On the way out, he pulled the trailer door tight, an instinctive gesture to protect the boy's possessions while he was away.

At their meeting place on the river, Morrison found him.

Coming toward the sea wall he had half-expected—*hoped*—to find him slouching against a mooring post, blowing smoke from the corner of his mouth, his face breaking into a wide grin at the sight of Morrison. What he saw, though, what first drew his attention, was the rope coiled around the post.

He hesitated before leaning over the water, hesitating again before touching the rope, tugging on it, feeling its awful weight. What he couldn't see because of the darkness was the blood on the water which, in thinking back on it later, he knew must have been there. At that moment, though, it was the weight at the end of the rope that pre-occupied him, the boy's head breaking the surface first, the rope tight around his neck then looped in a harness under his arms and across his chest.

It was only when he had pulled the body onto the hard ground of the landing that he saw the razor-like slit across the boy's throat, his eyes frozen wide in disbelief, staring up at Morrison as if asking him *why*.

----TWENTY-TWO----

JOHNNY-O RETURNED FROM MAKING HIS call. At the bar he leaned between Rowan and Aggie. He turned her stool, taking away Rowan's view. Then he edged closer and nuzzled her neck. She giggled appropriately, pulling her head back and squirming as if she were ticklish.

Cute, Rowan thought. Teenagers in love. Real cute.

"So what you two been up to?" Johnny-O said, having re-established his territory. He stood behind her, hands on her bare shoulders, massaging them with a hard affection as if digging in sand.

"Stop, Johnny. You're hurting me." She shifted her shoulders to ease the pressure.

He stopped digging but left his hands on her, palms flat on her shoulders. "Sometimes she likes it rough. Not tonight, I guess." He winked at Rowan, man to man. "Women. They change with the wind, don't they?"

"Some guys feel that's part of their charm."

"You hear that, baby? Mr. Nick here finds you charming."

"We were only talking, Johnny."

"A friendly chat," Rowan added.

"Well, now, I'm damn sorry I missed it." His eyes shone with a cold light. "The world needs all the friendliness it can get, way I see it."

Aggie leaned back against him. "Nick thinks he might be able to help me out."

"He does, does he?" Johnny-O nodded slowly, taking it under consideration

"Used to be good at that. In my old life." Rowan was working him, figuring a way to ingratiate himself. Because Rowan could recognize desperation when he saw it and this one, like Morrison, was sure as hell desperate. Takes one to know one, right? He laughed at himself. Desperate people were needy people, and he wanted to take advantage of the man's need—whatever that was—find a way to make it profitable. If it meant scoring dope for baby doll here, he was more than willing to do it. He squared his shoulders, showed his teeth. For a moment he felt his old swagger: the fool who thought he'd conquered the world. "Finding product, we called it. Back in the hood."

"Always interested in finding product for my baby." Johnny-O squeezed her shoulders, more affectionately this time. "Anything to keep her happy, right?" He gave Rowan an earnest look, briefly letting his guard down. "I'd be, let's say more than grateful, you could put me in touch with a reliable source or two." He leaned to kiss Aggie's shoulders. "We'd sure make it worth your while, wouldn't we, honey?"

Aggie smiled coyly. "I'm a girl who appreciates kindness."

"That you are, baby." He tried to nuzzle her again but she pushed him away.

Rowan reached for his beer. "I'll see what I can do."

"Much obliged, man. 'Cause you see, baby here's a little on edge. Things didn't go exactly as I'd planned, and we're a little behind schedule. So she needs a little something to help her chill out."

"Had a little setback myself today," Rowan said.

"Enough bad luck to go around, I guess." Johnny-O offered his hand and Rowan shook it. "Gonna check out what's happening down at the pier. Then we got a little business to take care of, me and my honey here. We'll catch up with you later on tonight." He gave Rowan a knowing look and turned the stool to help Aggie step down, holding her hand like a real gentleman.

Rowan, watching them walk through the dining room, knew that once again he'd made a pact with the devil.

JOHNNY-O had his arm around Aggie's waist, keeping her close. They were standing on the porch, looking at the river. Rowan moved to the dining room door for a better look. He didn't figure them for the piano bar sing-along type.

They were watching a man at the river, his back to them,

staring at the water. An unremarkable sight really, except perhaps for how still the man stood, as motionless as the pelican on the mooring post beside him, and the fact that in this weather he wore a suit.

It was Morrison.

Johnny-O leaned close to Aggie, telling her something, and she nodded. Then he was ushering her along the porch, his walk easing into a saunter as they passed the piano crowd.

His grin said it all: she's totally *mine*, boys.

Rowan realized why he disliked him so much. It was like seeing himself when he was living the high life. Easy money, easy women. Brass balls, baloney for brains. He laughed again at himself. In a matter of days he'd fallen to the bottom of the earth, this hellhole for mosquitoes and gators, but he sure had a clearer view of the man he was trying to leave behind.

He looked at the strange madness around him in the bar: this trophy room from a bygone era with its animal heads growing out of the walls. Everywhere you confronted bared teeth and fangs, eyes that gave you a chill with their dead cold look. He imagined the Mob version of this: instead of animals, the bloodied remains of contract killings, ear-less heads, bullet-holed eyes, mouths without tongues. And here he was, the newest member of the club, because now *he* could have a trophy room of his own: Fat Tony, Mookie Wells, Vincenzo with the face like ground beef, and the nameless black man on the pier.

I must be getting drunk, he thought, taking his seat at the bar. I *am* drunk. He spun around on the stool to avoid the leering face of the bobcat.

"Need another beer?" Rayelle said behind him.

He shifted in the seat, grinned at her. "No offense, but this place brings out some serious weirdness."

" 'Bout like anywhere else, I'd say. 'Cept for those murders tonight."

"Who else?

"Guatemalan kid. Found him upriver."

Rowan's heart thumped hard against his chest. What had he gotten himself into now? He forced a laugh, tried to regain his cool. "See what I mean? It's this place. Serious weirdness."

She rapped her fingers on the bar. "You want that beer or not?"

"Why not?" When she brought it he said, "Take me, for example."

"You ain't going philosophical on me, are you?" She said it lightly, half-chiding, half-amused.

"Nah. Nothing like that."

She leaned on the bar and watched him with steel-blue eyes.

"Been thinking about my old man," Rowan told her, "all day. That happen to you? No reason, you just keep thinking about someone who's gone?"

"Like they're talking to you? Like they're right there in the room with you?"

"Yeah, like that."

"He die this time of year maybe?"

"I think it's more the situation I'm in. He would of related."

"Maybe he's tryin' to give you some advice."

"Could be." He raised the bottle to his lips, stopped. "Listen, can I buy you a drink?"

She glanced toward the dining room. "Boss don't like us drinking on duty."

"Later, maybe?"

"Yeah, maybe."

"My old man," he said, as if he'd been telling the story straight through, without a break. "Thought everyone was laughing at him. Thought everyone saw him as a fool. So he was always using his life as an example, to show me what I shouldn't be doing." He stared vacantly at the glasses gleaming in a line along the mirror.

"That the end of the story?" She shifted her weight from one foot to the other, seemed in no hurry to tend her other customers.

"Makes me sick to think I never took his advice. He died thinking he'd wasted his life because I hadn't learned a damned thing from the mistakes he made." He glanced at her to see if she was still with him, but he was talking to himself now. The story would come out, with or without her.

"He had this terrible fear of fire. All his life he was convinced that was how he was going to die. And one night, the building he lived in burned to the ground. All five floors. Everyone got out but him. I still wonder about it; I mean, he worked for some bad people. The other tenants survived. Why not him? Bad luck? Fate? Or does the thing we fear get us in the end? Is there some way *we* make it happen?" He searched her face: the tired lines around her eyes and mouth, the clear hard focus of her gaze. "What do you think?"

She stared back at him evenly, but her eyes had softened. Or so he thought. She brushed a lock of hair out of her eyes. It seemed a long time before she spoke. "Important things, things that matter most, we never know why they're the way they are. We just don't." Her eyes fell away from his.

Her face *had* softened, no mistaking it this time, and in the moment before she moved away down the bar, something of her own story flashed across the blue steel surface of her eyes.

As she came toward the cash register, she tried to blink away the moisture in her eyes. She didn't want DeeDee to see, didn't want to talk anymore about the mess her life had become. Nicky's story—she wasn't even sure what the point of it was, if it even *had* a point—had reached dark, faraway places she couldn't name.

Try as she might she couldn't fool DeeDee who seemed to know something was wrong before Rayelle made it halfway down the bar. She had stopped ringing up the last of the dinner checks, the sympathy in her moon eyes exactly what Rayelle didn't want to deal with now.

"So what are you gonna do, Ray?"

She picked up a rag and began wiping the polished bar surface. "About what?"

"You know. What you told me. About you and Bobbie."

DeeDee's presence hovered behind her. She drew the rag down the bar to give herself some distance. "I don't know."

"You're gonna talk to him, right?"

"Am I?"

"You got to do that, Ray. Give him a chance to explain."

"Do I?"

"Sure you do."

She was wiping in circles now, cleaning what was already clean. "Explanation's job is to clear up a confusion. I'm not confused about anything."

"Maybe there's more here than meets the eye."

"Like what?" She said it so harshly she could feel her friend freeze beside her.

"I don't know, Ray. I'm only tryin' to help."

"I know you are, honey. It's just that, well, some things can't be helped." She stopped wiping then, stood there with her head bowed, biting her lip.

DeeDee leaned close, curled her arm around her waist. "You

want to go in the ladies room a while? I'll cover for you."

She stiffened, said, "No, I do not want to go to the ladies room." She bent down, began washing glasses in the sink, setting them to drain on the mat.

Absently, DeeDee watched her friend's hands move in and out of the sink. "I don't know what I'd do if Lonnie ever did that to me. I'd like to think I could find it in my heart to forgive him. Maybe if you talk to Bobbie he might say something that, you know, makes you feel more kindly to him."

"You don't have any meanness in you, honey." Rayelle was bent low over the sink, her hands turning red from the sudsy water. "But I'm not good like you. There's a line that once you cross it there's no way you can go back. Bobbie and me's been drifting toward that line a while now. Yesterday he stepped over it, is all."

She straightened up then, took the rag to dry her hands and glanced toward the door. "Seems like I'm not the only one looks like death warmed over tonight."

----*TWENTY-THREE*----

MORRISON STOOD IN THE DOORWAY, grave and hesitant. It appeared he might turn and bolt, swaying uncertainly as he was, but he held his ground, even took a step forward into the soft light of the room where voices rose around him like an offer of comfort and a woman sang on the jukebox about love gone bad.

Images jerked across his mind: *The stuttering light of a police cruiser. Emilio's body lifted on a stretcher. The short procession across the landing. The closed doors of the van removing him from sight. Night descending again undisturbed over the black river.* He had watched it all from the shadows at the pier's end.

The images made him dizzy and he stepped back against the door frame for support. It seemed he had made a mistake, that he didn't belong here after all.

A voice spoke to him out of the smoky darkness. A shape attached itself to the voice, a bright blue shirt with palm trees dancing across it at cock-eyed angles, and then a face above the shirt.

"Been looking for you, man," Rowan said. "We need to talk."

"I don't know if I—I should be going." But he stayed there against the wall, solemn-eyed, swaying unsteadily and staring into the room.

"You all right, man? You sick?"

"No, I—"

He took Morrison by the arm. "Come on, let's grab a seat." They moved toward the French doors where there were empty tables facing the pool.

When the girl brought the whiskies, two doubles that Rowan had ordered with the authority of a doctor prescribing medicine,

Morrison drank deeply, eyes closed, attempting to push away the vision of Emilio staring up at him from the damp ground. He set the glass down but kept his hands wrapped around it, as if, even in the holding of it, there would come an easing of grief.

He felt he had lost his voice so he sat there in silence and stared at the pool. The muscled rivulets of the waterfall sent ripples across the surface of the shimmering green water.

"You Bible salesmen live on the edge."

Morrison's face remained unchanged, beyond the reach of irony or wit. "You don't understand."

Rowan rested his arms on the table and leaned forward. "Enlighten me."

Morrison grimaced at that. If only I could enlighten myself, he thought. Was Emilio killed because his co-workers found out he was a rat? Had Morrison made him even more vulnerable by pushing him too hard for information, by not insisting he flee when there was still time?

Or was it Morrison's enemies in the Division tightening the noose, cutting him off from his sources, the way they had cut him off from Krebs? Or—and this possibility hurt him the most—had he sealed the boy's death warrant himself by not defending him to Caruso, by leaving the impression that he too thought Emilio had double-crossed him? No matter how he looked at it, one thing was clear: he hadn't given the boy the protection he needed.

"I sacrificed him to the enemy." He said it as if talking to himself.

"What enemy?" Rowan angled his chair so that he faced Morrison head-on. "Those same guys who were after *you*?"

"The enemy," he said again, as if the phrase explained itself.

"Who's *him*?" Rowan's eyes flashed with impatience. "Who you talking about? That Guatemalan kid?"

Morrison took another drink, the whiskey slamming him hard as a fist, and for a moment the veil of grief lifted. He stared at the man listening to him.

Who was he and what was his angle?

Because he looked like a guy who'd worked lots of angles. Deep-set eyes that seemed always in motion, working the room, working a deal. The flippant curl of his lip, always on the cusp of sarcasm. But even in his disordered state Morrison saw there was something else, too, hiding back in those deal-making eyes, something more serious and complicated. "Who are you?"

"The guy who saved your ass tonight, remember? I figure you owe me."

"What is it you want me to do?"

Rowan looked bemused. "Maybe we can help each other."

"How's that?"

"Give me answers, for one thing." He eyed Morrison warily. "You're some kind of Fed. I can smell it."

"I work for myself now."

"Drugs? That your game?"

"No."

"I'd lay odds you're in the trade—one end or the other."

"It's not what you think."

"What do I think?"

"What*ever* you think."

"That guy, the one who ran away, he gonna come after us?"

"It's not safe to be seen with me, if that's what you want to know."

"Too late for that now, isn't it? Small matter of a dead man on the pier." He regarded Morrison with a mixture of curiosity and impatience. "Besides, the way I figure it, I'm the only friend you've got."

"How would you know that?"

"You're sitting here, aren't you? You could be anywhere right now, but you're here."

Morrison stiffened, his old defenses standing at the ready, but he lacked the will to muster them. He said in a weary voice, "You don't know anything about me."

"I know you're into something pretty heavy. I know that much. I know we're walking down the same road."

"What road?"

Rowan chuckled. "The No Name highway. The road to Terminal Junction, crossroads to oblivion."

Morrison raised his glass and drained the last traces of whisky. He spoke quietly, wearily, without rancor or belligerence. "You're a self-assured son-of-a-bitch, aren't you?"

"No man, not really." He settled back in his seat, the bright green light of the pool illuminating one side of his face, giving it the look of a garish mask. "It's just the way I learned to play the game."

He called across the room for two more doubles.

Rowan went to the men's room. Morrison sat alone at the table when the girl brought the drinks. She set the glasses down carefully, then stepped back, her ponytail swinging as she moved.

"Will there be anything else, Mr. M?"

"I don't think so, no."

She smelled of something sweet, strawberry or cherry, something only a young girl would wear. Her face was round and cherubic. Too wholesome, he thought, for a place like this: this region of festering marshland and intrigue. "We'll be closing up here soon," she said, "but the piano bar is still open. And the Tiki, of course."

"Yes, thank you."

She turned to leave and he called out, "Miss?"

"You don't have to be so formal, Mr. M," she said, smiling down at him. "You can call me DeeDee."

"DeeDee—" The name felt awkward on his tongue. He shifted uncomfortably in his chair. "There *is* something—"

"Sure, what do you need?" She stepped close to the table, her head tilted in his direction, her bright eyes awash with wonder and innocence.

He stared into his drink, cleared his throat. It had been a long time since he'd had a conversation with a girl so young. Of course there were the waitresses in diners, in bars like this one, but he had never gone beyond the formality of placing an order.

He cleared his throat again. What should he say? He wanted to ask her for something to make him feel less alone, to release him from the questions that hounded him.

Had he been wrong to distrust the boy?

Had he himself been the real cause of his death, either by pushing him too hard for information or by forsaking him with his doubt?

Then he caught himself. He was being ridiculous, wasn't he? How could she possibly appease his guilt? And yet her innocence, what at least he imagined to be her innocence, and her hopefulness seemed to call him to judgment.

Forgive me, he wanted to say. *Forgive my lack of faith.*

Her moon eyes watched him, a rapt expression on her face.

He shook his head slowly. "Never mind," he said. "It's nothing."

He drank his whiskey alone. The fool, lamenting. What kind

of solace, he asked himself, could he have expected from one so young? She had but one thing to offer: the gaudy trickery of youth: finding hope in the truly hopeless. Which was, of course, what he most needed now. He watched her walk away. As if she were another of his children going forth into the world, he thought with great sadness. One day she would know the truth and its darkness. One day she would know how it feels. And as with Emilio, he would not be there to offer her comfort.

Behind him Rowan said, "Fooling around with jail-bait, are we?"

"I wasn't—"

"Lighten up, man. I was putting you on." He stood behind his chair without bothering to sit, and reached for his glass. "She *is* cute, though," he said, watching her move to the bar. "It's that little bit of baby fat, wouldn't you say?"

"I'm afraid I've never thought much about it."

"What *do* you think about?" Rowan asked sharply.

"My job, mostly."

"Your job." There was a layer of sarcasm in the way he said it. "Whatever *that* is." He took another swig of whiskey and set the glass down. "Come on," he said, "they're closing this place down. Time to move on."

----*TWENTY-FOUR*----

AT THE PIANO BAR, ROWAN stopped briefly to check out the scene and for the first time Morrison took a close look at the crowd gathered there. Their eyes intrigued him: the eyes of fugitives. For the first time he counted himself among them. Like them, he couldn't face the silence of the room waiting for him.

At the Tiki Hut they found standing room at the bar, facing the dancers, and Rowan ordered whiskies. At first Morrison clenched himself against the hard-driving music, every muscle in defense mode, but there seemed no way he could keep it at bay so he quit trying. Soon the pounding from the jukebox became an odd sort of temporary relief, beating away at his memories, beating them bloody.

"Back where I'm from," Rowan was saying, "clubs were a way of life."

The man had New York written all over him but Morrison asked anyway. "Where was that?"

"The Big Apple. And you?"

"St. Louis. A lifetime ago."

Rowan nudged him with his elbow. "See that wasn't so bad, was it?"

"What wasn't?"

"Sharing personal detail. Getting to know each other." He nudged him again.

Morrison, in spite of himself, smiled. "Just don't call me Walty."

"Huh?"

"Private joke."

When the drinks came, Rowan lay a twenty on the bar. "On

me tonight," he said, handing a glass to Morrison who had turned to watch the dancers jammed tight on the small patch of battered plank flooring. "You get to repay me later."

The sides of the Hut were open and the cooler air of the river filtered through. In the crowd a short Guatemalan man danced with a tall red-haired girl. Under other circumstances their physical incongruity would have been a source of mirth, but the man looked vaguely enough like Emilio for Morrison to reach for his whiskey and down it quickly. The numbing effect of the music was wearing off. The boy's face stared at him again from the river landing. *Why?* the eyes were asking. *Why?*

"What do you think of Rayelle?" Rowan asked.

It took Morrison a moment to shift ground. "I can't say I know much about her."

"You're so diplomatic, man. Come on, give me your honest."

"She's going through a rough time. You can see it in her face."

"She intrigues me." He turned toward Morrison, resting an elbow on the bar. "She's not your typical barmaid, I can feel it. And you're right: her eyes are the giveaway. They've seen more than their share of bad times." As he drank, he watched Morrison over the rim of his glass; he seemed to want to convince him of something. "I've invited her over here for a drink, when she's through. In case."

"In case of what?"

"In case I don't get another night like this." Rowan smiled faintly. "Then you and me, man, we got to do some serious talking."

MORRISON finished off his third—or was it his fourth?—whiskey. He'd lost track. It had been a night of shocks and jolts, and now he was alone at the bar with a terrible emptiness. Rowan had gone off to a corner table with Rayelle where he sat hunched forward, talking earnestly and non-stop. Morrison found himself missing the man's company.

He ordered another whiskey and stared through the Tiki Hut's open shutters at the river, silent and dream-like beyond the room's din. A breeze ruffled the fronds of the thatched roof, the sound of paper being shuffled. It was then he noticed Aggie among the dancers. In a clinging red dress, her body moved with a sinuous grace, slower than the beat of the music but mindful of it all the same, pairing its rhythm with a rhythm of her own.

The man she danced with couldn't take his eyes off her but she paid him scant attention, keeping her eyes on herself, as if monitoring her movements for imperfection, for any trace of imprecision. When she looked up she caught Morrison's eye and smiled, and he stared quickly down into his drink. Then she was standing in front of him, her hand reaching for his. She took the glass away, set it on the bar, and pulled him into the crowd.

Even if he had wanted to disengage himself, the words of refusal would not have formed in his mouth. It was as if he hadn't yet learned the mechanics of speech, floating as he was in a realm of pure sensation: the soft firmness of her hand wrapped around his, the bared back and delicately sculpted shoulders that he walked behind.

When she turned, her eyes watched him with faint amusement. "You can't guess how glad I am to see you here. I've danced with these local boys enough for a lifetime."

"I'm not very good at this."

She cocked her head and smiled at him sweetly. "We haven't even started yet. How do you know?"

He reached awkwardly to take her hand but she slipped her arms around his neck and leaned against him. "It's nicer *this* way."

He stood still, hands at his sides, as she swayed in time with the music which was slower now, as close to a ballad as the jukebox had played.

"You can put your arms around me, you know. It's only a dance."

Still he hesitated before extending his arms, wrapping them tentatively around her waist, his fists closed so as not to feel the full impact of the thin clinging fabric of her dress and the skin beneath it.

He could not remember the last time he danced with a woman. Years now. Once at his wedding reception and, before that, sometime in his youth. For a moment it seemed no time had passed since then: he was a boy taking lessons at his aunt's insistence, the small studio near the train station, the excited tittering of the girls as they waited to be asked to dance, the teacher—Miss Van Houten—placing the record on the turntable, lifting the needle and setting it gently onto the spinning disc, that first hiss the signal for the boys to begin their approach, he always the last among them to move, so that his partner would be whichever girl had not yet been asked.

He could hear himself muttering the formal invitation Miss Van Houten insisted upon, "May I have the pleasure of this dance?" and the girl, because she had no other options, would naturally accept and then would begin the sweaty contact of palms, the hand placed firmly but respectfully around the waist, the fumbling and self-conscious footwork executed to the strains of the Glenn Miller Orchestra, Miss Van Houten's favorite.

He felt the same awkwardness now and he moved stiffly, too quickly. She said, "It's more fun if you slow it down. Just stay in one place and sway a little. Like I'm doing. Nice and easy."

It was as if he had to rein himself in, restrain the skittery beating of his heart, the nervous twitching impulses of his muscles. He adjusted his pace to hers, tried to imitate the subtle, shifting movement of her hips. In doing that he found himself giving in to desire.

To distance himself he closed his eyes but that only intensified the smell of her perfume and the warm pressure of her head against his, the insistent heat of her body.

Her words came muffled against his ear. "That's better, isn't it?"

They were barely moving. He was simply holding her or, more to the point, letting himself be held by her, while everything around him seemed to be in motion—the room, the dancers, the swirl of voices. They were the calm at the center of the storm. *Aggie holding him was the calm.*

What he felt both disturbed and astonished him.

Need, like a hungry infant, was crying out to be fed.

So when the dance ended and she said she'd left her purse in the room, would he mind walking her back, he said, no, of course he wouldn't mind.

Rowan, deep in conversation with Rayelle, winked at him and mouthed the word, *Later,* but Morrison barely noticed. Nor did he notice the envious, disbelieving looks of the single men at the bar. Suddenly there was the stillness of the river path, the slow purling of water against the pilings, their footsteps rising in the silence.

It occurred to him, of course, that he might be being set up. But for what purpose? What could this woman and Johnny-O possibly want from him?

Aggie leaned against him, slipped her arm around his waist, but he kept his distance. "If it's Johnny you're worried about, you can put your mind at ease," she said. "He's gone."

"Where?"

"Back to Alabama."

He looked at her for an explanation.

"We broke up. No big deal. It's been coming a while."

"I'm sorry."

"Don't be. I'm better off this way. Free as the breeze." She pulled at her dress, exposing more of her breasts than the scooped neckline already revealed. "Not that there's ever enough of a breeze down here." She stood close to him and used her hand to fan herself. "How *do* these people stand it?"

When they reached the bungalow, she said, "Why'nt you come in while I freshen up?"

----TWENTY-FIVE----

ROWAN AND THE WAITRESS TOOK the service stairs at the far end of the hotel lobby. For Rayelle it was like the old days, accompanying men to their rooms after a night of dancing at the Tiki, the two of them sneaking up the long stairs, hushing their voices, choking back their giggles, because Mrs. Lowry had strict rules against her waitresses fraternizing with the guests.

The stairwell still smelled the same, dry and airless, and the hall on the third floor still smelled of wood polish. Its floors gleamed in the dark. The faint red EXIT sign glowed at one end; at the other a trail of moonlight fell in fractured pieces through the window's latticed glass. In the old days she would hold her breath, remove her shoes, lean gently against the man she was with as they moved down the hall.

Now she didn't care if the entire world knew she was here.

What mattered most to her was taking control, finding a corner of her world where she could exist without Bobbie. This man walking down the hall with her would help her get there, on *her* terms.

At one time or another she had been in every one of the rooms on this floor, each door opening wide as a promise, and she had stepped through carrying her illusions like a purse. Now she carried neither a purse nor illusions. This was only what it was: a man and a woman alone in a room, an hour, more or less.

When the door swung back and Nicky stood aside for her, she hesitated. What she saw was exactly what she remembered: the pale gold and green coverlet on the double bed, the braided throw rug, the dormer window with its tiny piece of night sky.

She couldn't, she thought. Not here. Not again.

"I've got a better place," she said.

She led him along the river. At the construction site she stopped and let her gaze wander between the posts and beams. The carpenters had been busy today. Along the side of the house a new stairway lifted to the main level.

"*Here*?" Rowan said. "I didn't know you southern girls were so kinky."

"We have our unconventional side."

He glanced at the neighboring houses, several hundred feet away and dark. "The neighbors?"

"Asleep. And the river doesn't care."

"Why here?"

Because, she thought, *I'm saying goodbye*. "Personal thing, that's all."

She led him up the new stairs that were spotted with sawdust. Moving through the maze of posts, yellowed and smooth and smelling of wood dust, was like finding her way in a carnival funhouse. Everything was illusion, a trick of the eye: rooms and walls and ceilings, even the house itself. The maze led nowhere, meant nothing.

In what would be the master bedroom she walked the perimeter as if measuring it in her mind and stopped at the wide glass-less picture window that would someday have offered she and Bobbie a three-quarters view of the river. "*Here*," she said.

They began by standing up against the window frame and gradually found their way down onto the floor where their clothes served as a mattress. He was slow and methodical, not anything like Bobbie who was always in a hurry no matter how much he denied it; and what was even more upsetting to her was that she always knew *exactly* what he was in a hurry for—a beer, to catch the last innings of a Devil Rays' game on TV, to go to sleep or, more often than not these last weeks, to attend to the "business" that would supposedly secure their future here on Easy Street—he was *that* simple to figure out.

Nicky would never be that easy, she sensed. At any one time there were always two or three things going on in his head. She could see it in his eyes and the way he would jump quickly, sometimes in mid-sentence, from one idea to another, his mouth trying to catch up to his brain.

Even now, attentive as he was to her, she thought he might be thinking deep thoughts and she worked harder to bring him back to her: using her hands on his shoulders and at the base of his spine, using her hips in that swiveling way that drove guys crazy in her Tiki days. Because she needed him to be with her a hundred percent on this, for as long as it took. After that he was free. *Absolutely no obligation to buy*, as they said in the TV ads.

Bye-bye love.

That was the way she wanted this to be. No illusions. No tomorrows.

The boards were hard on her back. They groaned like bed springs but she didn't mind the hurt, welcomed it in fact, because it helped her feel the act more. When she looked into his eyes this time she saw that they—Nicky and Rayelle—were traveling the same stretch of road, no double or triple thoughts going through his mind, no being in a hurry for a beer. She saw, too, how lovely he was, his hair wet and slicked back from sweat, his white skin glistening against her tan, his long thin body grinding Bobbie out of her life, burning him to ash, and what was sending everything up in a blaze of smoke and flame was his shaft, long and sleek like his body, searing the raw nerves inside her, burning them clean, scorching memory and wasted hope and useless desire.

He was with her now.

Nicky.

She saw something flicker in his eyes: fear or uncertainty; the child he once was, reaching out to her. Then it was gone, the child in him, and he was a man again, sure of his power, and she saw him the way she imagined he'd been in New York: at the wheel of a flashy car with an even flashier woman by his side. He was driving fast, incredibly screamingly fast, so fast they were going to die but nobody cared and then he was coming and she was coming and then time slowed to a crawl, they were breathing hard, lying still, and when she dropped her arms in sheer exhaustion she could feel the sawdust clinging to her sweaty skin, and the soreness in her backbone and shoulder blades from their merciless contact with the floor.

"You're still a little boy inside, aren't you?" she said when he was lying beside her and they were staring up at the black sky crowded with stars.

"Why do you say that?"

"I don't know. The way you looked before. Kinda lost."

"I used to think of myself as a tough guy."

"You were fooling yourself."

"I fooled myself about a lot of things." He reached for her hand, their arms wet against the wood.

"Like what?" she asked. "What were you fooling yourself about?"

"Everything."

"Me, too."

Her eyes were moist with sweat and tears. She blinked to clear them. The sky was too beautiful not to see. Enough stars to light her hopes and dreams for years to come.

At the bungalow, Morrison waited in the doorway while Aggie went inside. Beside the bed her shadow leaned to turn on the light. He heard the click and then her voice muttering in disgust, "Now the bulb's out." She went into the bathroom, flicked the wall switch there, and stepped back into the space where the light slanted into the room. "I have to use the ladies'. May as well come all the way in, rest your feet a minute."

There was no chair so he sat at the foot of the bed stiffly and stared ahead at the jalousie windows, slats opened to the night. The porch bulb threw a muddy yellow light against them. From outside came the buzz of insects, their shadows flitting against the screen, the sound of them suddenly cut off by the toilet's flush then the splash of water hitting the porcelain surface of the sink.

The room smelled of warm air and stale sheets, and the residue of her perfume stirred into life by the occasional movement of air through the windows. Feeling pressure in his shoulders, he shifted his weight on the bed and stretched his upper body taut from his waist. There wasn't a single part of him that didn't feel tight and constricted. In his rumpled suit he felt both hot and dirty. He thought he might go next door to shower, but that seemed too much of an ordeal.

From far away a boat horn sounded on the river.

In the room a door opened and she was standing in front of him in her red dress, barefoot and smiling.

Reaching behind her she felt for the zipper, the dress falling away from her breasts. She helped it with her hands, shimmying her way out of it, standing before him naked except for her panties, pale pink lace against her tanned skin. Never—not even in his imagination—had he seen such beauty.

She leaned forward to loosen his tie and undo the buttons of

146

his shirt. Kneeling on the floor she removed his shoes and socks, pulled away his pants. When he lay back on the mattress, when he felt warm breath between his legs, her tongue and lips calling him back to life, he was thinking of another room, another bed, years before: his wedding night.

That room, too, was at the edge of a river, in the shadow of a bridge the lights of which cast a blue-white pallor upon the bed where Helena lay waiting. Still in his tux he lingered by the window watching smoke form loose, unraveling clouds above the factories on the riverbank. In a white negligee that she had bought for this night, this moment, she lay spread out in the center of the double bed, calling to him, "Darling, My love," and when he came to her finally, when he lay naked beside her, the first time they were naked together—she had been raised in a deeply religious household and he had been too shy to overcome her resistance— he was filled with a profound emptiness, as if he had been cut off from everything and everyone in the world, as if he had already experienced the failure his marriage would become, the lonely road his life would follow.

Aggie had raised herself, straddling him now, watching him closely. "So who is she?"

"Who?"

"The girl you're thinking about."

"Is it that obvious?"

She laughed. "Guy's with *me* and his mind's wanderin', I figure it's got to be something heavy."

He liked her simple, unabashed self-confidence. You couldn't argue with her logic.

"Someone I knew," he said.

She gave the flesh of his belly a playful squeeze. "Do I have to guess?"

"My ex-wife. A lifetime ago."

"What happened?"

He closed his eyes and wondered if it was possible to condense three years of living with someone into a meaningful sentence or two. "I couldn't love her the way she needed to be loved."

"You mean you couldn't screw her good."

"That was part of it. I couldn't give in to love. I was always holding something back."

Aggie was working his sex with her hand. She lifted herself and slid him inside, holding him in place while she raised and lowered herself, riding him slowly to make sure the fit was good. Then she smiled and moved her hands to his hips, riding him harder. "Seems to be working real fine *now*."

Against the window's murky light her body arched above him, a slow rising and falling that for the moment overcame his resistance, his memories. Her beauty was more than his hands deserved—the delicately formed breasts and shoulders, the incredible curves—and for the first time he understood why some men would kill for a woman.

Then he had traveled beyond thought. He existed only as thrusting muscles, fingers groping flesh: his body a piece of debris drawn by the tide's undertow deeply and swiftly into ever-darkening waters, to some necessary place in the womb of the world where he would be welcomed and received, where at last he would find a home.

Above him a woman cried out, her head tossing side to side, waves of silky hair whipping her face, the motion of her hips becoming slow and measured, wrenching every bit of pleasure from the pain of surrender; then he was surrendering too: a fast and trembling rush.

Into the sudden stillness came the smell of sweat, his own and the woman's, and the drone of mosquitoes, far away. He thought he must be dreaming because he saw Emilio come walking out of the sullen light from the porch and turn his head in such a way to reveal his neck, the skin smooth and clean and brown except for the razor-thin slit filling with blood, the boy saying *te amo, te amo, I loved you, why*?

Morrison heard himself saying, "I loved you, too. I love you," and then Aggie's voice above him was saying, "Ah, honey, you don't have to say that. It was only sex, real good sex," and then he was laughing or crying, he couldn't tell which, because he saw how hopeless and irreversible it all was, how he had failed for the second time in his life to recognize genuine love and friendship when it had finally come to him.

No winners or losers as Caruso had warned him, only the lightless road ahead.

----TWENTY-SIX----

MORRISON THOUGHT HE MUST HAVE been asleep because when he opened his eyes the lights in the room were shining brightly and there was a pistol pressed hard into his skull. Red-faced with rage, Johnny-O stood over the bed, digging the barrel deeper into the thin flesh of Morrison's temple. "Walt, meet Little Walt."

It took Morrison a moment to make the connection. Little Walt, the Walther pistol he was now on intimate terms with.

"Jesus, Johnny, take it easy," Aggie said.

"Shut up, you." He swung his gun arm in her direction. She cowered against the wall, wrapping herself hurriedly with a sheet. "And put some damned clothes on. I'll deal with you later." He reached down for Morrison's pants, flung them at him. "You, too. I don't wanna have to look at your sorry naked ass."

Morrison pulled on his pants, thinking of the 9mm inside his jacket which had been thrown onto the floor. He cursed himself for his negligence and blamed it on his weakened spirit. Now he was paying the price. He looked around for the rest of his clothes. He felt ridiculous being naked in front of this man. "I'll need my shirt, too," he said.

He saw the motion before he felt the pain: a flicker in the corner of his eye, the raised shadow of Johnny-O's arm, then hard steel slicing across his temple.

Aggie cried out, "Stop it, Johnny," but the man was hearing only himself now. "*I'll* decide when you get your shirt."

Morrison raised his hand to his head. Blood dampened his fingers. Rage was building like pus in the kid's eyes and he thought he would be struck again. Instead, Johnny-O rocked back and forth on his feet, shoulders hiked in a tough guy pose, and again shoved Little Walt at him between the eyes.

"So what's the game? You come in here, *my* room, *my* bed, you screw *my* girl, maybe got her pregnant, maybe gave her disease. What's the game, Walter? You a back-door man, that what you are? Thou shalt not covet a man's girlfriend. You of all people should know that, Bible salesman like yourself." He jabbed the barrel harder into Morrison's forehead. "What you got to say to me on the subject, *Walter?*"

Morrison spoke softly, more to himself than to anyone listening. "It was a failure of judgment on my part."

Johnny-O let out a howl. "*A failure of judgment?* That what it was?" He turned toward Aggie, held the gun straight out at her. "What do you think of that, honey-bunch? *A failure of judgment.* That the way you see it? Was it *a failure of judgment* on your part, too? Is that what we got here? A simultaneous *failure of judgments?*"

Aggie had pulled on her dress. It hung off one shoulder. Her lipstick had smeared and her hair was bunched sideways at an awkward angle. She looked like a broken-down kewpie doll. "It's not like I planned it. It happened, that's all. It just happened."

"'Course it did," he said in a mock-comforting, sugar-coated voice. "Kind of like you got carried away, right? Swept up in the moment."

She stood with her shoulders slouched, eyes watching him blankly. She wasn't sure what she was agreeing to. "Yeah. I guess."

"That's what's wrong with this country. Nobody takes responsibility anymore. Not the President. Not the damn congress. *Nobody.*" He was pacing alongside the bed, lunging menacingly between them, waving the pistol. When he spoke his voice was high-pitched, mocking, the voice of a helpless woman: "I don't know what came over me. I got carried away. *It just happened,* that's all. *It just happened.*" In his normal voice he said: "What's the hot-damn problem here?"

"No problem, Johnny."

"Not for you, pussy-cat. You just got laid. But that don't mean there's not a damn serious problem here." He cocked the hammer, held the gun on her. She let out a breathless cry. "It's pathetic," he said. "The whole damn country's done lost its moral character. What I want here is some honesty. I want the plain and simple truth. You gonna give it to me, honey-pie?" He stared down the barrel at her. "Are you?"

"Sure, Johnny," she said in a choked voice, "whatever you want."

"Good. That's good. 'Cause nothing tastes better to me than a heaping bowlful of the good old truth." He grinned at her malevolently. "So here's what I want to hear you say. I want you to say, 'I fucked him, Johnny, and I liked it.' "

She hung back against the wall, her eyes pleading with him. "No, Johnny, no."

"*No, Johnny, no,*" he said, mimicking her. "I'm only asking for the truth, sweetie-babes. That's not too much to ask, is it? I mean, we all got a right to the truth. We're in America here. We got constitutional guarantees." His face turned hard again and he took a step toward her, Little Walt at arm's length. "Talk to me, Ag, or would you rather be talkin' to the angels?"

She tried to speak but what came out were sniffles and sobs.

"Can't hear you, baby. The truth don't want to know about tears. The truth ain't got time for cry babies."

She had moved against the wall behind Morrison. He heard her voice, a whisper no louder than the buzz of mosquitoes against the screen. "I fucked him . . . and I liked it."

"That's better," Johnny-O said, "but it ain't quite there yet. What I told you to say is 'I fucked him, *Johnny*, and I liked it.' Not too much for your brain to wrap itself around now, is it? I mean, you got so much heat down below, you'd think a little of it would warm up them teeny-tiny brain cells of yours. Now try it one more time."

She was sobbing again, murmuring, "No, no."

"*Say it!*" he screamed.

She choked back her tears and spoke again, barely audibly. "I fucked him, Johnny, and I liked it."

"Louder."

"I fucked him, Johnny, and I liked it," she said, her voice shaking, but at normal volume.

Johnny-O nodded. "So be it." His face had visibly blanched and he swallowed hard, as if trying to digest her words. "Nothing humbles a man like hearing his baby doll speak the truth." He seemed to be contemplating the ramifications of that when he turned sharply on Morrison. "What do you think, Walt? Should I believe her? Or is she lying to save her ass? I mean, she lied to me once already tonight. Said she just wanted to go out dancing and I find her curled up all nice 'n' cozy here with you. So how

I know she's not lying to me right now? What's your opinion on the subject?"

Morrison stared straight ahead at the bathroom door, still partly open the way she had left it. Her red purse sat on the counter next to the sink.

"Hard to say, isn't it, Walt? Could go either way. Fifty-fifty. Six a one, half a dozen of another. And the hell of it is we never really *do* know, do we? Stranger on the street or a loved one, *'specially* a loved one, it's all a matter of faith. We hear what we wanna hear."

He was looking at Morrison, thinking hard over something. "But for the sake of argument, Walt, what would you do? If she was *your* girlfriend. Because in a way she is, isn't she? I mean, you were the last to be rammed up inside her. Squatter's rights, so to speak. Possession is nine-tenths of the law, or however the hell that saying goes. So, you see, you've got a stake in this, too. If you see my point. So if you were in my place what would you do about this mutual *failure of judgment* you two just had?"

"I'd let her go."

"Hear that, Ag? You've got a hero for a boyfriend." He seemed amused by that but a moment later the amusement had fled his eyes. "That's a little too nice 'n' easy for my taste, though, Walter. I mean the way I see it, an injustice has been done to me and someone's got to pay the consequences. That's only fair, right? I'm standin' here wondering who's going to pay. That gonna be you or her? You willing to take the rap for both of you?"

"Yes."

"*Yes*?" He nodded his head in mock appreciation. "You picked a winner, Ag. You got a knight in shining polyester here." He turned viciously on Morrison. "How you gonna do that, huh? How you gonna make up for the terrible thing you done, this hurt I got to carry around in my heart now long as I live? I mean I got to think what's appropriate: eye for an eye, like the Bible says. What do you think would be *appropriate* compensation?"

"I don't know."

"Well then, let's go over the options." He leaned close, wiggling Little Walt in the general proximity of Morrison's crotch. "First and foremost, the most logical option using the eye-for-an-eye notion as a guideline is I blow your balls off one at a time. Law of the jungle, right? 'Cause we *are* in a jungle here, there's no denyin' that. And the law is the law: I hurt you the way you hurt me. Clean and simple—nothing to think about. Satisfies most people's sense of justice. We'd be just about even-steven."

He straightened up and looked over at Aggie. "Wouldn't you say so, baby-cakes?" His sneer went ear to ear. Slowly he sauntered around the bed, sidled up to her with a mock coziness, tickled her chin with Little Walt. "Wouldn't you say that'd make up for the terrible thing he done to you while I was out working hard for my baby, makin' sure I give her the best this little old world of ours has to offer?"

She turned her face away from the gun, twisted her body, moved farther along the wall. Johnny-O laughed, watching her squirm. He walked back around the bed to Morrison. "Option number two. I turn you over to Bobbie Dawson."

"What's Dawson got to do with this?"

"Eye for an eye, like we been saying. Word on the pier is you took out one a his men; he's looking for a return, in kind."

"What's in that for you?"

A smile oozed across Johnny-O's lips. "You know, Walter, you're a lot smarter than you look. You done hit it right on the nose, first shot. You done identified the problem. I'd say you done identified the problem *in a nutshell*. What's in it for me? That *is* the question. Say I drag your ass over to him right now. What kinda thanks am I gonna get? Or I take you out to the swamp, shoot you myself, bring back an ear for identification purposes or maybe that finger there with the nice gold ring on it. What's he gonna give me? Maybe somethin', maybe nothin'. Can't trust the man. Because he ain't givin' me nothing so far. And I come to him on account of a mutual friend we both have. I come to him with *references*."

"This friend—"

Johnny-O waved the gun at the air as if swatting a fly. "Don't matter about him now. Long and short of it, he don't show up when he's supposed to. Fell off the face of the earth, who knows? What matters is Bobbie Dawson won't do business without him here. Bobbie Dawson says he don't know me from a hole in the wall, looks at me like I'm some piece a scum blew in on the wind." He bent low in front of Morrison, spread his lips wide in an exaggerated grin. "That what I look like to you? Scum on the wind?"

Morrison stared back at him blankly, ignoring the clown routine. So maybe that *did* confirm his theory about the wildlife stash at the still: Dawson and Turner doing business on the side, ripping off from the cargo that passed through the Blue Lagoon. Their own private enterprise.

Think fast, he told himself. He leaned toward the leering face. "How do *I* fit in?"

Johnny-O straightened up slowly, the freakish grin gone, the edges of his mouth turned down as if he'd bitten into something sour. "Dawson's a stubborn son-of-a-bitch. No-deal Bobbie, I call him. Tells me go see you." He touched the barrel again to Morrison's forehead, drew a question mark on his face and dotted it on his chin. "He send me to the right place?"

"Depends what you want."

"Reptiles, birds, monkeys. Anything I can turn a profit on."

"How much are you looking to buy?"

"How much you got?"

"Enough."

"Whoo-ee!" He pumped his fist in the air. "See that, Ag, I knowed the man was into something heavy." He grinned down at Morrison. "Bobby Dawson knowed it, too. He knowed you used to be a Fed. Figured you'd tired a that, turned profiteer. Figured you're here setting up an operation of your own. Not that he told me so himself. But you be surprised what kind of stuff you hear down here if you get these Crackers drunk enough."

"What kind of stuff?"

"*All* kinds of stuff. Like, how none a them can believe a man would spend his whole life hunting poachers, in the effen W or wherever, without realizing he's crazy not switching sides to rake in all that easy money." His face was shiny with sweat, bright with self-satisfaction. "I *knowed* it. First time I seen you. It's you quiet, sneaky types got all the action. Ain't that right, Ag?" He waggled his hips obscenely. "He showed you some of what he's got tonight, didn't he?"

From his jeans he pulled a bandanna and mopped his brow. "Don't know about you cold-blooded types, though, how you could go at it like that, grinding away like hogs in a ditch, in this kinda heat." He shook his head in mock bewilderment. "Just can't figure it. True love, I guess. But you won't mind if I cool things down a little bit now, will you?" he said, reaching to the wall unit above the window and flicking on the A.C. It jumped to life with a deep-throated rumble. He turned to Morrison. "This business we gonna do—"

"I'll need a few hours, a day maybe."

"You got till tonight."

"These people I deal with," Morrison said. "They're going to want to see some money. They like to know who they're dealing with."

"I got my hands on more than a hundred grand. They'll see it when the time comes."

"I'll pass that on to them." Almost unconsciously he slipped into law enforcement mode, setting up a case against the man. He feigned deliberation, as if something troubled him. "This merchandise I have. I don't have papers for it. I can't guarantee any of it's legal."

Johnny-O bared his teeth in a laugh. "I could give a rat's ass."

"All right then." He glanced at Aggie who seemed less agitated at this point, watching him with a mild and distant curiosity from the shadows of the wall. Turning back to Johnny, he said, "Can I have my shirt now?"

When he was dressed he moved toward the door without looking again at Aggie. Johnny-O, a languid smile on his lips, slouched against the door frame. He raised his arm to examine Little Walt, turning it side to side in his hand, finally raising the barrel to his lips and blowing on it. "Your balls," he said. "One at a time. Remember."

FROM the door, standing in the porch's dusty yellow light, Morrison saw that his room had been ransacked. He'd come for the computer and a change of clothes, since he'd be spending what was left of the night in the hotel.

He stepped inside to flick the wall switch. Clothes spilled from the dresser drawers and the covers had been pulled from the bed; the bed itself had become a repository for the maps he'd kept stored in the desk. They'd been tossed there haphazardly in various stages of being unfolded. The maps—and his computer—were the only investigative tools he kept in his possession. Innocent enough items: nothing incriminatory. A salesman, or even your average tourist, might possess them. All other data he stored in his head—he had trained himself over the years to be capable of that: one of the assets that made him especially well-suited for deep cover jobs like this. The Division knew that. There would have been no reason for them to search his room.

The same went for Dawson and the crew at Blue Lagoon. They'd had plenty of opportunities before now. If they truly considered him a threat, they would have gotten to him sooner.

The box of Bibles he kept beneath the desk had been turned over. The books lay scattered across the floor, some opened. On the desk itself his laptop had been turned on. A blinking window on the display asked for his password.

Because he abhorred disorder of any kind, he moved around the room returning things to their proper place. When he was satisfied he packed a small bag with what he needed.

In the bathroom he used a wash cloth to clean the cut on his temple. Through the wall he heard Johnny-O carrying on his harangue. "You didn't have to like it so damn much. You didn't have to come like it was the end of the world."

Then Aggie's voice closer, as close—it seemed—as when she held him. "Give it a rest, will ya. Just give it a rest."

At least he knew now why she had bothered with him. The ransacked room explained that. What it didn't explain was why Johnny-O had waited so long to interrupt them.

----*TWENTY-SEVEN*----

ROWAN LAY ON HIS BED fully dressed and stared at the ceiling. He could feel, still, the hard boards beneath him, the imprint of sawdust on his wet skin. Lust, he thought, set things in motion but what waited at the end of the road was something else: grief or boredom or regret. If you were lucky, maybe some peace as well. Right then he was feeling something akin to contentment, reminding him of his long ago feelings for Regina: the point of measure for all his subsequent loves.

There was an odd light in the waitress' eyes when they parted. Sadness, he thought, but more than that too: a certitude. Something had been decided. "Got to get back now," she'd said, rising from the floor of that unfinished bedroom. A thin grey light etched the horizon; a mist was rising from the river. The air smelled river-damp, ripe with the anticipation of morning. "Things to do today. Whole lotta things."

He liked the way she'd said it, kind of gutsy in her low-keyed way, with the suggestion that the day might be tough going but she was up to the challenge. No sniveling. In so many ways, she reminded him of Regina. Same attitude. Same determination to beat her hard-luck past. As she walked away, he'd said: "If I'm here tonight, I'll take you out to dinner." She turned to him standing in the road and the faintest glimmer of a smile broke her lips. "If *I'm* here, I just might accept."

But he knew he had to be moving on.

A greyness smeared the window: day emerging in silence and fog. Into that silence, footsteps came. He took his gun and stood by the door. He recognized Morrison's purposeful, light-footed gait and opened the door slowly, to make sure. Then he lowered the gun, opened the door wider and motioned the man toward him.

Inside the room Morrison, exhausted, sank into the wicker chair and stared ahead at nothing.

Rowan regarded him with an amused curiosity. "What happened to your head?"

"Jealous husband."

"Jeez, you're lucky that two-bit punk didn't skin you alive."

Morrison smiled grimly. "He's planning to. I just bought some time, that's all."

"You promise to sell him an exotic bird, or what?"

"How'd you know?"

"His girlfriend let on he was in the market."

"She comes in handy," Morrison said dryly. He leaned forward with his face in his hands and rubbed his eyes with his palms.

"So tell me, I'm curious. How was she?"

"Dangerous."

"Women like that always are."

"She caught me off-guard."

"They're into some kinky stuff, those two. My bet is he gets off being tortured when she comes onto other guys. Then he gets off again punishing her for it. What do you think?"

"It was a failure of judgment on my part," Morrison said and laughed at the phrase, at himself for having said it. He grew quiet, thinking about the day ahead. He would have to line up the only resources he had: the Admiral for one, and RoyBoy for another. He would have to get out to the island. Hope Crimmins was there. Or at least enough evidence to use against him.

And he would need more ammunition. A hell of a lot more ammunition.

Sunlight cut through the morning fog and the room grew brighter. Rowan was the one who broke the long silence. "So, how we gonna get out of this?" he said, standing at the edge of the bed.

Morrison was struck by the word *we*. It was an unfamiliar word in his vocabulary. It hung between them in the room's silence like a promise.

PART FOUR: SUNDAY

----*TWENTY-EIGHT*----

AT NIGHTFALL, MORRISON WAITED NEAR the boat landing on the canal.

A pinpoint of light appeared above the dark water—a steady light, growing larger, but it was not until he heard the faltering putter of the engine that he was certain the boat belonged to the Admiral. He made his way down the sandy beach as the skiff's prow emerged from the shadow of the sea wall, the Admiral hunkered low in the stern, working the outboard. His face emerged then, too, his eyes shining with a solemn intensity as he guided the boat into shallow water.

"You bring your friend?" Morrison asked, once he was aboard.

The Admiral patted the cabinet beneath his seat. "And tonight, a little something extra, in case."

When they reached the bay, the Admiral opened the engine full-throttle, ignoring the no wake zone signs. They had, at most, ten or so hours before the siege of the fishery began. Morrison had informed him that this island excursion was his own idea, unsanctioned by his superiors. He told him, too, it was high risk and highly problematic, but there was a chance—albeit a slim one—to bring in Alexander Crimmins, who among his many other enterprises was most likely involved in one of the largest wildlife smuggling operations Morrison had encountered in his years of service. Which was more than enough to win the Admiral's cooperation. As both a naturalist and a conservationist, he felt committed to the cause. And the promise of adventure, as always, brightened the sparkle in his eyes.

When Morrison explained that there'd be no official back-up, the man had stepped up as Morrison thought he would. *I'll* be the back-up, he'd said without hesitation. Morrison hoped it wouldn't come to that, but the man's enthusiasm was comforting.

"So you're with the F&W?" the Admiral had asked.

"Customs."

"Would it have hurt so much to let me know that ?"

"It's in my nature to be cautious." Overly so, he thought now, in light of the man's willingness to help him out in his time of need.

"I'll say." The Admiral was laughing. "Never met a fellah played it so close to the vest."

"I've always kept to myself. Almost always."

"Must be real lonely livin' that way."

Morrison said that yes, it was. He'd never admitted that to anyone before.

In the windless night the air felt warm and heavy, even on open water. They passed several fishing boats and an in-bound yacht and then they were alone on the wide expanse of the bay. Soon they were moving among the dark shapes of islands. The moon had not yet risen so that visibility was measured in shades of darkness: sky and water and the murkier blackness of the floating mangrove forests.

Finally Hells Island took shape against the night sky. The Admiral cut back the engine so that the low puttering was barely louder than the water slapping the hull. From this vantage point, across open water, house lights were visible high on the hill, illuminating a narrow patch of open ground near the summit.

"Moon was out, we'd be sitting ducks," the Admiral said.

Morrison nodded. Breaks like that he was counting on. He'd need a lot more.

As they drew closer, the island looked more like a fortress with its steep sides and its house lodged on the pinnacle. Finally they were in its shadow, drifting along the southeast edge below the wooded hillside, looking for a place to put ashore. They had decided earlier in the day that using the boat dock was too dangerous, would leave Morrison with no cover as he made his way up.

The Admiral nudged the prow into sea grass that grew along the rocky shore. Morrison was able to step onto the rocks and maintain his balance, despite the slippery footing.

"Sure like to come with," the Admiral said from the boat.

"I need you to be ready with the boat."

The Admiral handed him the backpack. Morrison had put

it together quickly that afternoon. Emergency supplies—for a variety of contingencies. Bullets. An extra hand gun. A Taser stun gun. Manacles. A digital recorder that he slid now into his shirt pocket.

"You getting cell service?"

The Admiral squinted at his phone's display. "Two bars. Oughta do it."

"On the way out I'm going to aim for the boat dock. Easier than having to negotiate this hill again."

"I'll be there."

Morrison slipped on his night goggles, adjusted the backpack and began to climb.

The rock outcropping rose thirty feet or more above the water-line. For most of the climb he was able to pick his way from ledge to ledge. At one point, close to the top, the lip of rock running upward to the next ledge narrowed to less than two inches, the angle a sharp 45 degrees. When he put his foot against it, the edge of the lip crumbled, sending dirt and small pieces of rock skittering below. He drew in his breath and tried again, leaning his weight against the face of the wall, forcing his shoe as deep into the lip as it would go and using his palm on the ledge above as a brace.

When he reached the top of the rocks, breathing heavily, he glanced down at the Admiral who, from the rear of the skiff, gave him the thumbs up sign.

The hill rose steeply from there, thickly treed and path-less. With the help of his goggles, he wove his way between low-hanging branches and densely-matted underbrush. He hadn't traveled far when he heard the frenetic and breathless barking of dogs giving chase. He fumbled in his pocket for the Taser. He'd brought it to take out any guards quickly and silently, but it would come in handy now, sooner than expected.

He climbed steadily, sweating in the heat, swatting at mosquitoes. The barking was closer, somewhere off to his left. Two dogs, he thought. Maybe three.

About halfway up he reached a small clearing and stopped at its edge. The barking grew fiercer, closer. There was a thrashing noise in the trees on the far side of the clearing. A small deer came bounding into the open. It shot past him in a blur of tawny fur and flashing legs, vanishing again into the tunnel of trees, crashing its terrorized way through the underbrush. He'd heard that deer and raccoons swam miles to get from island to island, a feat that for whatever reason—maybe because it illustrated the desperate lengths an animal would go to forage—both surprised and fascinated him.

The barking had reached an hysterical pitch, vicious and deafening and close. It sent a chill through him and his mouth went stone cold dry, because he knew that even though the deer might have been the original object of the chase, *he* was the prey now.

The first of the dogs, a snarling over-sized Shepherd, broke out of the trees. He dropped it before it reached the midpoint of the clearing. The second came from his right, a shadow's flicker first that became a lunging assault weapon of bared teeth and bone. He jerked backward and shot it in mid-leap, watched it recoil from the impact, its head snapping sideways as if to bite away what struck it. The body, having gone suddenly loose, became oddly unraveled and sprawled meekly on the dirt several feet from its cohort.

Morrison, breathing heavily, scanned the trees around him half-expecting the assault to continue but the hillside had settled into silence. Above him the dense forest stretched toward the summit; below, the water was a long way down and at this angle, given the curve of the hill, he couldn't see the Admiral or the skiff.

He began to climb again. Within a few minutes he could see, built into the hillside, the square of tarmac with room for two choppers. Only one sat there now. The Crimmins' taxi, possibly?

From the cover of the trees he stared across the tarmac. There appeared to be no sign of a guard. He waited several moments to be sure before crossing the tarmac in the shadow of the retaining wall. From there he went directly to the stone stairs that connected the launch pad to the terrace.

He was coming up the stairs when he heard footsteps above, a man's voice shouting, "Baron! Maggie!"

A profusion of ferns, cascading from flower boxes on the balustrade, fell in tresses halfway down the wall. Morrison hid in their shadows.

"Here, Baron! Here, Mag!" the voice called. The footsteps came along the patio and stopped directly above Morrison. The smell of tobacco smoke hung in the air. The caller whistled sharply, first in the direction of the lawn, then toward the launching pad, the side of the hill where the dogs had gone after the deer.

The man waited for a response, his breathing a rasping sound in the stillness. He took a deep breath and exhaled. An arc of fire spun out of the ferns and the glowing cigarette butt sparked brightly against the bottom step. His footsteps sounded sharply on the stone tiles as he walked back toward the house.

Morrison moved quickly. He reached the patio at the same time the man heard him and turned, facing the Taser. The astonished face colored suddenly. His mouth opened in a choked-off cough as he stepped toward Morrison and fell.

The patio extended some fifty feet towards the house and Morrison, crossing quickly, had reached the end of it when someone came barreling around the corner of the building and nearly collided with him. There was a moment of shocked recognition when he saw that the man standing before him, raising his gun at him, was the driver of the second white panel truck, the man who had fled last night on the pier.

He held the Taser at the man's neck and fired. The dark-skinned man crumpled in a loose heap onto the tiles.

Quickly Morrison handcuffed and gagged both men then flung their weapons into bushes at the patio's edge. He stood near the house and listened. Nothing but the steady, riffling sound of leaves, the salt air tinged with the sweetness of jasmine. From here the views were endless in all directions: the bay with its smattering of islands; the unbroken expanse of the Gulf; and, on the opposite side, the long coastline that reached toward Florida Bay and the Straits.

From the porch he looked directly down at his intended escape route: the wide lawn that sloped to the sea and the boat dock. As he edged along the wall, the planks creaked beneath him and he stopped abruptly. A foghorn sounded at sea. He held his breath, his heart pumping hard, until the stillness of the night settled around him once again. At the first of the windows he looked into a narrow pantry. A dimly lit kitchen lay beyond that, though all he could see of it was a round oak table.

At the second window he looked into a large room with sliding glass doors open to the sea. A man in shadow, his back to Morrison, sat at a table writing in the light of a lamp. A cell phone lay open within arm's reach of him.

The table, dark and highly polished, seemed more appropriate for an executive office building than a rustic Florida homestead. Clearly, it was the room's centerpiece. The few odd straight-backed chairs placed here and there in the corners seemed an afterthought.

Morrison watched the scene a while before leaving the porch to follow the wall of the house. The two bedroom windows were closed and dark, shades drawn. He listened for a moment then came back to the porch. The man had not changed position. Whatever he was writing, occupied him completely.

The cell phone rang and the man reached for it quickly, not bothering to look first at the display. "Yes," he said, "yes. . . .I'm here. Yes, on schedule." He set it on the table, then walked to the sliding glass doors to watch the sea through a pair of field glasses. He was a tall man in a short-sleeved dress shirt, his bearing stiffly military and vaguely familiar to Morrison who tried the handle of the porch door.

It wouldn't turn. He would have preferred coming in on the man from behind, but he had no choice now. He came around the house. Through the glass doors he saw, with an ugly jolt of recognition, that the man—back at the table now—was Pendleton. His superior's head jerked up in shock when Morrison stepped into the room, leveling his 9 mm. at him.

"Morrison, what the hell—?"

Morrison's eyes had already taken in the kitchen; he moved quickly toward the bedroom door, holding his gun on the Division chief. "Please, nothing rash, Major. It wouldn't be in your best interest." He pushed open the bedroom door. The room was dark, the twin beds empty.

"Morrison, what the *hell* are you doing?"

"I might ask you the same thing, sir."

"You work for me, remember? You answer to *me*."

Morrison laughed. Even with a gun in his face, the man couldn't comprehend the meaning of the word *humility*. He sat there, back straight as a board, his silver hair and thin, angular face the picture of arrogance. "Things have changed now, Major. Wouldn't you say?"

"What are you talking about? What are you doing here? Nothing's changed. You've got an operation on the mainland in less than nine hours."

Morrison set his backpack on the table and smiled. "You wouldn't hold it against a man if he didn't show up at his own execution, would you?"

"What in *hell* are you talking about?"

"You know what I'm talking about."

Pendleton stared at him with blank, implacable eyes the color of gunmetal. "You're way out of line here, Walter. You're jeopardizing a strategic operation—"

"And what are you doing nice and cozy in the house of an international flesh peddler?"

"I advise you, Morrison, to cease and desist immediately. You're in violation of your sworn duties. I can have you brought up on charges—"

"We're way beyond that now, I'm afraid." He reached into his bag for a set of handcuffs.

Pendleton stared back at him incredulous. "What is wrong with you?"

Morrison stood behind him and pressed the barrel of the pistol into his neck. Pendleton stiffened but refused to cringe. Even seated, he was an imposing figure. "Your hands, sir."

Pendleton put his arms behind him and Morrison cuffed his wrists before patting him down. He removed the derringer strapped to the man's ankle and slid it into his backpack.

"What is it you think you know, Walter?" he said in a softer, conciliatory voice. "What is it you think you're accomplishing here?"

"My job, sir. My sworn duties. To investigate and report on a Florida-based wildlife smuggling operation."

"And you think I'm part of that?"

Morrison pulled the ledger closer, squinted down at the most recent figures recorded in a meticulous hand. "September 15—150 *o*, 100 *hm*, 50 *sm*. . . . Morrison was familiar with the shorthand: ocelots, hyacinth macaws, spider monkeys.

September 28—24 *cap*, 35 *tap*, 20 *por*, 32 *ant*. . .capybaras, tapirs, porcupines, anteaters.

October 9—300 *tou*. . . .toucans.

October 27—550 *afp*, 20 *bpy*. . . .African parrots, Burmese Pythons.

"You think I'm part of that?" Pendleton repeated.

"The evidence would suggest so."

Next to each entry was a name in Spanish. *La Casita, La Flor Azul, La Casita*, again. Ship names? Was that what Pendleton was looking for with the field glasses? The carrier of tonight's shipment? Other notations filled the margins—the abbreviation P.O.O. (point of origin?) followed by what appeared to be the names of places: Buenaventura, El Valle, Jurado. There was an occasional surname with a phone number scratched next to it.

He looked down at the last entry in the book. "October 30— that's today, isn't it? 200 *py*?"

Pendleton scowled at him, his tone one of mild annoyance, as if scolding a wayward child. "I'm simply recording my estimations of what has passed through the Blue Lagoon since you began monitoring their operation. The entry for today is only a guess at what we might find in tonight's raid. You'll notice it's penciled in, with a question mark. Subject to revision."

"Pretty specific for a guess, wouldn't you say?" He scanned the ledger again. "*La Casita.* How would you know the name of tonight's carrier? Even I don't have that information."

"We've been monitoring all cargo ships passing through the Gulf. That one is a known carrier of contraband. And it's *in the Gulf* tonight. It was a simple deduction to make."

"Some of your entries pre-date my arrival in Mangrove Bay. Were those simple deductions to make, as well?" He closed the ledger, stuffed it into his backpack.

"That's government property." Pendleton's face reddened. He strained forward in the chair. "That constitutes a theft of government records."

Morrison moved around the room in search of anything he might use to bolster his case. In a kitchen drawer, he found a sheaf of invoices. He scanned them quickly, noticing a series of deliveries to Laroo's, to various game parks and pet stores across Florida, then stuffed the sheaf in his bag. He opened the kitchen cabinets, checked the dresser drawers in the bedroom, but found nothing else of use.

At the table, he reached for the lamp switch and plunged the room into darkness. He didn't want to be surprised by the helicopter pilot or whoever else might be on the grounds.

"What are you doing *now*?" Pendleton's voice came from the dark.

Morrison settled at the end of the table with a view of both the porch and the sliding glass doors. "We'll wait for the person you're expecting."

"And what creature of your imagination would that be?"

"Alexander Crimmins."

"You're out of your mind."

"Why? He owns this place, doesn't he?"

"You have no idea what you're doing."

"I know Crimmins owns this island. I know he was headed for South Florida this afternoon. I know you're alone here in the man's house. Those are facts. What you always insisted we had to have before drawing conclusions."

"Facts." Pendleton spit out the word. The darkness had lifted enough to reveal his shadowed face, contorted with outrage. "You still think the truth is something you can put your hands on, something with a beginning and an end. You wouldn't know what a fact is if somebody shoved one up your arse. You're being a fool, Morrison. You're a danger to yourself *and* to the Division."

Yes, he thought, he was a fool. Not to have seen he'd been deceived as well as manipulated. Not to have realized why his investigation was being shut down.

"You've been a loyal and steadfast agent these years," Pendleton was saying, conciliatory again, tempering his voice with reason. "Don't throw it all away over some crazy notion of yours. For God's sakes, man, don't throw away your future."

"I wasn't aware I had a future."

"Why would you even say that?" Pendleton asked, as if it was the most preposterous of assumptions. "You're letting your imagination run away with you."

He considered reeling off his litany of suspicions, but he knew the Major would dismiss each of them. He was a master of manipulation. Stories had come back about what he was like in the Gulf War. And he knew first-hand how reasonable the man could sound. He'd seen him in action as Agent in Charge of Special Operations for nearly five years. More than once he'd gone out of his way to admonish Morrison. You're reading into things, he liked to say, you're letting paranoia, an agent's worst enemy, get the best of you. The same thing he was saying now.

What Morrison finally said was, "Why did you have Emilio killed?"

Pendleton stared back at him, unblinking. "Dawson killed Emilio. For obvious reasons. He'd figured out he was feeding you information."

"And you had nothing to do with that?"

"Of course not." He watched Morrison with the same unblinking stare.

"Then why is your guard out there one of Dawson's cohorts? Is he F&W, too? *Or Customs?*"

Pendleton's face remained unchanged. He wore the mask of

implacability like skin. "Sometimes a man plays more than one role in this game. You should know that."

He's playing with your head, Morrison told himself. *He'll run you in circles, push you deep into the vortex. He'll beat you at this game, if you let him.*

"For argument's sake," Pendleton was saying, "if Crimmins *were* to show up here. What are you planning to do?"

"Take both of you to the Sheriff's office in Mangrove Bay for starters. Then I'll put through a call to Taylor McCormack at the *Herald.* I think he'll have some interest in this story."

"That left-wing pansy. He's done more to undermine our work at Customs than anyone I know."

"He doesn't see it that way."

"Journalists, they have no idea what we're up against with wildlife trafficking. You should know that. How difficult it is to build a case, how many years it takes—" His eyes brimmed with a venom even the shadows couldn't conceal. "The Blue Lagoon is one small blip in Crimmins' organization. That's why *I* had to get involved. As you can see, I've successfully worked my way in. He needed someone like me to run the U.S. sector. And this is how we're going to bring him down. From here, I'm building a case against the European and Asian sectors of his operation, as well."

He watched Morrison with a mixture of disdain and menace, as if gauging how much of this was sinking in. "That's why we're shutting down your investigation. Because in the big picture it doesn't matter. In the big picture you're jeopardizing our ultimate goal." His voice cracked and for a moment it seemed he might choke on his own bile. "And *you,* myopic fool that you are," he said, shoulders thrust so rigidly forward Morrison thought he might topple from the chair, "are gumming things up yet again."

But hadn't Krebs said Crimmins *wasn't* under investigation? Or had Krebs simply been misinformed? "Trying to do my job," Morrison stammered. "That's all."

"Your job is to follow orders."

Morrison hesitated. What if the man were telling the truth? What if once again the bulldog had seen only the bone, not what was beyond it? For surely his vision had been a flawed one. His loner mentality, though a main reason for his success as an undercover agent, had been a hindrance, too, limiting him in ways he was only now beginning to see. In depriving himself of close personal contact, hadn't he eliminated the tempering effects of human discourse, allowed his mind to run amok with its preoccupations? Or were they, more pointedly, *delusions*? Was the man sitting across from him, like Caruso, the voice of reason, and he—as he had been labeled—the myopic fool?

"Why did you allow me to begin my investigation if it was so insignificant?"

"It seemed harmless enough, your puttering around down here with these low-lifes. Running down your pathetic little leads, chasing shadows through the swamp. And we needed *some*one to do the grunt work, to add to the evidence to support our case."

To support *your* case, Morrison was thinking. The data I collected you could use as leverage, if Crimmins ever decided to turn on you.

Pendleton grinned malevolently. "And maybe I was hoping some gator would take a chunk of you, send you out on disability. Who knows?"

"Then why shut it down? Why not give the gator more time?"

"Because you've become a nuisance and an embarrassment. People are getting killed needlessly, a government agent among them. That's why."

"Or maybe I was getting too close. Maybe the trail I was following would have led to you."

"Don't flatter yourself. You were a long way from finding me."

Morrison gestured with his hands to indicate their present situation. "Not such a long way, I'd say." He was thinking that no matter what side Pendleton was really on, his arrangement with Crimmins was a perfect fit. Who better than Pendleton—a man who knew the wildlife laws inside and out, and hence how to get around them—to run the oil man's smuggling venture. And, of course, Pendleton came with a bonus: advance warning on any moves the law might make.

What was it Johnny-O had said was the local credo? It wasn't possible for a lawman to spend his whole life hunting poachers without realizing he's crazy not to switch sides.

And yet he himself hadn't switched sides. Wasn't it possible that Pendleton, *Major* Pendleton, who'd had a long and distinguished career in the military, had remained true to his commitment, as well?

In the jaundiced light from the patio he studied the man's face for cracks in the façade. The chiseled face, the cool bloodless grey eyes, the relaxed lips. No trace of anxiety.

Soon, though, the man's patience wore thin. "If you're waiting for Crimmins, you're wasting my time *and* yours. He never comes here. That's why he has me. He's much too smart to get anywhere near the hot stuff. Besides, he'd rather spend his weekends hunting."

"At Indian Point?"

Pendleton let slip an amused smile. "Another of your great discoveries. You nearly got yourself killed that night, you know. If the guard had his way—"

He seemed then at a loss for words. He glared hopelessly at Morrison. Finally he said, "This is about that boy, isn't it? You developed some kind of attachment to him, didn't you?" He drew his lips back in a sneer. "If you only knew. He was the worst kind of opportunist. The only reason he was cooperating with you was to get his citizenship. He wanted out of Guatemala at any cost. He would have whored himself for any country that would take him in."

"I don't think that's true," Morrison said softly. "He believed in America. The ideals it stands for—or once stood for."

"Hogwash—"

Pendleton rambled on about how Morrison was throwing away his career, his pension, everything he believed in for some misguided affection. But Morrison had stopped listening. Something had caught his eye on the patio. He stared through the glass doors at the tree tops on the hillside and beyond that the dark waters of the Gulf. Something moved again and this time a man with an assault rifle appeared in the doorway, calling out, "Major? Are you in here, sir?"

"I'm being kidnapped," Pendleton shouted. And the man— another of the guards, Morrison assumed, or perhaps the pilot of the chopper—stepped into the room and Morrison fired the Taser at him point blank.

"Good God Almighty!" Pendleton said behind him. He stood with his lips twisted in disgust, leaning over the table for a better look at the fallen guard. "Look what you've done."

Morrison knelt over the man and pulled away his rifle.

"You maniac—" Pendleton's rage was interrupted when his cell phone rang. The display glowed blue on the dark table top. "If I don't answer that, they'll know something's wrong. They'll be on this place like flies on dung."

Morrison leaned across the table to read the display: a *D.C.* area code. The insistent ringing cut into the silence like an alarm.

When the phone went silent, Pendleton said with a smug satisfaction, "Now, you've done yourself in. That was Headquarters."

"Play back the message."

"There won't be any."

Morrison shoved the 9 mm. at him. "Your mailbox code, Major."

Pendleton gave it to him and he punched it in. There was no message.

"It's enough that I didn't answer," Pendleton said. "They'll be reinforcements on their way within a matter of minutes. You can kiss your Boy Scout heroics goodbye."

Another bluff? Possibly.

But then there was a nearly equal chance that in this case Pendleton was telling the truth.

Either way, it was time—Morrison knew—to be on the move.

"If you leave now and fulfill your required duties tonight, we'll forget all about this," Pendleton was saying. "Chalk it up to an error in judgment. No hard feelings."

Afterward, Morrison would conclude his decision to take him prisoner was based as much on this as on any other factor: the cold bloodless look in the man's eyes when he had talked about Emilio—the lack of any concern or feeling whatsoever for the boy or his death.

He flicked the light on and took one quick look around the room for anything he might have overlooked. With his cell, he took some quick digital photos of the room, the felled guards inside and outside, and finally the man sitting at the table.

He swung his backpack over his shoulder and nudged Pendleton toward the door.

"You're a dead man, Walter. You sure in hell are one very dead man."

On the porch Morrison hesitated, his eyes scanning the sky as if he expected a fleet of military choppers to descend at any moment.

Below them the grassy hill fell away to the sea; the white caps' dull silvery creases sliced the black surface of the water.

Pendleton, his hands locked behind him, moved sluggishly despite Morrison's prodding, as they started down the hill in the direction of the boat

----*TWENTY-NINE*----

WITH ITS NOISY CARGO, ROWAN'S Caddy rocked and jounced over the rutted road that led to the highway. Around him marsh grass grew wild and thick, his battered car, this imperfect road, the only escape from miles of bottomland that stretched, without relief, into the night. He was late for his meeting with Johnny-O, who waited on a dead-end turnoff a mile to the east; but he couldn't make up any time, not on this road, the condition it was in.

From the beginning he'd been behind schedule. First, because Johnny-O was late showing him the cash. After dinner he'd waited in his room nearly forty minutes before the kid finally showed up with a sun-bleached leather suitcase. No apology— nothing but his dumb laconic smile and the lame offering that he'd gotten "tied up." Judging from the hickeys on his neck, it didn't take a genius to know Aggie had been the one who'd done the tying.

He'd opened the suitcase on the bed, let Rowan finger a stack of fifties then snatched it from him, dropped it into the case with the rest of the banded stacks, snapped the locks tight and muttered that he wanted to get on with things. Rowan figured there wasn't nearly the hundred grand that Johnny-O said there was, but there was more than enough to get out of the country with, and to live on a while.

Then he'd gotten lost searching for the stash of animals. Morrison had taken him out there in the afternoon, but it was another thing finding it in the dark. He'd found the highway turn-off all right but he'd taken a wrong turn on this dirt road, found himself dead-ended at a cypress slough deep in the swamp. Then, after working his way back to where he *should* have been, he had trouble locating the creek; and once he did, once he'd gotten to the still and the shed, it had taken him longer than planned to load the Caddy to capacity. He'd had to walk, a cage in each hand, down the long hill from the still to the Caddy. Eight trips, alone in the dark, stumbling his way along the ridged and cratered path. So that now the trunk and every available space inside the car, save where he was sitting, was piled high with crates and cages. Around him, birds and snakes and dog-sized rodent-like creatures made a racket: hissing, cooing, grunting, chuffing and whining.

Fortunately at least, Leach wasn't on guard this night. At first he'd thought that odd but the location was so remote, he figured, it would be unlikely for someone to stumble upon it by accident, especially at night. Hell, it was hard enough to find it when you knew it was there.

Through a break in the grass he saw the highway ahead. As he eased the car up the grade, he yelled at the menagerie around him to pipe down.

This time of night the highway was dark and empty as it cut eastward. He passed the blue and red neon sign outside BUBBA'S BLUE CRAB CAFÉ. That was how he'd identified the rendezvous point for Johnny-O: the turn-off at the broken down billboard exactly 1.2 miles east of Bubba's.

When he reached the billboard, he turned onto the dirt horse shoe that looped behind it. There, shielded from the road by what was left of the rotting board, Johnny-O sat on the hood of a Jeep with a U-Haul attached and watched him pull in.

Again Rowan cursed the way the evening had turned out.

He'd expected to be here well before his buyer; the last thing he wanted was to give him any ideas. If the kid had his eyes open, he could have seen the Caddy's headlights cutting through the tall grass, then the car itself turning onto the highway.

Before leaving the car he adjusted his over-sized shirt to conceal the pistol wedged beneath his belt. He glanced toward the billboard's shadows in case Aggie was hiding there.

When Rowan stepped away from the car Johnny-O said, "Thought you and the suit stood me up."

"Your turn to wait."

"How come *he* ain't here?"

"He's busy. I've got what you want."

Johnny-O pulled himself off the hood. "Lemme see."

"Let me see the money first."

Johnny-O gave him a toothy grin and swung open the Jeep's rear door. The faded leather suitcase rested on the seat.

"Open it."

He leaned in and unsnapped the latches, raising the lid enough to expose the banded packs of bills. His grin had a *See, so up yours* look to it that Rowan didn't like. "Out of curiosity, tell me how a punk-ass kid like you gets into the wildlife trade?"

"That's my business. But let's just say I got people interested in what I got to sell. *Rich* people." He snapped the latches in place. "Now lemme see what you got for me."

Rowan opened the Caddy's back door and the kid peered in. "That all?"

"There's more in the trunk."

The trunk held two suitcases of baby tortoises. Star tortoises, Morrison had called them. Rare and extremely valuable. The little buggers crawled over one another in a writhing orgy of slow motion.

Johnny-O rubbed his chin and stared, his brow furrowed as if he might be counting them. "Help me load this stuff into the U-Haul."

"Bring over the money first."

"Sure thing, boss." He turned away then swung around pointing the Walther at Rowan's head. "Load this stuff, man, I ain't foolin'."

Rowan groaned. He leaned his head against the hand that held the trunk's lid aloft. The kid patted him down and pulled the gun from his belt.

"Come on, Johnny, we had a deal."

Johnny-O cocked the hammer, the sound lost in the rush of a passing car, its lights flashing briefly through holes in the billboard. "*Load it!*"

When everything had been transferred, the trailer was only half-full. Johnny-O closed the doors and motioned Rowan to the driver's side of the Jeep. "Get in. Got me a feelin' you guys got plenty more where this came from."

"That's it, I swear. You have it all."

Johnny-O grinned back at him. "Got me a feelin'."

Rowan stared sullenly across the dark grass. He'd been lucky twice out there already; a third time would be pressing it. Who knew what manner of night crawlers would be skulking around as it got later, or what they might be moving under cover of darkness? "Oh, man, you don't understand, it's gonna be dangerous out there."

"I ain't feared of the dark," Johnny-O said.

RAYELLE had spent the day making herself beautiful. When she woke, first thing she did was have her coffee in the back yard, sunning herself to give her face some color. Then she'd driven to Homestead to have her hair and nails done and to treat herself to a make-over. On the way back she stopped at a drugstore to pick up a bottle of perfume she'd seen advertised.

When she'd come strutting into work at five, carrying her jewelry box in the bottom of a shopping bag, she'd turned a few heads in the lobby and even Mrs. Lowry gave her a begrudging nod of approval from behind the desk. *Damn right*, she'd thought. *I look good and I feel even better.*

DeeDee had said, "You must of worked things out with Bobbie, huh?"

"Oh, I worked things out, all right."

The truth was it had been two days since her discovery, since their fight in the street, and he still hadn't said one thing about it. She hadn't either, waiting for him to bring it up, waiting to see how long it would take. She'd found a grim satisfaction in thinking, *just like all the men she'd known.* The whole world could be falling around their feet and they'd look the other way, talk about that new left-handed reliever the Rays just acquired or the twelve pound snook they pulled out of their secret spot in the St. Thomas.

"I could tell," DeeDee said, "I could tell you were in a good mood the minute I saw you."

"You got that right, honey."

It was later when things slowed down that she pulled her jewelry box from beneath the bar. She'd come into work wearing her ankle bracelet but neither Mrs. Lowry nor DeeDee had noticed. Now, at the far end of the bar, she began putting on each of the arm bracelets Bobbie had given her.

DeeDee saw what she was doing and left the register to come to her. "You know Mrs. Lowry doesn't want us showing off our jewelry here."

"Don't want to send the wrong message, girls, now do we?" Rayelle said, mimicking Mrs. Lowry's deep, crusty voice. "The

River Hotel's a respected name in this town."

DeeDee couldn't help herself and joined in, doing her own throaty version of their boss' voice. "We earn our living *honestly* here."

"Not like *some* in South Florida." Which was Mrs. Lowry's reference to the area's rich history of smuggler types. Rum-runners, dope peddlers, arms dealers—and the latest variety, the Noah's Ark crowd.

DeeDee giggled. "I will not let my hotel's reputation be sabotaged by a bunch of low-life outlaw swamp rats."

"Hey, watch that, lady," Rayelle said in her own voice. "Them's our boyfriends you're talkin' about."

They both broke out laughing, DeeDee glancing down the bar to make sure no one heard. "Seriously, Ray, you shouldn't be wearing that stuff in here."

"Tonight I want to play by *my* rules."

"We got to keep up appearances. We got to look poor and honest."

"Appearances been killing me." She held up a gold necklace with its garlands of leaves and flowers and diamonds. "Men have guns, we have this." She turned it so the stones reflected the blue bar light. Her birthday present from Bobbie last month. "Makes a statement, doesn't it?"

"It *does*," DeeDee said breathlessly.

"Question is, *what* statement does it make?"

"A true love statement."

"I used to think so."

DeeDee frowned. She didn't understand. "I thought you and Bobbie made up."

"Feel this." Rayelle held out the necklace.

DeeDee lifted it like she was testing its weight then reached to set it back in the box, but Rayelle gently tugged it from her hand. She turned to the bar mirror and held the necklace across her neck to admire it.

"No, Ray, don't."

"My rules tonight, remember?"

DeeDee looked at her friend closely. "You and Bobbie did make up, didn't you?"

"We came to an arrangement." She held her head high, feeling the weight of the gold on her skin. "No words necessary."

"You're being weird tonight. You're scaring me."

"Times are changing, is all. I got to change with them."

"What are you telling me, Ray?"

"Writing's on the wall, honey. That wall right there. Got the history of this place spelled out for anyone to see." She nodded toward the end of the bar, the trophy wall. "We had gar, we had snook, we had catfish. We had bear and deer and wild pigs. We lived off the land, did whatever. Didn't have much but we got by. Folks driving around in old beat-up pick-ups, drinking beer and shots at the Shack. Guy takes you out, guaranteed he's gonna smell like the sea. Till something besides marine life started floating through the rivers and bays. Now all our boys are driving fancy cars, paying for their coffee with hundred dollar bills, and not too many of them smell like fish anymore."

"That's good, right?" DeeDee asked hopefully. "Everybody's living better. I mean, I *know* it's helping Lonnie and me. He's putting away the money he makes on the side for when we get married."

She shook her head sadly. "You don't get it, do you? You don't understand the law of expanding opportunity."

DeeDee stared blankly at the empty jewelry box, a bad feeling uncoiling in her stomach. "What don't I get?"

"Some poor kid's livin' in the swamp out there. Just one river nearby and that river don't have many fish, but it's all he's got so he throws his line in and a long time goes by before he even hooks one, and when he does it's all scrawny and small, most likely a bottom feeder but he's hungry and he's happy he's got *some*thing, so he takes it home and eats it."

"So you're saying you and me, we're some kind of scavenger fish?"

"I'm sayin' the guys around here got all of Miami to test their rods in now."

DeeDee shook her head no. "Lonnie's not like that."

"Why you think those Hollywood people keep getting married and divorced every other minute? Opportunity—too much of it. Opportunity's like a balloon. Expands till it pops."

"He's not like that. Not my Lonnie." Her eyes turned dreamy in a way that made Rayelle's heart stop with the knowledge of what she'd lost, or maybe never had.

"He's so tender with me," DeeDee was saying. "When we're alone, I mean. The two of us. The way he looks at me, the way he runs his finger 'cross my lips. Makes me feel I'm the only woman he sees."

"You've got a sweet way of looking at your world, Dee. A real sweet way."

Tears filled DeeDee's eyes and she looked at her friend the way she might look at a statue in church, a holy figure to pray to. "I hope I never lose that, the feeling I have for him. And right now I swear, no matter how tough things get, I'll hang onto whatever shred of love I can find. I'll stay with Lonnie till the end, 'cause I can't separate who I am from how I feel about him. If those bad feelings ever come I'll hold them to my heart like naughty children, till they stop their fussing and behave."

She blinked to clear her eyes and touched Rayelle's hand. "What do you think, Ray? You think I'm ever gonna lose that?"

ON the boat ride from Hells Island Pendleton rode in the prow with his hands cuffed behind him, eyes fixed ahead on the low, dark rim of the mainland. The wind, Morrison observed, barely disturbed his carefully oiled silver hair. On the surface he seemed his usual unflappable self. There was more than a hint of rage, though—an unyielding determination—in the rigid cast of his shoulders.

When they reached the outer limits of the bay, the steady drone of the engine at full throttle and the *rap-rap-rap* of the waves against the hull settled Morrison. Enough, at least, for him to consider the situation in more detail.

If he assumed for the moment that Pendleton was telling the truth, that he was merely the infiltrator that he claimed to be, then he, Morrison, was making an irreversible mistake. Certainly his career in government services would be over, and most likely at the very least he'd be facing serious jail-time. But then his career was going to end tonight anyway, wasn't it, if his calculations were correct? Either way he would be, as Pendleton had predicted, *one very dead man.*

If, on the other hand, the man *had* been corrupted then bringing him to justice would be the most significant accomplishment of Morrison's career.

You don't have a solid enough case yet for that, he reminded himself. The man is far too intelligent, far too *slippery*, to go down so easily.

But if he could bring the press into it, if he could get a spotlight turned on the man, then he would have accomplished *some*thing.

And who knew where that might lead?

That might be the best he could hope for. That might be what he would have to accept: the "real world" that he was always being accused of not understanding.

But if he were a smarter man, he chided himself, if he understood more of what was going on here, wouldn't he be more effective?

For instance, how was the F&W involved? Was the black man who was guarding the island house a double agent, as Pendleton hinted? Had Ned Turner been one, too? Or had they both simply, along with Pendleton, gone to the other side?

And who else in the F&W was involved? Who else in the Division? Was Caruso a part of it? Or simply another pawn, like himself? Did the corruption go even higher than Pendleton?

And what was in it for Pendleton besides the obvious, the money he was making?

Power?

Morrison speculated that could be the case. The desire for power was something the man had never been able to conceal. It was common knowledge that he had never gotten over his failure to make General, and that his aspirations had always been set higher than regional Division commander. If he couldn't be a top dog in the government, then he'd be one in the criminal world? Could he be that egomaniacal? The thought that a man whose job it was to protect earth's creatures would be willing to forsake that to satisfy his need for control, revolted Morrison and he had to quell the impulse to push the man overboard right then and there, let him founder hand-cuffed and helpless in the murky water of the bay.

You're being naïve again, he could hear both Pendleton and Caruso chiding him. You don't understand how the system, how human impulse, works. Men have been raping the earth for their own needs since time immemorial.

Thank God he didn't understand, Morrison offered in his own defense. Thank God he hadn't yet become numb. Because once we lose our capacity for outrage at injustice we're doomed, aren't we, as people, as a nation?

His mind reeled with questions, possibilities. He would have put a gun to the back of Pendleton's head and demanded answers but the man's rigid bearing at the prow, the intractable set of his jaw signaled that he wouldn't give up a thing right now, not a damn thing, not even if he had to die for it.

When they reached the still waters of the canal, the Admiral cut back the engine. Morrison sat beside him and explained as much as he knew. When he finished, Pendleton twisted his body and sneered at him. "The man's delusional," he said to the Admiral. "Conjecture, supposition, paranoid fantasies. That's what he's feeding you. He has no idea of the scope of the Division's activities in this situation. No idea, whatsoever."

The Admiral tugged at his beard, directed his wide-eyed stare at the man half-turned in the front of the boat. "Why don't you explain it to us, then?"

"That's classified information. I can't divulge any more than I already have." His eyes glared with the indignity of the request. The chiseled lines of his face had tightened; it seemed, at any moment, the face itself might crack from the rage it held. "And you, sir, you're aiding and abetting in the kidnapping of a federal officer, can't you see that? You're in violation of both your security clearance and your oath as a government sub-contractor."

The Admiral guided the skiff toward the boat landing, not looking at either of his passengers. From the fixed set of his face Morrison knew the man was weighing his options, and for the first time it occurred to him that he really couldn't be sure whose story he would believe. If he had only confided in him on those nights of surveillance in the swamp, if he had only made him feel more a part of the operation, explained more of the intricacies. . . .

It wasn't until the skiff touched land that the Admiral finally spoke, directing his question to Morrison. "You planning on bringing him over to Sheriff Olsen?"

Morrison sighed with relief. Considering everything else he had to deal with, he didn't want the Admiral against him, too. "That was the plan. But the man I expected we'd be bringing back was Alexander Crimmins, not a guest in his house."

"Plan B then, huh?"

Morrison walked up the sandy incline looking for Rowan's car. He checked his watch. The man was supposed to have been here with Johnny-O's cash by now.

He came back down to the water and pulled Pendleton from the boat. On the embankment he cuffed the man's right hand to the metal loop of a mooring post. He would be able to sit or lie there but wouldn't be able to stand.

Then he called Taylor McCormack's number and had him

paged.

"What's up?" the Admiral asked from the water-line, red-faced and heaving from the exertion of having pulled the skiff onto dry land.

Morrison stood on the road, deciding. "I'm worried the Sheriff won't have enough to hold him. Anyway, I can't take the chance. I put a call through to McCormack at the *Herald*. If he gets on this story, if it gets into the papers, well, at least something might come of it."

"I've been reading his column on the environment for twenty years." The Admiral's eyes glowed, the red in his face now from giddiness. "Finally I'm gonna get a chance to meet him."

Morrison glanced again at his watch. "I've got to check on a friend. Will you stay in case McCormack gets here before I come back?"

"Damn right, I'll stay." He reached down into the cabinet beneath his seat and pulled out his 30.06, smiling like a kid about to play a war game.

"I don't think he's going anywhere," Morrison said.

The Admiral held the rifle up, one-handed. "This'll make sure he don't."

Morrison was driving toward the highway when McCormack returned his call. He filled him in briefly on what he thought he had.

"I'll be there soon as I can," the reporter said.

---- *THIRTY*----

ROWAN WORKED HIS WAY UPHILL towards the still, Johnny-O breathing
heavily behind him. Their shoes scraped against the crisp, dried
leaves underfoot.

Soon as they had begun their climb, the kid started in with
the breathing. Way too out of shape for someone his age and for a
while there Rowan considered making a run for it. Too chance-y, he
decided, even with the darkness, even with his captor's respiratory
difficulties. It would take him at least two or three seconds to get
lost in the trees, enough for the kid to catch his breath and aim.
Better to bide his time, wait for an opportunity later on. The kid
wouldn't know how to find his way out of here on his own. So
Rowan figured he would more than likely be safe until they got
back to the highway. *More than likely*. Those were the best odds
he could give himself.

He walked as quickly as the wooded terrain would allow. At
one point Johnny-O stopped behind him, his breath rasping in the
thick air. "Slow it down, will ya?"

Rowan ignored him. "You want to get there or not? I told you,
it's not safe out here."

"Wait for me," the voice behind him pleaded, high-pitched,
almost a squeal.

"Hurry up, then."

"I should blow your head off."

"You won't, though." Rowan kept moving. Behind him came
the clatter of rasping leaves and short, gasping breaths as the man
hurried to catch up.

When they reached the still, Johnny-O stared in disbelief.
"Well, I'll . . . beat me, fuck me, call me Ruth. You suckers are

into moonshine, too."

Inside the shed Rowan showed him the remaining crates and cages.

"Turn on the light," Johnny-O said.

"What do you think? This is the Ritz-Carlton?"

"Light a match."

"Don't have."

"How'd you see in here before?"

"Flashlight. Left it in the Caddy." Actually, he'd thought about it before they left but he sure as hell wasn't going to make things easier for the hillbilly.

Johnny-O's breathing had settled down. He dug in his jeans pocket, came up with a pack of matches and shoved it at him. "Light one."

Rowan held the match in the dark building but the cages remained in shadow.

"Move closer so's I can see."

He stepped toward the cages and lit a second match. Johnny-O stared at the faces staring back at him. Rowan had no idea whether he knew the worth of what he was looking at, or even what in hell kind of animal some of them were. Except for the monkeys, Rowan surely didn't know. The smell alone kept him leaning away from the caged critters.

Rowan had lit four matches before Johnny-O said: "Take one of them monkeys and that there ugly thing." He pointed to a tailless, rodent-like creature with web feet. It was so ugly, in fact, that Rowan had deliberately decided *against* taking it earlier when he was loading the Caddy.

"*You* take it. That thing scares hell outta me."

Johnny-O's arm shot up. He pressed the Walther to the back of Rowan's head. "Take the damn thing."

Gingerly, Rowan reached for the cage and held the tail-less monster as far from his body as possible. The monkey, on the other hand, seemed a hell of a lot friendlier-looking.

"I'll take this here red monkey and that there baby lizard," the kid was saying. He managed to hold the monkey cage in one hand, and both the gun and the lizard cage in the other.

"Fine, then. Let's get out of here."

"Not so fast."

In the silence he could hear the kid's brain working: *How can we take more of these things?* But even greedy punks think clearly *some* of the time. There was no way they could carry more. Maybe, Rowan thought, he was planning to come back another time on his own.

They were standing in front of the shed, ready to strike out through the woods again when something screeched behind them: a piercing human sound, so close, so loud that Johnny-O cried out, dropped the lizard cage and fired blindly into the darkness. There was a wild flapping sound, wings beating air, then silence.

"What in hell was that?" the kid said.

"How should I know?"

"Birds. Some crazy-ass birds." He sounded as if nature had a personal vendetta against him.

"Let's go," Rowan said.

They had gotten as far as the still itself when a second scream broke the silence: this one louder, more agonized, a sound neither animal nor human. Rowan turned to see a shadowy form lunging at the kid who had dropped *both* cages this time and was stumbling backward, swinging his gun hand to fight off whatever it was.

Rowan dropped his cages and took off running down the hill. Behind him he heard a thrashing sound, the kid crying out, the awful primal screaming of whatever sub-human beast had materialized out of the night; and then he knew what it was, from what Morrison had told him. *That crazy man, Leach.*

A shot rang out. Then two more in quick succession.

He battered at tree limbs and vines, whatever came at him, hearing nothing now but his own rasping breath and the splashing sound his feet made in the leaves, until he stumbled at last into the clearing where the Jeep was parked. The momentum kept him going and he fell against the hood, splaying his arms across the metal to brace himself.

He heard thrashing sounds coming down the hill, and he thought *the keys, the keys, if only the kid hadn't taken back the keys* and then the kid was there, staggering out from the trees, clothes torn and muddy, blood streaming from his eye, from a gash across his chest where his shirt had been ripped open. With a bloodied hand he waved Little Walt vaguely in Rowan's direction. In the other he held the cage with the lizard, at arm's length.

He wiped his bloodied hand across his face to remove what was leaking from his eye. "Who. . .what—?" he said between breaths. "Who *was* that?"

"The keeper of the treasure."

"Why didn't you tell me?" He sounded disappointed that Rowan had let him down.

"You weren't listening."

"I—I coulda been killed."

"I warned you."

"And that damn monkey got loose. Swiped me with its nails. Tore your gun right outta my hands."

Rowan thought the kid might break down and cry right there. But he waved the Walther in the air. "Get in the car. You're gonna drive me back." The way his body wobbled on the uneven ground it seemed he might plunge forward at any second but he managed to keep himself upright.

Rowan held out his hand. "The keys."

In the Jeep, Johnny-O set the lizard cage on the rear seat then huddled against the door, cradling himself. With every bounce and lurch of the car he groaned, kept telling Rowan to slow it the hell down.

When the highway was visible, Rowan thought about bailing ship but the kid seemed to sense something and straightened up. He waved his gun hand to the right, as if Rowan didn't know the way.

When they pulled in behind the billboard there was a yellow Mustang convertible sitting there, top down, Aggie behind the wheel. She got out as soon as they drew near, came toward the passenger side in stiletto heels, a tight tank top, an even tighter skirt. "Where the hell you been?" she said to Johnny-O. She saw Rowan staring at her and tugged down her skirt which had risen dangerously high from sitting in the car. She turned again to her boyfriend. "Thought you ditched me."

"I wouldn't do that," he mumbled weakly. Then he turned and she got a full look at his bloody eye, the condition he was in.

"What in—?"

"We ran into a little trouble."

She glared at him, white-eyed and furious. "What kind of trouble?"

"The bad kind," he said with a feeble laugh.

"You had a simple job to do. You get the man's goods, you clear the hell out. What's so hard about that?"

"There's *more*," he said. "A hell of a lot more stashed away out there." He nodded toward the swamp then looked to Rowan for help. "Tell her."

"Sure, man, what do you want me to say?" He was calculating the distance to the bushes along the road. Through the billboard's gutted spaces he watched car lights race by, then a slower set of lights as if the driver might be lost and looking for directions.

"We don't have time for this, Johnny," Aggie was saying. "How long you think it's gonna take for them cops in Mobile to figure out where we are?" She yanked open the passenger door. "Now get on out here."

Using the door for support he lowered himself to the ground and stood in front of her unsteadily. "You're pitiful," she said, looking him up and down. "Give me the gun."

He handed it to her meekly and sat down in the dirt, too weak to keep himself upright. Side-stepping him, she held the tiny Walther on Rowan. "You, Slick Nick, I want you out too."

He climbed down slowly, thinking: women like her, they'd always been his downfall, so why not now too?

"I want you to take a little walk with me out in those bushes there."

He smirked at her. "That mean I won't be getting the money I was promised?"

"I'm no murderer," she said. "Just want to see you walking the other way, putting some distance between us. Then I'm gonna blow out your tires and we're gone."

"The money. We had a deal."

She gave him a tight-lipped, amused smile. "There's the deal you make with your mouth, and the deal that's in your head. The one in your head's the one that counts."

"I was depending on that money. You might say it's a matter of life and death."

"Think of it as another bet you lost. Like that one in New York you were telling me about." She cocked her hip and leveled the gun at him. "Start walking," she said.

With his hands raised, he stepped into the tall grass. "How far?"

"Till I tell you to stop."

He turned then to gauge the intent in her eyes. She stood stone-faced with her feet apart, gun hand pointed directly at him. Behind her the shadows shifted along the base of the billboard. A figure materialized against the rotting wood frame.

"Keep moving," she said.

Then Morrison was behind her, his arm around her neck, his

hand twisting hers to dislodge the gun. She cried out and kicked at him with her stiletto heel, bit into his arm, but he held her tight until she whimpered and went limp in his arms.

"Bastard," she said. "All I want is my little piece of the dream."

MORRISON moved quickly. He handcuffed her to the Jeep's door handle, did the same with Johnny-O on the other side, using the last of the manacles in his bag. "You can't just leave us here," the kid whined.

"The Sheriff or one of his men will be by before long. They'll be interested in taking a look at your papers, I imagine, for what you've got in the U-Haul."

Rowan pulled the suitcase out of the jeep and walked toward the Caddy. "Come on, man, we've got our ticket out of here."

"You go."

Rowan stopped mid-stride, turned back to him. "You're not coming?"

"Unfinished business."

"It's getting on, man." He checked his watch:10:20.

"Wait for me long as you can."

"Let's get out of here now."

"Can't yet."

"You sure?"

Morrison nodded yes. Some choices were made a long time back before you even knew you were making them. He had to finish things with Pendleton. And Crimmins, too.

Rowan set the suitcase on the ground. "Here, take some money at least, in case."

"Keep it. If I get stuck here, it won't do me much good anyway."

A playful smile lit up Rowan's face. "What if I get greedy? What makes you think I won't leave you flat?"

"Guess I'll have to trust you." The words felt odd on his tongue. But there was something he'd come to like about the man, despite his rough edges.

"Didn't think you were the trusting type."

"Doesn't come easy, but I'm learning."

Rowan opened the Caddy's door, lifted the suitcase onto the front seat. " 'Least let me drive you to your car."

"It's right there. Past the billboard."

Leaning against the door, Rowan ran his hand through his hair and shook his head in disbelief. "Johnny-on-the-Spot, that's you."

"Do me a favor, will you? Find me a name with a better association."

Rowan smiled. "Gotcha." After a moment he nodded, acknowledging something. "Guess we're even now."

"Only if she was going to do you in."

"You think she would have?"

Morrison looked across the dirt yard at the woman chained to the Jeep. She stood in her heels, hip thrust out, skirt hiked to allow a near hundred percent view of her long sleek legs, her free hand fluffing out her hair, getting ready for whoever was coming to bring her in.

When he cuffed her to the door handle she'd leaned close to him, whispered in his ear: "You'll never have anything this good again." He could still feel her warm breath burning his neck.

"If I was a gambling man," he said, "I'd say your odds were 50-50."

---- *THIRTY-ONE*----

THE ROAD TO THE BOAT launch was free of cars which meant McCormack hadn't yet arrived. The Ford's head lights swept across the sandy beach, the Admiral's skiff, and then the Admiral himself, bleeding in the dirt near the canal wall.

Pendleton was gone.

He knelt beside the old man who groaned and opened his eyes. Across his waist, and along one arm, blood seeped through his shirt.

"The son of a bitch got loose," the Admiral said in a thick voice. "Thought he was having a heart attack. Said he couldn't breathe. Said he had pills in his pocket he couldn't reach. I *thought* maybe he was faking it. So I was extra-careful, ya know, holdin' the gun on him, keepin' my eye on him. But he got me anyway. 'Fore I know it, he tears a gash in my arm with a damn shell and he's pulling the rifle out of my hands. The bastard shot me, but I got him with the .38." He raised his hand to show Morrison he still had the small gun. "Crawled off into those bushes there."

Morrison looked toward the area of thick grass and stunted trees that grew along the marsh edge. The man was nowhere in sight. But he did see the rifle lying on the ground several feet in front of the grass. At the base of the mooring post, beside the blown-apart manacles, lay the bloodied, ragged shard of an oyster shell.

This proved the man was guilty, didn't it? Otherwise, why would he have anything to fear from a country sheriff's questions, or a reporter's?

He called 9-1-1for an ambulance. "Hang on, old man. All right?"

192

"You bet your ass I'm gonna hang on." The Admiral's voice, hoarse and garbled, trailed off momentarily before he continued. "Wouldn't let an arrogant prick like that beat me."

In the faint light from the boat launch lamp, Morrison was able to pick out spots of blood in the dirt. Wading into the tall grass he could see where it had been flattened in places, where the blades had been stained dark. He reached into his pocket and again flicked on the recorder.

He found Pendleton at the edge of the marsh, curled against the base of a tree beaten bare by sun and wind, its dry and disfigured limbs reaching out.

His silver hair had been streaked with mud and fell in thin, untidy strands across his forehead. Blood leaked from his mouth, darkened the expensive white cloth of his dress shirt. Morrison held his gun on him, though it was clear from the man's position, from the limp heap of him, that he was too weak to be a threat.

His eyes watched Morrison with contempt. "Pull the trigger, Walter. Eliminate the enemy. Be the hero you always dreamed of." He coughed, choking on the blood in his mouth; then Morrison realized it wasn't a cough at all: the man was laughing at him.

"You wouldn't do that, though, would you? That would offend your moral conscience, your sense of justice and the law. You're the good cop. You think you're saving the world. But you have no idea anymore what the world is. Because in *this* world, the one we live in *now*, there's no room for heroes. There's no such thing as moral choice, no right and wrong. That's all been replaced, Walter, and what's replaced it is *necessity*. You either yield to it or you get chewed up and destroyed by it, like what's going to happen to you."

His body shifted in the dirt. His legs twitched, as if the desire for motion hadn't left him even though the power to do so had. "The whistleblower, right? The human alarm bell. But nobody loves a rat. Not even a good rat. It violates the American spirit, our sense of freedom and fair play. Whistleblowers end up isolated and alone, running out the clock somewhere in fear of retribution." He began choking or laughing again, Morrison couldn't tell which. His legs kicked involuntarily at the dirt. "And you know what's funny, you know the funniest thing of all, it's how little you really know."

"I know enough to know you're dirty. Otherwise you wouldn't be lying like this, half-dead in the dirt. I know that much."

"There you go again. That right and wrong bullshit. No matter what you think you know, I'm trying to explain how you're going to be *perceived*. As a clumsy, bungling fool who disrupted a strategic Division initiative. You'll die as you've lived: alone."

"Not if I bring down Crimmins."

Pendleton choked out another laugh. "And how do you propose to do that?"

"I'll find a way."

"With his security force, you won't get within a hundred yards of him." His eyes had turned venomous. Spittle formed on his lips. "But I hope you try. I sure as hell hope you try."

"To what extent is the F&W involved in this?"

Pendleton stared at him smugly. "Why should I answer that?"

"Who else in the Division?"

"One more thing you'll never know." He was speaking more slowly now, his breath coming harder, his words forming with greater effort.

"And Dawson?"

"Dawson worked for me, of course." There was a clear note of triumph in his voice.

"You authorized him to kill Emilio, didn't you? And tonight *he'll* be one of the casualties of the raid." He tried to find some flicker of admission in the man's stony face. "You knew he was stealing from you?"

"Of course I knew." The note of triumph had gone from his voice. What Morrison heard now was fatigue, maybe even indifference. "Go tell that to the world, Walter. You and McCormack. See who believes you." He leered at Morrison. "Necessity, Walter. It's *every*where."

Morrison paced in the open space along the marsh edge, trying to answer the questions still hanging in the air.

"Out of curiosity, Major, when was the decision made to terminate me?"

"In my mind, you've been digging your own grave since—"

"Since— *when*?"

But the Major had no more to say. Blood trickled from his mouth. From deep in his throat came a sound like gargling. His head jerked sideways and he lay still.

Morrison knelt beside him and grabbed him by the shoulders to shake him. "Who else was involved? How high up did this go?" Pendleton's eyes stared back at him, lifeless as glass.

The sound of car tires on gravel behind him, and the sudden sweep of lights across the marsh grass, told him McCormack had finally arrived.

MORRISON reached the Hunt Club before midnight. He had told his story to McCormack, given him the ledger, invoices and tape then waited for the EMS to arrive before he headed north on the fifteen mile jaunt to this forest at the edge of the Glades. The odds were long that anything good would come from this. Put yourself in danger enough times and sooner or later you come out on the losing end. He had no illusions about that. He was pushing his luck, and for a moment back there at the boat launch he'd considered letting it go, leaving it in McCormack's hands. But he owed it to Emilio, if not himself, to finish this.

One way or the other.

He cruised the dark road past the locked gate, following the high tensile electric fence nearly a mile until it turned away from the road and ran back into the woods. In the Ford's trunk he kept a small supply cabinet and he removed from it now a pair of long-handled wire cutters. On his person he still had with him his night goggles, Taser, a small high-intensity flashlight and, of course, his 9 millimeter. Before leaving the car, he doused himself with repellent.

He walked a short distance into the trees and knelt next to the fence, a more or less standard version of the permanent high tensile type: high tension wires strung between wood posts. These posts stood close to six feet in height, high enough—Morrison figured—to contain whatever big game roamed within. Only certain of the wires, not all, were electrified. The giveaway was the black insulator that surrounded the wire where it passed through the post. No insulator, no electricity. He clipped the non-electrified wires and, moving slowly and delicately, was able to slip through without being jolted. He left the clippers there and moved through the trees in the direction of the gate.

The forest, though thick with yellow and loblolly pine, was easy enough to move through with the help of his goggles. The relatively cool night, the light breeze, the time of the year, helped keep the mosquitoes to a minimum. A sweetness filled the air, a dreamy stillness that under other circumstances would have brought him comfort.

Walking quickly and as quietly as possible given the conditions, he worked up a sweat. Fear drove his temperature even higher. He held the Taser ready in case the shadows that shifted around him suddenly leapt in his direction. What type of game animals had been brought here, other than cats, he could only guess at; but knowing Crimmins' penchant for adventure he could safely assume there were any number of aggressive nocturnal stalkers on the loose.

Through a break in the trees, he spotted the white sand of the road, a short distance from where he calculated the main gate should be. If he stared hard enough in that direction he thought he glimpsed the faint glint of the gate's metal rails. For several minutes he stayed in the safety of the trees and listened.

Scuffling sounds in the underbrush.

The soft soughing sound of wind in the pines.

The cry of a night heron somewhere off to his right.

He thought it safe enough to leave the sanctuary of shadow, follow the road to whatever waited at its end. Silently, he slipped through an opening in the trees and stepped onto the sandy roadbed. Instantly the night turned bright as day around him and he was staring into the blazing headlights of the security van.

The engine growled into life, headlights moving toward him, a man with an assault rifle leaning from the passenger side door, shouting: "One move, I keel you."

----THIRTY-TWO----

WHAT WAITED AT THE END of the road was a log cabin-style lodge with a wide deck on the second-level, accessible by a stairway at either end. A guard with an assault rifle stood at each of the stairways, and a hundred feet or more beyond the lodge stood a second and smaller barracks-style building. A cleared, open area surrounded by a tall, chain-link fence extended from the buildings outward until it met the tree-line some two or three hundred feet distant.

The driver of the van and his rifle-bearing cohort, both dressed in paramilitary gear complete with camouflage uniforms and boots, pulled Morrison from the back of the van and shoved him toward the nearest stairway. The guard there, dressed in civilian clothes, spat at him as he was being led upstairs. The two guards who had found him escorted him to the center of the deck where Crimmins, whiskey glass in hand, sprawled on a lounge chair. On the table beside him, next to a bottle of imported Scotch, the remains of a cigar had been mashed into an ashtray. The smell of smoke still hung in the air, erasing the sweet fragrance the forest offered.

"Well, well, if it isn't Mr. Morrison, " Crimmins said. "I was wondering how I'd entertain myself tonight. My guests won't be arriving until tomorrow, but now I have you."

He had put on considerable weight—he was easily two hundred seventy-five pounds, Morrison estimated—no longer the trim, dapper adventurer pictured in the Sunday supplements. He wore an open-necked khaki shirt that revealed the thick hair of his substantial chest. His matching shorts encircled thighs the size of tree trunks and his feet, two wedge-like chunks of flesh with over-sized toes, hung over the edge of the chair. With the accumulation of weight, his dark eyes had receded into the meaty excesses of his face. The commanding arrogance of their I'll-take-on-the-world look had been replaced by something more menacing, the languid and indifferent look of the truly decadent.

"I found these on him," the driver of the van said, setting a small vinyl bag containing Morrison's recorder, gun and other accessories on the table.

Crimmins barely acknowledged them. "No wire?"

"No wire."

Crimmins motioned with his finger pointing to the ground.

"*Arrodillarse*," one of the guards instructed Morrison. "Kneel."

When Morrison did so, Crimmins nodded approvingly. His added weight had a curious effect on his pock-marked face. It gave his skin a distended, oatmeal-like texture. "Always gives me pleasure to see one of you game wardens on your knees."

"I'm not a game warden."

"Sure you are, Gamey."

Instantly, the mockery in the big man's eyes lost any trace of playfulness. "I *know* who you are." Then his eyes grew languid again as he thought something over. "At ease, boys," he said to the guards who stepped back away from Morrison and sauntered to the deck's far end where they leaned against the railing and looked on with empty, dispassionate faces.

To Morrison he said in a lowered voice, "Actually I'm glad to finally get a look at you. I've heard so much about you from your superior. He thought you quite the nuisance." He smiled briefly at the recollection. "But I think he missed the point, don't you? With your focus on the Blue Lagoon, you might have taken care of a few of our problems. Like Dawson, for one. I don't take kindly to a man stealing from me, even if the amount is negligible. You see, I believe in justice and sooner or later you would have gotten around to taking out the man. Like you did with Turner. And as far as the rest of those swamp rats in Dawson's crew—all of them put together don't have the brains of a cow. I'll be happy to see the whole place go up in smoke. Tonight's not soon enough for me." He sipped at his drink and eyed Morrison over the rim of the glass. "By the way, was the good Major the one told you I was here?"

"No. He was your loyal servant."

"Good, good. I'm sure glad to hear that. 'Cause he hasn't been answering my calls tonight. Thought maybe he had something to hide. But let's get back to you. 'Cause I'm real curious about a guy like you, how a guy like you thinks. That's why you're still alive right now, kneeling here on my deck. Otherwise you would have been shot out there in the woods. For trespassing. Signs all up and down the road. Or maybe you would have been killed because you were mistaken for—for whatever. This is a hunt club, after all. Some of our members hunt at night, gives 'em that extra jolt. Easy to see how an accident could happen."

He leaned over to pour himself more scotch. "So tell me. You thought you could just walk in here with impunity. You thought you could walk in here and do—*what*? You gonna mount a one-man case against me? You got a search warrant? You want to look at my stock? 'Cause I've got papers for every imported animal out there."

"I'm sure you do."

"You calling me a liar?"

"Papers can be bought and sold like anything else, as you well know. Most of the time they prove nothing."

"They exonerate me in the eyes of the law."

"Yes, in the eyes of the law."

"But clearly not in yours."

"I'm just a man doing his job."

"But if you know I have papers, if you know you've got no case against me, that the Customs Service has yet to build a case against me, then *what*?" He hauled his massive frame up in the chair, leaned menacingly toward Morrison. "You were going to take me down, *assassinate* me? That why you're here?"

That thought had certainly occurred to Morrison—do what the law couldn't, or wouldn't: remove him from the picture—and it was even more tempting now that he had met the man, experienced first-hand his brand of callous smugness, his assumption that right was on his side. But an act of assassination wasn't in his nature. He had come for less tangible reasons. He wanted to confront the man who, ultimately, was responsible for Emilio's death. And tucked away in the recesses of his capacity for hope was the possibility that maybe, just maybe, he'd find something to incriminate him that he could pass on to Taylor McCormack. "Let's just say I'm here as a matter of conscience."

Crimmins slapped his leg, a sharp cracking sound, and howled. "A matter of conscience. I like that. But let's get more precise.

Whose conscience? Not mine, cause my conscience is at peace. Way I see it, I've done nothing wrong. I'm just a member of a hunt club, enjoying my weekends best I know how. No government's got a right to take that away from me, the way I see it. So it's got to be *your* conscience with the problem, wouldn't you say? It's got to be *your* problem."

It was the self-assurance with which the man said it that most disturbed Morrison. Not the law, certainly not an insignificant "game warden," not even personal conscience, would stand in the way of his will. Sprawled there in his lounge chair, with the world at his feet, he was a man who took his power for granted. He knew the government had not yet built a case against him, would most likely not devote the time or resources it would take to build such a case. And even if they did, if they were able to connect him to the vast smuggling enterprise his underlings ran, what would his punishment be? A fine? A six-month jail term? A slap on the wrist, at best. Nothing he couldn't handle.

And there again was the languid and indifferent look in his eyes. He had lived to excess. He had gorged himself with the best life had to offer. Consequences no longer mattered to him. He simply didn't care.

"Yes," Morrison said, shifting his weight to ease the hard pressure of the boards on his knees. "It's my problem. The same problem I always have when I see people breaking the laws heedlessly for their own pleasure. Especially when it involves endangered species."

Crimmins leaned forward in the chair, the better to glare at Morrison. "You self-righteous prigs still manage to astonish me, you know that? Everything's black or white to you. You're a throwback from some other time. A vestigial organ that's lost its use. It's a grey world out there now. Real grey. That's the morality of the twenty-first century. *Greyness.*"

Morrison wasn't sure whose ethical system he disliked more: Pendleton's worship of necessity, or this man's elimination of the line between right and wrong. With what artful convenience, he thought, we find a way to justify our behavior.

Crimmins started to push himself up. "Come here. I want to show you something."

The guards rushed forward to help him but he waved them away. Under his own power, huffing and straining, he struggled to his feet and told Morrison to follow him. At the edge of the deck he looked out on the cleared area of grass and dirt. A pen of some sort, Morrison could see now, the chain-link fence around it a good ten feet in height. In the far corner, some two hundred feet from the lodge, he could make out in the newly risen half-moon's light dark forms moving along the fence. Four of them, he thought. Cats. One adult, three cubs.

"*Carne*," Crimmins said to the guards.

One of them, the driver, went to a trunk-sized cooler near the door and brought back two hunks of raw red beef. Crimmins rapped a stick against the metal railing. He stopped then rapped again, harder this time. Two of the cats, the adult and the largest of the cubs loped toward them. Now Morrison could see for certain what they were: black jaguars.

By international treaty, Morrison knew, all trade in jaguars or their parts was prohibited, and they were protected here in this country under the U.S. Endangered Species Act. But, as always, there were loopholes. Trophy hunting was still permitted in Bolivia, and both Ecuador and Guyana offered no legal protection to jaguars. So via those countries there was a "*legal*," if not *moral*, way for a man like Crimmins to obtain papers for the two specimens that prowled now beneath the deck.

"Even wild things are creatures of habit," Crimmins said beside him. "They know when food's on the table. Not the other two, though, the babies." He indicated with a nod of his head the far end of the pen. "They haven't learned the drill yet."

So the two still out there were the new arrivals, Morrison figured. What he had seen being delivered two nights back.

"You see," Crimmins was saying, "I'm a man who loves nature as much as anyone else. In fact, I love it so much I want to get as close to it as possible. That's why I had this pen built the way it is. So these astonishing creatures can come right up under the deck here. So nature lovers like us, like you and me, can look right down like this into their iridescent eyes." With undisguised appreciation, he watched them parade restlessly back and forth below the deck. "That's Big Mama," he said of the larger one. "And that's her baby, Princess. You ever see two more beautiful creatures on God's green earth?"

"*Endangered* creatures."

"Most assuredly, but I think you're missing my point." He turned to the guard holding the meat. "Ernesto. Appetizer time. Give them a taste of what's to come."

The man came forward and flung the first piece of meat to the right side of the pen where Big Mama began to devour it. The second piece he threw to the left side, at the feet of the cub. In a matter of moments the meat was gone and the two sleek animals had resumed their silent pacing beneath the deck.

"Magnificent, aren't they?" Crimmins said.

"All the more reason they should be protected."

Crimmins rambled on, ignoring the comment. "They're called the 'ghost of the forest' because of their stealth, and yet they're the only kind of jaguar that can roar. One of nature's sweeter ironies, don't you think? Both the Mayas and the Aztecs believed the jag had magical powers, that it could shape-shift. And one or the other, the Mayas *or* the Aztecs, believed it could facilitate communication between the living and the dead."

"The Mayas."

"I'm impressed. I like a man who knows his facts." He nodded his head approvingly, but it was clear to Morrison that compliments were the last thing on the man's mind. "What I find most remarkable is the way they kill by biting directly through the skull of their victims. Their bite is so enormously powerful they can pierce the armored shell of any turtle, any reptile and pulverize even the heaviest bones. So you can imagine what they can do to a man." He stopped himself then and offered Morrison a cold smile. "Not that I'm telling you anything you don't know."

"No, you're not," Morrison said evenly. "But while you're mentioning the cat's attributes, you might want to include that it's considered an 'umbrella species' because it's so damn vital to the survival of the hundreds of smaller species that depend on its habitat."

"Point well taken," Crimmins conceded. "But it's not only about the animals. The way I see it the good Lord put them here on earth for man to use as he sees fit. After all, we *are* the superior species. We have needs, too. And one of those needs, at least for some of us, is to pit ourselves against the strongest forces in the animal kingdom—bulls or elephants or lions or tigers or black jags—to prove how strong we really are in a fight to the death."

"Not exactly a fair fight when you're using high-powered rifles, is it?"

"Our weapons merely compensate for the animal's greater strength. And if they give us a slight advantage, well, I'd say that's of minor concern in light of the aggression we're able to release.

Because it's my unflinching belief that man, like all animals, has a need to kill. Under the right circumstances, when his aggression level is high enough, he will most certainly kill, as we well know. So by bringing in worthy opponents like these cats here, I'm really doing a service to mankind, the way I see it. A man kills one of these, maybe he doesn't go shooting up some office building or some school full of innocent kids. Maybe he doesn't beat his wife at night." He laughed, only partly in jest, at his own beneficence. "Who knows how many lives I save?"

He was gloating when he turned from the pen and leaned against the railing, contemplating Morrison. "Which brings us to you, my friend. *I hope you're up to the Challenge.*"

The Challenge, *El Desafio,* was a ritual engaged in by the Mayans, Crimmins explained. Morrison knew of the ritual but he listened as if hearing about it for the first time. If a man alienated himself from society, either by a criminal act or other serious offense, he was sent at dusk into the jungle alone. If he survived until daybreak, if he eluded both the beasts of the night and the hunting party sent to kill him, he was allowed to return to the community without further punishment.

"You'll be given a five-minute head start. Then we set the jags loose. Five minutes after that, me and the guards begin our hunt." Crimmins explained this in a matter-of-fact way, as if giving directions to a house party. He said he assumed Morrison would head for the break in the fence where he entered. That would make sense. That was clearly his best option. But to up the ante, to make the Challenge a bit more exciting, he would have the voltage raised in the electrified wires. A body touching any one of them would no longer simply be stunned but temporarily immobilized. And, well, Morrison could imagine, couldn't he, what might happen to an immobilized man when there were hungry jaguars on the loose.

"If the jags get you," Crimmins said, "they'll be nothing left for the police to find. And if the search party gets you, well, then it will be one of those unfortunate night hunting accidents. A matter of a man being in the wrong place at the wrong time."

"Oh, and by the way," he added, "*I'll* be the one hunting you. Just so you know. If we get to you before the jags do, I'll be the one who pulls the trigger." He laughed then, a deep-throated laugh. "Help me with my aggression problem, you know?"

Once again it was the arrogance of the man, his smugness, that infuriated Morrison. Here at the club nothing could touch him, or so he assumed. He was in control, the game would be played according to *his* rules. No way he could lose. He was damn sure of that.

"It's playtime, Gamey."

----THIRTY-THREE----

MORRISON WAS HALF-WALKING, HALF-STUMBLING toward that section of fence he had cut his way through earlier. It was difficult without his goggles, without light of any kind save for the occasional dappled spill of moon glow where the tree canopy thinned. His arms were bruised and bleeding from swatting away branches and vines, and his breath came in heated gasps.

At times the forest seemed impenetrable with its knots of trees, its tangled vines, the cloying grip of underbrush.

He stopped at the edge of a dense thicket of pines and bent over, hands resting on his knees as he drew in air. His mouth was dry and raw, as if he had swallowed sand. The simple act of breathing had become painful. In the heavy air, mosquitoes swarmed around him and he strained to hear beyond their dull buzz.

Nothing of human origin.

Nothing but the pulsating energy of the night forest.

Then, far off, what sounded like a buzz louder than mosquitoes. A car's motor?

Morrison checked his watch. The faint green glow of its hands told him he'd been on the move for nearly twenty minutes now. Which meant that the jags had been on the loose for fifteen minutes already, the human hunters for only ten—*if* they kept their word. And what guarantee did he have of that?

He listened for the sound of the motor but heard only the noises of the forest. Rather than belabor his way through the pine thicket he skirted its edge in hopes of finding a way around it. When he'd been set loose from the lodge he'd struck out in what he calculated to be the most direct route to his entry point:

a diagonal line which should at least bring him close. Then it would be a matter of following the fence until he reached the cut wires.

That had been his plan. As Crimmins had said, it seemed to make the most sense. His other options had appeared less appealing. If he'd followed the road to the main gate, he would have—without his wire cutters—no way of negotiating the fence. If he had doubled back and sought refuge in either the lodge or the barracks, he had no idea what he would have found there. More guards, most likely. But even if both buildings had been left unguarded, what was the likelihood he would have found weapons lying around? And without weapons what kind of a stand could he have made?

So it had come down to this: head straight for his entry point in hopes he could beat them and the jags there. A simple enough plan, though he was certain he'd gone off-course.

The question was how far.

In following the perimeter of the thicket now, he was going even farther astray. But at least this way he could make better time. He could save himself the effort of blindly feeling his way around protruding limbs, of being gored by the pointed tips of broken pine branches. This way there was at least marginally more light to guide him.

A thrashing sound came from somewhere on his left and he froze. The sound grew softer, died away altogether. Not one of the jags. Something smaller. *What?* A panther's preferred diet, on dry land, was deer, peccaries, capybaras, tapirs. He was pretty sure Crimmins was the kind of man who would have stocked his land accordingly. Anything to keep his cherished prey—*the strongest forces in the animal kingdom*, as he called them—happy. Anything to keep them primed for *the fight to the death.*

So it might have been any one of those quadrupeds hustling away. Or any of the smaller species native to this part of Florida. What he was sure of was that it wasn't one of the big cats. With their retractable claws, their soft pads and the fur between their toes, jaguars were silent stalkers. You would not hear them before they were on you.

And what was it Crimmins had said about his two most prized cats? "Don't be fooled by the smaller one. She's more vicious than her mother. She'll be on her own before long. She'll be a holy terror, I promise you." He had left Morrison with one more parting shot. "I'm sure I don't have to remind you that black jags are the strongest climbers of all the cats. They give the phrase, *Death From Above*, a whole new meaning."

In the branches above, shadows and thick foliage made it impossible to see what might be waiting there. As he moved beneath the entangled limbs of live oaks and hackberry trees, his shoulders instinctively hunched. Despite his fear, he found grim amusement in the futility of his natural reflexes, as if such a gesture as hunching his shoulders would offer any safeguard against the roughly two hundred pounds of pure muscle that might come descending upon him.

He had reached the end of the thicket where the dense cluster of pines had given way to more navigable alleys between palmetto plants and wax myrtle. He circled the outer edge of the pines in hopes of re-joining his imaginary diagonal line to the fence.

Veiled moonlight fell across the way ahead. He stayed to the shadows and when the darkness closed around him again he saw, through a break in the trees, what he thought to be the dull shimmer of a roadbed. The sand was not nearly as white nor as exposed as the road from the gate, pine needles darkened it with a brown veil, but as he moved toward it he was certain it was a road.

He'd drifted father off course than he'd realized.

Keeping within the tree cover he followed the road's curve. Somewhere ahead he heard a motor's low throb. Several hundred feet farther on, around a long bend, the road dead-ended against a wall of trees. Engine idling, parked sideways as if the driver had begun to turn it around then quit, was the security van.

So they had gotten here before he did. No surprise. The rules of the game were in their hands to make or break. They had guns, a car. They knew the layout of the land. Which meant that somewhere ahead, between where he stood and the fence, Crimmins was waiting to intercept him.

MORRISON made his way closer to the van. He could make out the shadow of the driver slumped against the door. Asleep? Dozing? There was a good chance of that since the man wasn't moving. Or maybe he was awake, simply resting.

On his knees, he swiped away mosquitoes with one hand while he felt around for something he could use as a weapon. It took him several minutes before he found a piece of branch the size of a night-stick.

The driver still hadn't moved. Morrison crept closer until he was within ten feet of the van. Crawling out from the tree-shadows and crouching low, he moved along the side of the idling vehicle until he reached the door. He raised his arm and yanked the handle sharply, the driver cursing and squirming as he tumbled outward. Morrison clubbed him as he fell and clubbed him again when he hit the ground until the man lay in the dirt bloodied and still. On the seat an assault rifle rested against the console.

He had taken the rifle and stepped away from the van when he heard from a distance, from what he thought was the direction of the lodge, a full-throated roar that shattered the forest's stillness. In its wake the silence grew deeper. Even the smallest sounds, the buzz and murmur of insects, had been erased.

He stood there as if mesmerized, scanning the trees in the direction of the sound, before taking the bloodied stick which lay beside the guard's motionless body and beating it against the metal of the truck's hood. He wanted to draw the jags closer. If the sound of wood on metal was their call to dinner, he hoped they would come for the feast. He was putting himself at greater risk, for sure, but if Crimmins awaited him somewhere between here and the fence as he most likely did, then it was a risk he had to take. Balancing the odds, was the way he thought of it, giving himself some leverage.

Another roar broke the silence.

Closer this time.

The jags were moving this way.

Again, he rapped the stick against the truck's hood. Again the roar, closer still. Now he wasn't the only one being hunted. Crimmins and his guards would be fair game, as well. The hunt would no longer be as one-sided.

He rapped on the hood again. This time when the roar came it was close enough to make his blood run cold.

HE was moving quickly along a deer trail that led away from the van. He thought the fence must be ahead of him, not far, not more than a quarter mile at most. But he couldn't be certain.

Holding the rifle across his body he ran hard into the deepening darkness, away from what little light the road had offered. Around him the forest seemed a vast, spinning thing, without beginning or end. And then without warning the trees opened and he was standing in a clearing of sorts, an area of knee-high underbrush, at the far end of which he caught the glimmer of metal in light stolen from the moon.

The fence. He'd reached it at last.

He remained there, crouched in the brush, assessing this visible section of fence which stretched some fifty feet ahead. Was it to the left or right of where he'd entered? He thought it was to the right, but again he couldn't be certain. On both sides of the clearing deep pockets of trees blocked his view of the continuation of the fence. If he crossed the clearing he'd be an easy target for anyone hiding in the trees. So he waited. Straining to hear in the stillness, to smell in the air the presence of other beings.

Something twitched at the edge of his vision. A ragged-edged point of light broke the darkness, along with the sound of automatic rifle fire, then he was on the ground crawling through the brush, seeking refuge finally in the shadow of palm fronds and fern-like bushes.

Another round of rifle fire shattered the fronds around him. He lay still. When the silence took reign again, he pulled himself into the deeper and darker safety of the woods. He drew himself to his feet against the smooth bark of a bayberry tree. On the opposite side of the clearing a shadow flitted from tree to tree. Too swift to be Crimmins.

Morrison fired.

A man's choked cry. The shadow of an arm raised, then falling out of sight.

Nothing moved between the trees.

How many other guards were here? Morrison had seen four at the lodge. But in what he assumed was the bunkhouse building behind it, there might have been others asleep, waiting for their shift. So he couldn't be certain who else, besides Crimmins, was out there.

He moved through the trees along the edge of the clearing until there was no more cover. Twenty feet of open space stood between himself and the fence. Staying within the tree cover he walked in what he hoped was an easterly direction, toward the county road.

It took him several minutes before he reached another area where the trees thinned and the light was marginally better. He thought he recognized this sparsely treed patch of ground, that he had crossed it earlier on his way to the lodge. He was close to his entry point now; he was sure of it. Darting from tree to tree he traversed the relatively open space, a distance of seventy-five feet perhaps, and stopped to rest in a cluster of pines on the far side. He was sweating so much he thought his smell might give him away.

Kneeling in the dirt he heard it again: the jaguar's roar. Deep and full-throated, the voice of Big Mama, shattering the stillness. And then the cub's roar, not as deep, but chilling nonetheless. They were in the thick woods beyond the area he had just crossed. How far, he couldn't be sure. But close enough to send shivers through him.

They were moving with him.

Mosquitoes swarmed around him, braving the fading residue of repellent, biting his face and neck and hands as he crawled toward the edge of the pines. Sweat ran liquid on his skin, blurred his vision. When he blinked it away he saw ahead of him, across the cleared swath along the fence, what he'd been looking for. Dangling wires. And on the ground beneath them the long-handled wire cutters.

At last.

Something trembled between the trees on his left. One of the guards appeared, rifle raised, and Morrison swung the butt of his rifle at the man's face, sending him backwards with blood bubbling fountain-like from his mouth. On his back, arms flung wide, the man lay inert on the needle-blanketed ground. Dead or alive, Morrison wasn't sure, but the man was definitely out cold.

He waited in the shadows, listened. No animal or human sounds. Looking out from the trees, he watched the twenty foot swath of open space to the fence. A no man's land. A dead zone too dangerous to navigate.

When he looked back across the sparsely treed area he had crossed, he saw movement again. Only this time it wasn't human. He saw the baby cat slouching along the tree-line, in stalking mode. Which meant Big Mama was close by, too.

He glanced again at the twenty feet of no man's land between where he knelt and the fence. He couldn't chance making a dash for it. No way that Crimmins didn't have that patch of ground in his sights. Most likely from the trees to his right, beyond where he'd seen the shadow of the cat. His only hope, Morrison knew, was to draw the man out, force him into the path of the jags.

The guard he had felled was close enough to Morrison's size to pass—in the dark, at least— as his double. Quickly he pulled the man's jacket off, replaced it with his own. Blood still oozed from his mouth which made a gurgling sound when Morrison lifted him to his feet and dragged him to the edge of the tree-line. The man was coming to, his eyes opening and rolling back in confusion as Morrison held him propped up there a moment before pitching him forward into the no man's land of open ground.

Crimmins' voice tore a hole in the night's uneasy calm. "Gamey!"

The first shot followed immediately. Not a hundred feet farther along the fence, where Morrison had estimated he'd been hiding, the big game hunter stood in the cleared swath of ground and opened fire a second time, the guard spinning toward the fence and falling.

Before Morrison had time to get off a shot, Crimmins had swung around, rifle raised at the pocket of trees behind him. Instinct maybe, a hunter's sixth sense. But it came too late. He fired once into the darkness before the impact of the baby cat forced him back against the fence, his enormous frame doing a half-spiral as he went down, clutching the rifle which struck one of the electrified wires, his prostrate body shaking with spasms, then suddenly inert.

In the next moment, both cats were upon him.

---- *THIRTY-FOUR*----

WHEN RAYELLE CLASPED THE NECKLACE around her neck she checked herself again in the hotel bar mirror. She was wearing every single piece of jewelry Bobbie had given her—earrings, arm and ankle bracelets, rings—and she turned to show DeeDee.
"What do you think?"

"You look like a million," DeeDee said, even though her heart was breaking.

"I *feel* like a million." And she did. Because for that moment and for the rest of her shift everyone in the River Hotel bar and dining room, from Mrs. Lowry to the lowliest busboy, would know how much Bobbie had loved her, *once*. She wondered if Nicky would come by so she could show him, too.

When the bar closed she hugged DeeDee who couldn't stop crying. She told her she'd write, that she'd *definitely* come back for the wedding. Then she walked out to her car. It made her sad to think all her worldly possessions—those that mattered, at least— could fit inside a single automobile, even if it was a big one.

One more time she checked the trunk to be sure she had everything. Behind the gasoline cans, behind her suitcases, was the leather satchel she'd taken from beneath the floorboards in the bedroom she'd shared with Bobbie. His private stash—what he couldn't or wouldn't put in the bank. She'd left him the two others in the crawlspace. She thought that was fair, generous even. Normally when a couple broke up they split things 50-50. She'd only taken a third.

She glanced around the parking lot one last time for Nicky. Looked like the man was going to be a no-show.

She drove along the river to the construction site and pulled

212

into what one day would have been her driveway. With the engine off she sat in the dark and listened. Across the river the frogs and gators were croaking and grunting up a storm, but it was the wind through the grasses that she listened to: a steady sound at first that began to shape itself into words. First one voice, then another and another, sometimes in unison, sometimes separately, gently hissing *Who are you? Who are you? Who are you?*

Then she was crying because she couldn't answer, had nothing to say. She had been Bobbie Dawson's girlfriend, and before that she'd been her mother's daughter. Always she'd been defined in terms of someone else. That's why she had to leave this all behind. To find out who she was.

She opened the trunk, reached for the two gas cans, and carried them up the steps of the house. The voices had ceased. The wind, at that moment, seemed to be holding its breath in anticipation. She listened a moment before emptying the cans.

Driving out of town, crossing the Mangrove Bay bridge, she passed a line of police cars coming from the opposite direction. There must have been at least fifteen in all: lights flashing, no sirens. Something's up tonight, she thought, something big. But her mind was on other things. Whatever happened in Mangrove Bay from now on wouldn't matter to her.

She was thinking about herself, the new life that was beginning. She was thinking if anyone was standing back there on the bridge watching her drive away this is what they'd see: two dots of red light on the highway, then she'd be gone.

A POLICE cruiser, lights swirling, had already sealed off the main road into and out of the Mangrove Bay airport. Approaching on a side road, Morrison watched a uniformed officer pulling closed the airfield gate. The place was too small, too lightly trafficked to have a tower, so that this was the best they could do to shut it down.

At the east end of the airstrip he left his car in a weedy field and jumped the chain-link fence, running toward the idling plane.

He hadn't expected to see Royboy's Cessna still here. He'd assumed Nicky had long since bailed, left him for dead. But that was his deep-rooted distrust of his fellow man kicking in again. He figured that, in light of recent developments, this one among them—namely that the man had waited for him this long, had in fact saved his ass a second time—he would have to modify that distrust.

The Cessna, parked on the grass, had its props whirling. The small plane teetered onto the runway and stopped to wait for him. He ran harder, his body—in what seemed to be every last muscle and joint—aching from the night's ordeal.

Farther down the field, the officer shouted, struggling to free his revolver from its holster as he ran toward the plane. Morrison climbed aboard, Rowan pulling at him with one hand and reaching to close the door with the other, Royboy already having begun his take-off.

The officer had stepped onto the runway. Frantically he waved his arms for them to stop. When he saw the plane bearing down on him he dove sideways into the dirt, the Cessna airborne by then, Royboy chortling to himself, muttering "That'll learn ya" as he concentrated on clearing the trees at the runway's end.

"Didn't your mother ever tell you not to leave things to the last minute?" Rowan grinned from the seat behind Morrison. Then, leaning forward for a better look at him, he said: "You okay?"

"Better than okay."

"Better than okay." He nodded his approval at that and winked at Morrison. "A man could do worse than that in this world."

"Glad to have you aboard again, sir," Royboy said.

The plane made a long, slow bank above the river. Morrison saw flames rising from a burning building. At first he thought it was the Blue Lagoon until he noticed the police cruisers farther upriver. Red and blue flashers piercing the darkness, they were forming a ring around the Lagoon's complex of buildings. It chilled him, looking down like that on what would have—in the next few minutes—become his tomb. Who would his assassin have been? Caruso? Dawson, before it was his own turn?

One more piece of the puzzle that would remain missing.

"Hey," Rowan said from the back seat, "you had me worried, you know that?"

"Had myself worried." Morrison was surprised by the sense of kinship he felt with Rowan, his unlikely ally. "Would have hated trying to swim my way out of here."

The plane banked again and headed west toward the Gulf.

When they landed, he would try to get through to Krebs again, tell him about the animals left at the turnout off Highway 41, and those still warehoused at Dawson and Leach's place in the woods.

Failing that, he'd contact his friend at the wildlife shelter in Homestead. It was unlikely the animals would be returned to the wild in their country of origin—too expensive an undertaking for one thing, and the babies would have already begun to lose their survival skills—but at least they'd be well-cared for at a sanctuary or reputable zoo.

As they were approaching the open water of the Gulf, marsh and mangrove spread out below: a vast and lonely bottomland— as much, it seemed then to Morrison, a state of mind as a place. If you could leave a place then maybe you could leave behind the state of mind connected to that place.

Right now he needed to see his life with different eyes. He wanted to view his fellow man the way Emilio had, not oblivious to his capacity for cruelty and deceit, but not obsessed with it either. He wanted to find room for the warmth behind the boy's smile, his openness to wonder and beauty. So he would walk in his shoes, explore the streets of Santiago Atitlan, climb into the mountains, live for a while among the farmers there. He thought it might repair his faith in the world and his own ideals.

But first he would visit Emilio's family. Tell them what a courageous man their boy had become in America.

Philip Cioffari has authored three previous books of fiction: the novel, JESUSVILLE: the mystery/thriller, CATHOLIC BOYS; and the short story collection, A HISTORY OF THINGS LOST OR BROKEN, which won the Tartt First Fiction Prize. His short stories have been published widely in commercial and literary magazines and anthologies, including *North American Review, Playboy, Michigan Quarterly Review, Northwest Review, Florida Fiction*, and *Southern Humanities Review*. He has written and directed for Off and Off-Off Broadway. His Indie feature film, which he wrote and directed, LOVE IN THE AGE OF DION, has won numerous awards, including Best Feature Film at the Long Island Int'l Film Expo, and Best Director at the NY Independent Film & Video Festival. He is a Professor of English, and director of the Performing and Literary Arts Honors Program, at William Paterson University. www.philipcioffari.com